Pickled in Love

Gina N. Brown

NovaHeart Media

This book was written in the ancestral territory of the Mi'kmaw people called Mi'kma'ki.

Book cover design by: Peggy & Co. Design

NovaHeart Media website design: Crystal Picard Design & Marketing

Author photo: Mallory Brisson Photography

Your task is not to seek love, but merely to seek
and find all the barriers within yourself that you
have built against it.

Rumi

Dedicated to
all the romantics who are still open to love at any age.

Also by Gina N. Brown

Lucy McGee's Moment of Truth
The Sugar Bowl Feud

Editor

Cross-eyed Optimist: How I Learned to See in 3D and Straight-
ened My Eyes with Vision Therapy.
Written by Robert Bryan Crockett

Chapter 1
Jenn

Jenn's breath shortened into sharp puffs, and her heart pumped so fast it could keep the beat with an ABBA song. Her fitness watch pinged to congratulate her on achieving her maximum target heart rate, yet she was standing still. Debating whether she needed to get a grip or head to Emergency, she breathed deeply for several rounds until her heart rate calmed down.

Welcome to yet another first date in your fifties. Jenn didn't like them one bit, and second dates weren't much better. She recalled that in her twenties, dates were fun and she didn't worry one whit about how they might go beyond that evening. Worse, she applied no filters, such as whether her dates seemed interesting, kind or sane. And she showed no discrimination, because, let's face it, after 2 a.m. and multiple cocktails, every guy looked amazing, as if enhanced by an Instagram filter for partiers.

Fast forward thirty years, and first dates were the opposite. She preferred starting with a daytime coffee date in a public café, so now they were fueled by caffeine instead of alcohol. She overanalyzed everything, constantly considering the guy's every move, glance and opinion. Instead of finding common ground, she was more likely to focus on why they might not be a good fit as a couple. Maybe it was from too many years of practice, but she felt like she could sense dating disasters quickly and preferred not to waste anyone's time.

That's why she created a first-date ranking system, like a baseball player at home plate. One infraction was Strike One, which she would let slide. But if the irritation continued, she could hear an umpire in her head, one that sounded like her Dad's embarrassing hollering when he was the ump for her childhood softball league. Each time, he insisted on swinging his right arm in a full circle, then pointing to the plate and yelling, "Steee-rike Two!" in a you-better-believe-it tone. And while the guy on the date didn't know it, he was now on official notice: one more troublesome gaffe, and he was out.

Once again, thanks to her friend Maggie's uncanny talent for digging up first dates (including some older guys who looked freshly dug up), Jenn was back at it. And with a bit of tough love coaching from her friend, Jenn reminded herself that first impressions were important and positivity was key. "Oh well, nothing ventured, nothing pained," she thought as she arrived at the Jumping Bean Café on Agricola Street in Halifax. Tufts of frost danced around her face as she blew out the cold air. She peeked through the large window, which looked cozy on a brisk winter morning. She loved the café's soundtrack—the grinding coffee beans and hissing espresso machines all mixed in with the happy hum of conversations. It was her kind of shop.

She tried not to look obvious as she searched for her next "dating debacle," as she would later describe it to Maggie. Funny, Maggie was happily married with four kids running rampant, yet she was always meeting someone new for Jenn to date.

Meanwhile, Jenn, who had been single for years and met lots of people every week, was rarely invited on dates. How did Maggie do that? For one thing, Maggie was relentless. Jenn barely had time to get over one guy before Maggie was foisting another on her. Jenn was never in such a hurry, and lately, she nicknamed her friend "Naggie," which was code for "you are pushing too hard, girl." Maggie would laugh about it, agree to do better and then settle down... until she found another "perfect" guy for Jenn.

She spotted her date off to the side. He was a pleasant-looking guy, dressed in a casual marine blue sweater. His hair was brown and curly, and he had a trimmed, short beard. He looked busy on his phone, but his tapping leg and foot told her he was giving himself something to do while he waited.

When Maggie told her his name was Ed, Jenn said, "Ed? Ed? That sounds unusual for a guy in his fifties." Maggie looked sternly at her and said, "Now that's just nitpicking. Give the guy a chance."

Jenn checked the text that Maggie had sent her with the date profile, which frankly, sounded the same as all the others: super nice guy (Maggie always started with that), divorced (so was Jenn and no biggie), a business manager (let's assume he's good with money) and, he has a heartbeat (Jenn laughed because Maggie usually added something cheeky to see if she was still reading). The rest was up to Jenn to figure out.

With a background in psychology and a hint of intuition, Jenn had learned to suss out dates quickly. It was a process that began decades earlier when she realized early on her marriage wasn't going to work. However, from that marriage came the best gift ever, her twenty-six-year-old son Kyle. So she had no regrets. But it made her cautious.

She hadn't remarried and felt worn down by the hits and misses from dating in her thirties and forties. Now, as she raced through her fifties, she observed that it had become too easy to write off guys before giving them a chance. After dates and reporting back to Maggie, she often heard herself say, "he's almost a great catch." She had met many lovely men who would be perfect for someone, but not for her. So why waste time?

She caught her reflection and remembered that as she was bolting out the door, she had swapped out her stylish beret for a chunky wool winter hat with a bouncy pompom at the top. She pulled it off, revealing a hairdo like a bird's nest with strands pinging in every direction thanks to the static build from wearing a hat. Her hair cried out for a comb. That meant she had to make a beeline to a mirror before she made her way to Ed's table.

Fortunately, she noted the washroom was on the opposite side, so she snuck in with an arriving group and strode to the bathroom. After fixing her hair, stuffing the fat hat into her side pocket and applying lip gloss, she walked back into the bustling café. "Umm, Ed?" she asked, now unsure if that was him. "Yup," he said, looking up with a stingy smile, which caused her muscles to tighten. Unsure of what to do (a light greeting kiss like they do on dating shows? No thanks), she stuck her hand out to shake his, and instead, he passed her a small bag. "Oh," Jenn said, "what's this?"

"Don't say I never gave you anything."

Sure, it *sounded* like a joke, but Jenn sensed an edge to his tone. She opened it and pulled out a gift-sized chocolate bar in a plain blue wrapper—a triumph of quantity over quality. *Nothing says I picked up a last-minute gift at the pharmacy like a generic chocolate bar.* "Thank you," she gushed, unsure of what to think or say. She set it on the table, then removed her coat and draped it over the back of the chair. "Should we get a coffee?" she asked, trying to fill the awkward moment.

"What would you like? My treat," he added.

"Lovely," she smiled. "I'll have a small latté." She settled into her chair and watched him walk to the counter. He looked confident, which she liked. She also observed how he treated the staff, which provided insight into who he was as a person. Jenn noticed a brief exchange between him and the server, with him pointing at the cash screen several times and then paying. He nodded to the barista and walked to the table. He set the lattés on the table.

"Well, that was a new one for me," he said, sliding the latté toward her.

"Oh yeah, what was that?"

"I just paid twelve bucks for two coffees."

Puzzled, she said, "Yes, when you add the tax and tip, that's the ballpark. Why is that new?"

"I've never bought a latté before. I drink a small coffee at McDonald's. Much better value."

Steee-rike Two! It was a date, not a takeaway on his dime for everybody in the office. She sensed he might suffer from what she called 'the grumpy gene,' so she thought she should try to cheer him up. "Yes, but consider the caffeine experience," she said with a hint of joking, as she waved her hand across the table. "Look at the fancy mugs, the sweet design on the foam and the fun atmosphere." Jenn stirred her latté and noticed he looked unconvinced, so she went a step further.

"So, tell me about yourself, Ed." She could see that she'd landed on a topic of interest to him. Unfortunately, Ed forgot that conversations were meant to be two-way. Once he started, he'd inhaled a breath deep enough to talk for twenty minutes without taking a breath.

Jenn tried to insert an occasional joke or comment, which he barely noticed. Even when she interrupted him, it was clear he was keeping his mind blank while she talked so that he wouldn't lose his place in the story. She tried to keep in mind that people were often nervous on first dates and might ramble on for a bit until they felt more comfortable. It usually corrected itself within five minutes. Not this time.

By nature, Jenn was a listener. Her home organizing business had taught her that letting the client talk was the best way to understand who they were and what they wanted from her services. That, she believed, was her special way of delivering excellent results.

But that was business and she was being paid to do it. This was a date. This guy acted like he'd been locked in a room for months and she was the first person to crack open the door. And not only had he avoided asking her any questions, but he actively blocked her from contributing and complained nonstop about his life. Steee-rike Three!

Jenn couldn't wait for the "date-disaster" alarm to ding in a few minutes. She set it as a one-hour backup plan for first dates.

If she were having a rollicking good time and the alarm went off, she'd apologize and turn off the phone. If it were dismal or downright irritating, she'd say she had a meeting soon and had to leave.

When the phone reminder started, set to the sound of a chorus of harps, it jolted him out of his lengthy description. "Ah gee, Ed," she said, fetching her phone, "I have to run to a meeting."

"Uhm, okay," he said, looking confused. "Geez, the time flew. I was just getting warmed up."

"Sorry, I need to go to a meeting across town and you know what traffic is like in Halifax on a weekday," she said.

He nodded and stood up. "I had a great time, Jenn."

No wonder. You talked about yourself nonstop for an hour. While she wanted to hurl a few insults his way for breaking every first-date rule—hogging conversations, complaining about work, family, and ex-partners—she took the high road. "Thanks for the latté," she said, keeping her hands busy with packing to avoid a handshake, or worse, a hug.

"Don't forget your chocolate bar," he said, sliding the bar toward her. "And do you want to meet again?"

"Let's wait and see," she replied, appearing to take his request seriously while trying to lift the bar with her right-hand mitten. Finally, she swept it off the table and shoved it in her pocket. "Take care, Ed," she said, pleased with herself for not insulting him.

"Wait!" he said. "You don't have my cell number."

With her back already turned, she pretended not to hear him and bolted out the door before having to reply. Jenn had forbidden Maggie from ever giving out her cell number unless she okayed it, in case it was a 'thanks, but no thanks' date. She sat in her car, taking a few deep breaths, while she checked her messages. Then she called Maggie to ask what she was thinking. Jenn described how he talked for an hour straight. Maggie gulped and said, "Hmm. Now that I think about it, he's a bit long-winded at school committee meetings. But I figured that was only because it was a public forum and he had strong opinions."

Jenn was discouraged. She had an in-depth profile of his life, yet he hadn't asked her a single question. Why couldn't she meet someone with a quick wit, a sense of humor and a reasonable level of curiosity? As a fifty-something singleton, was she too picky?

Chapter 2
Mark

MARK RANG THE DOORBELL at the home of Mindy Lee, the instructor for the cooking class. He held a baguette in a long, narrow paper bag in one hand, and a bottle of wine in the other. Inside, he could hear chatter and laughter coming from the kitchen. Mindy swung open the door and smiled. "I can't believe you came to the potluck, Mark Russell!" she chirped.

"Neither can I, Chef," he said as he stepped over the threshold. He handed her the baguette with the open end facing down and sighed as the bread slipped out onto the floor. "Sorry," he said, bending over and picking up the stick. He dusted it with his scarf before handing it to her.

"Five-second rule," Mindy joked. "Our dirty little secret."

She wasn't too far off. He remembered he'd rubbed his dog with his scarf earlier that day. "You might want to heat that bread for ten minutes," he laughed.

She rolled her eyes and waved him into the kitchen. "Hey, everybody, Mark's here!" she shouted to the group. They all turned and said hi. He could smell the incredible aroma of delicious dishes on the counters. He set the bread beside the buffet.

"Did you make that?" teased Shari.

"No, I bought it myself," he zinged back. He understood his role as the hopeless cook—somebody had to play that part. Out of twelve people in the cooking class, he hovered at the lowest rung of the competency ladder. His idea of a triumph was learning how to make hard-boiled eggs without burning them. If he'd been on a reality show, like "Best Cook in the Kitchen," he would have either been turfed out in week one or kept on as the hapless disaster everybody watched for laughs as he messed up.

He was the only guy in the cooking class; the other two dropped out after the first week. Mark had also considered ducking out of the culinary debacle. In week one, he kept one hand on his car fob in his pocket in case he needed to make a fast getaway. Yet when he thought about it, he had nothing going on at home, so he stayed. He liked all the women in class and enjoyed their friendly teasing. Always ready for a laugh, he remained a good sport, deflecting their insults and sending some back.

The class was called "Entreés for One," which he had been railroaded into by his daughters. When they first suggested it, he said absolutely not. He rhymed off the types of participants that would fill the group: never married, separated, divorced, or widowed. He sighed when he opened his Christmas stocking to find a gift certificate to attend the class, with no refund. They had him in a corner; the two scheming sisters knew he wouldn't want to waste the money they'd spent. He finally agreed.

And since he showed no interest in or potential for cooking, he suspected the real motivation of his daughters was to find love for him. When his wife died suddenly three years earlier, he was shocked into a new lifestyle. Although he argued he was fine, everybody else felt differently.

For thirty-some years, his wife Annie had cooked and baked, while he happily cleaned up the kitchen. Both claimed they got the best deal. They had divided the household chores, mostly agreeing who was doing what—except for vacuuming, which for some reason he detested ("Can't make me," he'd joke). They had settled into a comfortable domestic life, with the occasional flare-up, but otherwise were clicking along like a passenger train, hitting a happy rhythm of moving forward.

While the cooking at home without his late wife Annie presented tough challenges, the much bigger issue was the loss of his special love, friend and companion of so many years. They were in a groove together that might have appeared a bit shop-worn to others, but it was full bliss for him. They both had their own lives, sets of friends, and activities, and they did lots together. He pictured them still doing things at eighty, and now, here he was, in his late fifties, alone.

The worst times were the quiet evenings, speaking to nobody except the dog. He and Annie had shared some traditions they both loved. After he cleaned the kitchen, they'd sit down to do their daily Wordles competing against each other's timing, then crosswords and cryptic puzzles or Scrabble. They'd wrap up in time for *Jeopardy*, trying to shout over each other to hit the imaginary buzzer. He had even made a score chart, which they filled in after every show. While he won a few more times over the years, they were pretty well matched.

Now he was in an unsatisfying rhythm of doing nothing in the evening. The crosswords and games had lost their shine and he stopped doing them. And while he still watched *Jeopardy* and sometimes shouted at the television, he only got the occasional puzzled look from his dog, Jack, curled up next to him.

As he predicted, there were no romantic results from attending the cooking class. Well, a few women had flirted mildly with him (he couldn't be sure that's what they were doing). He couldn't imagine they'd be interested in a retired gym teacher who had packed on a few pounds in the last three years. Worse, he had developed an annoying cough that freaked out some people in the class, even though he did a test and assured them he didn't have Covid. It didn't seem like a cold—the cough dwindled for a bit, then returned. He figured he was hardly a charming package.

As an active gym teacher and coach, he stayed healthy most of his life. He was used to conquering a cold in a day or two. But this cough was different. It wasn't severe enough to go to the doctor, but he worried about it.

Despite his misgivings, he stuck with the class. It had netted him a few new friends, occasional drop-off dinners, and the odd check-in from one of them to see how he was doing. He couldn't complain.

The potluck evening was fun, with a raucous round of trivia about cooking and foodie films. Then there were the end-of-season prizes for the best all-around cook—Cicely, not surprisingly, won that. There was also the Best Dish award, which Anita won for her Maritime Buddha bowl, full of fresh seafood, dulse, and rice. And when Beth was awarded the Most Improved, he complained that he hadn't won a thing. On cue, and laughing after a few glasses of wine, Patsy pulled out a handmade certificate bearing the title "Least Likely to Succeed as Chef."

He feigned hurt. "Yeah, yeah, yeah," he said, dismissing them with the flick of a hand. "You'll be lining up for autographs when I have my own cooking show." When the fun broke up around 11 p.m., he offered to drop off a few women who'd enjoyed a few too many drinks.

When he turned the key in the house door, Jack bolted down the hallway to greet him, acting like he'd been abandoned for eternity, not hours. Mark crouched down and petted him, then picked him up and carried him to the living room. Mark had gotten the dog only a year earlier; another of his persistent daughters' ideas, but it was a good one.

They campaigned and nagged him to get a dog. It was something he always wanted, but Annie didn't like the idea of a puppy messing up her house, so they never got one. But he warned his daughters not to bring a dog home. If he wanted one, he'd pick it out.

One quiet winter day, he began visiting the animal shelter and found a wee terrier that he immediately bonded with. He was only there for a few hours, walking and visiting other dogs, and the pup named Pookie wouldn't let him out of his sight. When Mark announced he was leaving and told the staff he'd think about it, the dog barked incessantly until Mark turned around and went back. The crate door was wedged open and the little dog jumped into his arms and wouldn't leave. Mark was well-known to the staff in the community, so, other than filling out a form and paying the fees, he was allowed to take the dog that day (they couldn't stand the thought of him barking forever). The first thing Mark did was change Pookie's name to Jack, which the dog seemed to appreciate—he *so* wasn't a Pookie.

Now fully attached to his human and settled in his home, Jack was barking furiously, which sounded like he was berating Mark for being out most of the evening. By the time Mark settled him down and carried him to the living room, Jack was happy again and the two sat quietly in the living room while Mark tried to watch an old movie, with a plate of crackers and a jar of peanut butter, even though he'd eaten at the potluck. A snack was his reset button when he felt untethered.

An hour later, Jack nudged his elbow, as if to remind Mark it was time to go to bed. He leaned forward in his recliner, ran his hands through his hair and put his feet on the floor. "And that, my friend, concludes another day," he joked to Jack as he arose from the sofa.

Chapter 3
Jenn

Jenn got up from her yoga mat and walked over to the wall shelving to stow the blocks and the foam cushion she had borrowed for the class. People in a hurry worked quickly around her, stashing their borrowed items on the shelves. In no time, the area was a mess. She smiled at the yoga instructor, Charlotte, who waited for everybody to finish so she could tidy the shelves.

"Funny, we just spent an hour relaxing with yoga, and now everybody is jamming things on shelves so they can race back to work, school, or their errands," said Jenn.

"So true," said Charlotte, juggling items.

Jenn stood back, assessing the mess. She felt sorry for the staff who had to reorganize the items umpteen times a day. "You know, there's a simple self-organizing solution so you and the team wouldn't have to tidy up after everyone."

"You sound like you know what you're talking about. Do tell!"

"All it would take is getting a multiple shelving unit with square box shelves—you'd need about thirty-six of them. You could also get a smaller version so that people can stow their phones and other personal items during the class. Gets more stuff off the floor, too."

Charlotte smiled. "Great idea, except I don't know about trying to buy and assemble them. Plus, they'd cost a lot."

"These units are always sold on marketplaces online. People move a lot. Some are unbelievably cheap. Tell you what, I'm in the biz. I can keep an eye out for them and I have an SUV to move them."

"That's right, you're the lady who organizes, right?"

"Yup, that's me," said Jenn. "I have a consulting business called Happy Space."

"That's cool. What do you do, exactly?"

Jenn went into her 30-second elevator pitch. "My goal is to bring peace to people's homes. I do that by clearing out, organizing items and maximizing the use of space. I organize, downsize and occasionally do home staging for selling a house." Jenn could see Charlotte's thoughts turning quickly in her head.

"Hmmm, that sounds amazing. You made me think of my Dad. His home is slowly turning into a mess. He does his best, but we lost our Mom a few years ago and he seems a little overwhelmed sometimes."

"I'm sorry for the loss of your Mom. It's not easy. I see these situations quite often."

Charlotte guided Jenn over to the side. "Really?" she asked. "My Dad could sure use some help. He wouldn't want to spend a lot of money, but he'd benefit from some support. There's a lot of clutter building up."

"It's not always about a big spend," said Jenn, getting into details. "When lives change, the use of a room may change and people may feel lost trying to figure it out. Sometimes it's just about clearing out clutter and reorganizing things."

Charlotte nodded enthusiastically as Jenn described the situation. "You know, my sister and I think my Dad would benefit from a home reorg. How do you work with your clients?"

Jenn took a deep breath. She had heard this story many times—well-meaning children pressuring their parents to make a change they weren't ready for. It was time for some tough love. "First, it's critical to determine if your father supports this plan. What we think is best for others is not always what they want."

"Good point," said Charlotte. "Dad sometimes complains that my sister Nicki and I have too many ideas." She chuckled briefly, sticking a block on the shelf. "Tell you what, Jenn. How about we talk to Dad, and if he's interested, how would the consulting work?"

"Well, there's a complimentary visit at his home. I'll walk through it with him and find out how he uses the space and what changes he'd like to make. Once I understand the functionality, I will present solutions to maximize the space and a quote to do the work." Jenn walked to her gym bag and got a business card, handing it to Charlotte, who was busy rolling her yoga mat before the next class arrived.

Charlotte stood up and looked at the card. "That sounds amazing and fair. Let me talk to Nicki first and then Dad. I'll get back to you. His name is Mark."

Jenn smiled and said she wouldn't do anything until she had a chance to interview him. She got these requests several times a year and found that the potential client wasn't always as interested in the project as the children were. But she never assumed anything and therefore was never surprised by the outcome.

She loved her job and especially enjoyed helping people sort out their challenges. She walked to her car to head across town for an appointment, then headed to her nearest pickleball court for a riotously fun afternoon.

Chapter 4
Mark

MARK SLUMPED IN FRONT of the television. Noise blared from the hockey game, and when it went to commercials, the noise grew even louder. He looked at Jack curled up in a ball of sleep and thought he should take him out for a walk. Suddenly, Jack's eyes opened as if he had read his mind. He jumped up and stretched, then stood at attention to show his interest in going outside.

He heard a faint voice from the kitchen calling, "Daddy? Are you home?"

Mark turned and smiled when he saw his daughter Nicki arriving, her arms full of stuff. "Hey honey, where'd you come from?"

Nicki set everything on the dining room table, which was starting to pile up. His daughters were constantly dropping things off that he didn't always know what to do with, so he left them there. He felt a little guilty that the slow cooker he had received as a birthday gift was still in the box. But the thought of endless chopping and prepping vegetables filled him with dread. He hoped Nicki hadn't noticed.

"I let myself in with the key under Mom's geranium pot. I knocked a bunch of times and even tried to call you, but no answer."

"Sorry, dear... I..."

Nicki walked over to the remote and muted it. "Geez, Dad, this is so freaking loud. Is your hearing okay?"

Mark coughed and nodded. "Hearing's fine. It's the commercials. They pump up the volume." He turned the TV off and smiled at her. "To what do I owe the honor of a visit during business hours?"

"Well," she said, "I have some exciting news. I finished my springtime line." She dug around the boxes, pulling out items. He had no idea what she was up to.

"Really? That's amazing." Mark was enormously proud of his two daughters, who were polar opposites of each other, and both successful in their own ways. Nicki, the oldest, was a moving target of energy—always looking for new excitement. While working remotely as a clothing designer for a company in Toronto, she went on maternity leave and discovered there was no daycare space when she was ready to return to work. Bummed out, she started doodling clothing designs for kids, which led to a new business, Pint-Sized Designs. A side-hustle had blossomed into a new chapter in her life.

Within a year, she'd created a process for clients to custom-design outfits for their kids. She did the design prep work, and then clients would go on her website to pick out various design elements: colors, fabrics and accessories. It was like the cut-outs that kids played with back in the seventies. Nicki then created bespoke clothing for her clients at a premium price. The business had taken off like a rocket and she had to hire people to keep up. She was soon running a mini-empire for people under a yardstick high.

"My social media channels are growing. I now have fifty thousand followers."

Social media wasn't his thing, but he knew that was impressive. "Get outta here!" he gasped. "You sure you don't mean five thousand?" He saw her beam.

"Nope, fifty thou, as in five-o."

They heard the door close and rustling in the kitchen, and Jack barrelled out to confront a potential intruder.

"Hi," Charlotte called out, walking into the dining room. "I was driving by and saw Nicki's car, so I thought I'd say hi." Charlotte kissed her Dad on the cheek, but her attention focused on the table. "OMG, Nicki, is this your spring line?"

"Yeeesss!" Nicki shouted, unable to contain her excitement. "Do you want to see it?" Before they could reply, she pulled out a child-sized mannequin that displayed clothing. "Wait. You two turn around for a minute. Let me get this outfit on the form so that I can do a proper reveal."

What the hell is a reveal? Mark wondered. He was used to her enthusiasm, so he knew to go with it. He turned to Charlotte and chatted about her yoga classes.

"Okay, turn around!" Nicki shouted.

Mark pivoted and saw the most stylish outfit he'd ever seen for a five-year-old. The form was sporting a pair of jeans with pressed creases down the front, copper rivets on the pockets and a sporty sweater over the jeans. Plus, there was a navy pea jacket with classy metal buttons. It was as if Nicki had taken a fashionable man, waved a wand and shrunk him by eighty per cent.

Mark realized he was far too practical. All he could picture was an active kid rolling around in the dirt at the playground or spilling a fruit smoothie on an expensive outfit. But she knew her market, so he supported her. "Wow, Nick," he said, trying to find the right compliment. "Every grandparent will want to buy their grandkids an outfit."

"You think?" she asked, sounding pleased. "The military look is trending at the moment."

"Oh yeah," added Charlotte. "You've developed something very cool. It's like each person gets to design a unique piece for their kids."

Nicki nodded. "And I'm getting tags designed. Although the brand is Pint-Sized, underneath, it will say, "Designed exclusively for Oliver Anderson.""

Mark's eyebrows shot up in surprise. "Wow, you sure inherited your mother's talent for crafts and sewing!" Then he looked at Charlotte, who sometimes placed second in the attention-grabbing role as kids, only because Nicki was a raving extrovert. "And you, my dear Charlotte, inherited my love of sports and recreation." He saw Charlotte's crooked little smile and knew she was okay with everything.

Nicki was already busy packing up things, preparing for her next appointment. "Thanks, you two," she said. "It means a lot to me that you like my stuff."

"Of course, you're the best," said Charlotte. "I'm still waiting for the kids' yoga line so I can sell them at the studio."

"I haven't forgotten, Char. Perhaps the fall line." She set the form up on its stand and turned to her father. "I'm leaving this outfit here for a bit, Dad. Mrs. Silverman, who lives down the street, said she wants to see it. She's got seven grandchildren and is hoping for one-stop shopping for the lot of them."

"No problem, hon," said Mark through a cough. It took a second to stop, which annoyed the hell out of him with his daughters watching. He grabbed his water bottle to take a sip.

"I don't like the sound of that cough," said Nicki. "Do you think you should have it checked?"

Mark shook his head. "Nah, it flares up now and then. Nothing to see here, folks," he said, trying to end the inquiry before Nicki asked too many questions. "While you were assembling the outfit for the next toddler fashion show, Charlotte was telling me about redesigning the yoga studio."

"That so?" said Nicki. "What's new?"

Charlotte laughed. "Well, it's no biggie. This nice lady, Jenn Morrison, gave me some great ideas to help improve the storage of all the equipment and the flow. It will improve the look and organization of the place and make my life easier."

"Cool," said Nicki.

"But the interesting thing, Dad," said Charlotte. "It got me thinking about your place."

Oh boy, here we go, Mark thought. When Charlotte and Nicki started dreaming up ideas for him, it meant disruption and spending money. "What *about* my place? I like it the way it is."

"Dad, we have noticed you are kind of letting the place... how shall we say it... idle," said Charlotte. "You haven't cleaned out Mom's things, and a lot of stuff is starting to pile up everywhere." She waved her hand throughout the dining room to prove her point.

Mark shifted. "I haven't had time," he said. He noticed the suspicious look his daughters exchanged when they disagreed with him, a look that had started during their childhood. "I'll grant you, there are a few boxes, the guest room has some items and you girls are always dropping stuff off," he said, but then regretted it. "Which I appreciate, by the way, but I don't always know what to do with."

"And that's why someone like Jenn could be helpful," said Charlotte, quietly returning to her pitch. "She'll help you figure out what to keep and get rid of, and more importantly, how to optimize your space."

"Why spend money on something I could do myself?" sniffed Mark. He saw both of them scanning the room and he could tell they were thinking.

"Hang on," said Charlotte. "There's no 'big money spend' going on here," she said, using air quotes to emphasize her point. "I asked Jenn, and she would come over for a complimentary visit. She'll look around, make some suggestions and you can choose to do them or not. You're handy. All you need is some shelving, and you could do it yourself."

"I'll think about it," he said, knowing it was better to show he was considering their suggestions than simply shutting them down. They'd only talk louder and longer. Yes, they meant well, but he had boundaries. As soon as Nicki started to speak, he raised his hand to prevent her from launching into more persuasive techniques. It worked.

"Okay, Dad, we'll leave you to it," said Charlotte, giving him a big hug, followed by Nicki.

Mark watched as they resumed chatting about kids' clothing as they exited the house and continued to the driveway. Then they stood talking for another five minutes, but he sensed the topic had changed because he could see them glancing back and forth at the house and plenty of handwaving. He had to be careful before they got too enthusiastic about yet another project.

Mark sighed and wandered around assessing the state of the house. The girls were right, of course. The place looked frozen in time and stuff was gradually building up all over. So much of it was Annie's, and he had no idea what to do with the things—all he knew was that he felt a bit of comfort walking into the guest room where her sewing machine was still set up. Unfinished projects were piled up beside the machine. He was always amazed how she would arrive home with bags full of fabrics and weeks later, new curtains would show up in the kitchen.

There were lots of things he could get rid of, but somehow, he couldn't get going. What was his problem? He wasn't sure why he couldn't let go. In his heart, he knew it was because he felt guilty about her accident. While he didn't think about it as often as he used to, it didn't take much for his memory to switch back to that cold winter day three years ago. Annie wanted to visit her parents, as she often did. He reminded her that winter weather was always dicey. But when her Mom called and said she needed help with something (there was always something), Annie, the dutiful daughter, automatically said yes. He should have offered to drive her, but he didn't. And much worse, he didn't stop her from going.

If only he could have pressed rewind on his life and stopped her. When she drove home that evening, the weather suddenly shifted into freezing rain. Her car skidded off the road and hit a culvert. She died instantly.

On bad days, the guilt got to him and he sometimes wished it had been him. She was the star of the family and the loving force that held them all together. He knew he shouldn't go there, so he had to change his thoughts as the grief counselor had recommended.

He looked at Jack and said, "Walk?" Jack bolted to the door and waited impatiently while he gathered the leash, clean-up bags, bright toys and treats to keep him in line. This dog required a lot of attention and exercise, which served as the best distraction for him at the moment.

As he eased the door closed, he glanced at the big chalkboard that Nicki had given them for the kitchen. In the early days, Annie would post the weekend meal plans, which Mark loved. However, over the years, it had evolved into the To Do board. He teased her and begged her to return to the meals. She said she would once all the chores were finished.

Yet every time he completed a project and drew a line of chalk through it for a dopamine hit, a new task would appear the next morning. One morning, he feigned shock and asked, "How did this turn into a To Do list? I much prefer the family meals." Annie didn't miss a beat. "Crazy thing. I discovered this board has special powers. Every time I add a task, it magically gets done. Why would I stop that?" He laughed and hugged her. "It reminds me of that sign in my Great Uncle Hamish's pub in Scotland, 'Free Beer Tomorrow'. Drove his clients crazy."

He looked back at the To Do list that still had chores with Annie's handwriting. He couldn't bring himself to erase it, even if it were a daunting reno project he didn't want to do. Jack yipped lightly to get his attention. "Yeah, coming, Buddy," he said to the dog and led them outside.

Chapter 5
Mark

Startled by the alarm, Mark woke up and stared at the ceiling, trying to clear the foggy feeling in his head. While he had slept through the night, he didn't feel rested. He had set the alarm for 7 a.m. so that he would have plenty of time to get ready for his doctor's appointment, which he was dreading. Usually, he bounded into the doctor's office because he had been healthy all his life. As a gym teacher, trainer and coach, he had always been fit and proud of it. And for anybody who would listen, he'd beat the drum about the importance of staying healthy.

When he turned forty, he was fit and happy. He didn't miss a beat. His fiftieth birthday had surprised him, but he still felt full of energy and healthy. The bigger surprise was that ten years felt like they were racing by him at warp speed. Soon, he'd be sixty. He had to adjust the old cliché to "time flies whether you're having fun or not." How many times did he reach for his toothbrush before going to bed and think to himself, "Didn't I just do this a minute ago?"

Each day seemed to vaporize, even when he had nothing going on after the accident. When talking about the past, his timeline was divided into two eras: "with Annie" and "without Annie." After her passing, he was shocked by the life changes he could never have imagined. He had no idea how much of a ballast she had been in his life. He'd always pictured himself as the model of being grounded, together and independent. Yet, over the past few years, he felt he had lost his way. While he had sometimes accused her of nagging too much, she knew precisely when he needed it. He missed being in sync with someone who understood how he functioned best.

One of the biggest changes was feeling lost daily. Earlier in his life, he'd been busy every minute, craving a long weekend. After the accident, his day was like a massive blank void that he was supposed to fill—but he couldn't get started.

He never would have retired early if he had known Annie wouldn't be there to share the time with him. When she died, he could have returned to work as a substitute teacher, but he couldn't face the thought of it. He told the administrators he would get in touch when he was ready, but he hadn't done so.

So here he was in his late fifties, without much going on, and unable to make himself crawl out of the hole he'd dug. Without his daily physical activities and less-than-optimal meals replaced with high-calorie snacking, he'd put on some weight around the middle. He knew that Dr. Singh would notice; besides, Mark didn't need a scale to tell him he'd gained fifteen pounds. In addition to feeling it on his body, his buddies in the dining out group had nicknamed him Pudge. He was many things, but being chubby wasn't one of them. This was all temporary. Plus, there was a persistent cough that lasted like the lingering smell of a leftover dish at the back of his fridge. What the hell was happening to his body?

Getting ready to leave for the doctor's office, he put the dog in his crate. Jack started with some whining that morphed into a near-howl as Mark left the house. He knew the drill with a Jack Russell: go about your business, remind the dog who was boss in the household and not make a big fuss about leaving. Showing any sympathy to a dog that demanded endless attention would not turn out well.

Mark sat in the chair at the doctor's office and stared at the pages of a magazine scribbled over by bored children. He was miserable about this visit. Finally, he was invited to walk down the hall to a mint-green room and was asked to sit. He tried to avoid reading all the posters covering the walls, which reminded him of the various diseases and conditions that could befall him.

Dr. Sanjay Singh walked in, breaking into a big smile. Mark had been his teacher in high school and he always knew the kid was brilliant. His nerdiness led to some teasing by his classmates, but Mark told him they only did that because they were envious of his brain and high average. And even though he announced he'd rather play chess than basketball, Mark reminded him that gym class was obligatory. Mark had used good humor and gentle coercion to help him find some exercises that he liked. Sanjay was now a respected family doctor in town. They had a healthy respect for each other.

"Hello, Mark," said Dr. Singh, shaking his hand as he always did.

"Hi. What's up?" Mark asked a bit abruptly, wanting to get this appointment over with.

"Let's slow down a bit," said the doctor in a velvet tone. "I want to review your recent blood tests, check your blood pressure and ask a few questions. Let's start by putting you on the scale."

Damn. He took off his shoes; he figured they weighed a couple of pounds. He didn't want to add to his woes.

As he stepped on, Dr. Singh glanced at his files, then at the scale. "Hmmm," he said, looking at Mark.

"What?"

"How shall I say this? You are the ideal weight for a man who is four inches taller than you."

Mark stepped off the scale. "So, I don't need to lose any weight; I just need to grow another four inches."

Dr. Singh laughed. "Still cheeky, I see."

"I know I've put on a few pounds. I need to get my butt in gear."

"Spoken like a true gym teacher," replied Dr. Singh. "I think you told me to do that a few times in high school."

Mark laughed, which triggered his cough. It took a few rounds before he could stop it. This was the last person he wanted to know about his cough. He foresaw humiliation in his future.

After the doctor took his blood pressure and reviewed his file, he looked at Mark. "Look, your blood work is fairly good. Your cholesterol levels have nudged up, but you can control them by eating a healthier diet and being more active. Your blood pressure is up slightly, but you look stressed, so that may explain it. It was always low, so it's not an issue."

"I know, and I will, Doc," he said, his tone laced with shame. He stood up until Dr. Singh motioned for him to sit down.

"While you are here, I want to check your lungs." He put the stethoscope on and listened. "How long have you had that cough?"

He grimaced. "A few weeks, I guess."

"Do you mean weeks or months?"

"Maybe a bit longer than weeks." Mark knew it was stretching into a couple of months but didn't want to admit to it.

"Feeling tired?"

Mark paused. "Well, tired or lethargic."

"Fever or chills?"

"Not as much now," he said.

"Shortness of breath?"

"No. Maybe if I went for a run, I might," he joked.

"Do you have any lung problems in your family history?"

Mark sighed. He told the doctor that his grandfather had died of lung cancer, but he worked in the Cape Breton coal mines and smoked constantly, often lighting the next cigarette with the butt of the last. He still remembered visiting his grandparents in the tiny house wafting with stale smoke. He loved his grandad, but Mark and his older brother were always on "thumping" duty. When his grandpa got into a coughing jag, they took turns giving him a good thump. It was terrible to watch and that image stayed with Mark forever. He never wanted to be that unhealthy.

He explained that his father had moved to Halifax and worked as a laborer, anything to stay out of the coal mines. But he smoked too and ended up with a respiratory disease and later cancer. "Am I doomed, Doc?"

"Not necessarily. You didn't smoke, right?"

"Never," said Mark.

Dr. Singh stood up. "Good. I'm going to send you for an X-ray to make sure all is fine. But don't worry about the results; it only makes you feel worse."

"Thanks," said Mark, shuffling out the door. Shocked with what had unfolded, he walked out into the sunshine and headed to Point Pleasant Park in the South End. Dr. Singh was right. Yes, he felt humiliated for being called out as a chubby sloth, but the doctor had a point. Mark understood the tough love concept and used it in coaching because it worked.

He would still fret over the X-ray—his family history worked against him—but he'd have to wait for the results. In the meantime, he could increase his walks with Jack. Jack would love him for it and he could start shedding the wretched spare tire clinging to his waist. No wonder his jeans felt a little tight. If he didn't smarten up, he'd be forced to go shopping for new pants. That alone was enough motivation to get him back into exercising.

Chapter 6
Jenn

JENN PULLED INTO MAGGIE's driveway and jumped out of the car. Maggie had sent her a cryptic text about an exciting business opportunity. Jenn loved working with Maggie—she was a professional stager, and Jenn was a space organizer. They never knew what contracts would materialize, so adventures ranged from staging luxury downtown condos overlooking Halifax harbor to managing interior film sets for some of the romance movies shot in the towns of Mahone Bay and Lunenburg. Nova Scotia's Victorian homes on the South Shore were always a treat to convert into picturesque inns.

Jenn knocked and strolled into the house. "Hello!"

"Be right down," shouted Maggie from upstairs.

"Okay," Jenn replied, heading into the kitchen to make coffee. She reached for her favorite mug, which had been custom-made for Maggie and said, "Organized people are just too lazy to look for things." She popped a pod into the machine, pushed a button and waited for a foamy latté. Then she made a mug for Maggie.

Jenn eyed the counter, piled up with the morning breakfast dishes from a family of six getting ready for work and school. There were abandoned crusts of toast, sludgy cereal bowls and glasses of milk and juice rings over every counter. Between sips, Jenn loaded the dishwasher and pushed the start button.

"Bless you," said Maggie, entering the kitchen. "I always plan to load the dishwasher as soon as everybody leaves, but the morning vaporizes before I get around to it."

"No problem, Mags. With Kyle away, I have it easy at home with dishwashing. So, I don't mind this."

"And how is your amazing son doing in Thailand?"

"Great," said Jenn. "Kyle and Achara are having a fantastic time. She's from Chang Mai in the north, so they are staying there while they figure things out."

"Is he still teaching English?"

"Yes, and so is Achara. That's how they met at the school. She was training to be an English as a Second Language teacher. I'm excited for them, but I secretly hope they move back to Nova Scotia."

"Do you talk often?"

"Oh yeah," said Jenn. "We use online phone and video apps. Plus, he texts me photos and messages all the time. I miss him every minute, but I'm so happy for him. He's twenty-six, full of energy and wanderlust, so it's the best time to travel."

"No kidding," said Maggie, walking to the dining table, eyeing the piles of paper, as if trying to figure out what to do with them. She pushed everything to one end and opened her laptop.

"Right, so what's so exciting, Maggie? Wait... this isn't another blind date, is it?"

Maggie laughed. "Sorry about the one last week. Would you rather I didn't keep an eye open for eligible guys?"

Jenn paused and sighed. While she regretted all the wasted time on first dates in cafés, she knew Maggie had her best interests at heart. "I suppose I won't meet anybody by standing back, while life rushes by, will I?"

"Exactly. I promise to be more discerning before I lunge at some poor guy on your behalf. It's only because the number of eligible partners dwindles after fifty and—"

"Don't remind me," groaned Jenn. "However, I'd rather wait for the right one than grab anyone off the shelf. Is it so hard to find a decent guy who's fun, interested in activities and sharing a laugh?"

"Careful what we try to manifest. Or is your memory that short?"

"Which one? There have been a few." Jenn blew a raspberry. "Do you mean when I set an intention to meet a guy who loved to dance?"

"I forgot about him. What was his name?"

"Charles R. Beauregard. Technically, he met the request—he was a fabulous dancer. But I soon realized we wouldn't be a couple. At the ballroom dancing classes, we called ourselves the *Gay-Divorcee* couple. He was gay and in his twenties, and I was divorced and in my forties. We laughed the whole season."

"Didn't you have nicknames for each other?"

"I called him 'Twinkle Toes' and he called me 'Wrinkle Toes.' We teased each other mercilessly."

"At least you had some fun."

"Yes, I still see him around. He's doing well."

"I was thinking more recently," Maggie said, sipping her coffee. "You know, Halston. Remember when we got cheeky with the vision board?"

"We? It was you!" Jenn thought back to four years earlier on New Year's Day.

She and Maggie had decided to create vision boards together. They had the essentials: colored markers, poster board and a bottle of prosecco. The wine wasn't the best idea because it made them bold, and Jenn didn't do bold. She left that to Maggie because it was baked into her DNA, like Maggie's Mom.

Jenn sometimes watched her fun-loving friend's behavior and wished she could be the wild one at the party, but she wasn't cut out for it. Jenn was more like the helpful guest on the sidelines, mopping up spilled drinks, replenishing crackers and cheese plates, and reorganizing nuts so the bowls would look full.

Mind you, she was no wallflower. Jenn moved lightly and happily through life, enjoying activities with her friends and thinking the best of people.

Unlike other years, when she created her vision board in January and looked back in December to review what hadn't been delivered, this session felt different. She and Maggie had taken a workshop and were coached to seek meta goals. "Aim higher and bolder, ladies!" urged the workshop leader. "Allow the universe to sort out the details."

After years of setting achievable and boring goals, she summoned the courage to focus on love. She conjured up exciting images of her dream guy with the two of them cycling, beach walking and watching sunsets. Of course, these were activities everybody mentioned on dating app profiles, but they rarely materialised.

After her second glass of prosecco and her personality getting bubblier by the minute, she had finished cutting out all the visuals they needed from the lifestyle magazines. However, something unusual happened with Maggie's visuals that changed everything. In the scrap pile, Maggie turned over a photo. On the back, she paused and said, "Well, well, what do we have here? Here's a random phrase that says, 'Date a royal.'"

"And this is important because...?" Jenn asked.

Maggie gulped from her glass. "I think this is a sign from the universe. What do you think?"

"News flash. You are married."

Maggie sighed. "Not me, you dork. You."

"Mags, it's a piece of paper from a scrap pile that has a random phrase on it. This is not a sign."

"You forget my Mom and Granny had the gift."

Jenn laughed. "I know *they* did, I'm not so sure about you. You have moments, but you haven't honed your skills, so your predictions can be a bit quirky and mixed up."

"Harrumph. Maybe a few have crashed and burned, but this feels different. Why not try it? What's the worst that can happen?"

"You aren't taking this vision board seriously," said Jenn.

"Of course I am. You are just chicken shit scared."

"Nope. I've learned a great deal about dating and failed relationships over the years. I'm practical." Jenn took another sip.

"Dare ya. Double dog dare ya!" Maggie teased.

Jenn blew out a breath. "Just like when we were kids, eh? You were always egging me on to do something I didn't want to do. Why is this so important?"

"The word 'prince' keeps pinging around my head. Humor me, okay?" she added, gluing the paper gently on Jenn's board. "Could be fun."

"Like I have a choice!" Jenn sighed as Maggie finished it.

"Happy New Year. And here's to new beginnings and some royal dude sweeping you off your feet," toasted Maggie.

Months later, the universe proved that Maggie needed more practice, and it had a sense of humor. Technically, it delivered a prince who swept Jenn off her feet—except his name was Prince, not his role in life. And unfortunately, she was standing on that rug when he whipped it out from under her. *Really, universe? Is that supposed to be funny?* Jenn sighed as she remembered how events unfolded.

Early on, she found the guy quite intriguing, which Maggie called her "prince win." Yet Jenn would learn a tough life lesson: when falling in love with someone who seems too good to be true, you don't jump headlong into something, ignoring red flags and nagging intuition. Yet that's what Jenn Morrison had done.

It all started when her girlfriend, Beth, invited her to spend the weekend at her cottage in Chester. A quick sprint from Halifax, Chester was a beautiful seaside resort hamlet on the Atlantic Ocean that slept quietly in the winter and blossomed into a sailing and party destination in the summer.

Sailboats dotted the harbor, bobbing up and down in the white-capped waters, with diamond sparkles pinging on the waves like starbursts in every direction. When the sun shone in the summer, people strolled through the village looking happy and relaxed. As a result, Chester became a magnet for wealthy people from other places. Summers were a frenzy of fun, sailing and partying that reached a feverish pitch during Race Week for sailboats. Jenn remembered these times fondly because she had lived there in her twenties and worked as a server in restaurants and bars.

Since Beth lived in Chester year-round, she received endless invitations to social events. While lots of gatherings were at people's homes and the yacht club, there was just as much socializing at the Mainsail Tavern. That's where Beth and Jenn had grabbed a late afternoon drink and were in full chat mode when Halston Prince walked by. He knew Beth, and as soon as she introduced Jenn to him, sparks flew.

In no time, they were swapping rapid-fire barbs. Halston invited both of them to his home for a gathering the next day. After he left, Jenn casually asked if he was in a relationship. Beth joked, "I think he's between flops." She couldn't remember if he was on his second or third marriage, and wondered if he even remembered. But as Jenn learned later on, there's nothing like the fog of multiple cocktails to make everyone look gorgeous and sound charming rather than alarming.

Before heading to the party, Jenn looked him up online and saw that he owned business projects in the northeastern U.S. When she and Beth turned onto the tree-lined road leading to his massive property on the ocean, she gasped. Beth explained it was only one of his places.

Halston Prince's custom-built home and sprawling acreage was designed by one of the region's top architects. She recognized the signature style. She was glad that she wore her favorite designer outfit, which made her feel confident, despite fighting the "I don't belong here" feeling that plagued her at rich people's homes.

When he opened the door, he looked happy to see Beth and even more delighted to see Jenn. He led her outdoors to the patio and invited her to grab a chair. He peppered her with questions. And when he found out she was a professional organizer, in no time, they were sharing drinks and Jenn was drawing ideas for him on the back of a large cocktail napkin. She couldn't help herself; when she entered a home, she immediately started looking for ways to improve or upgrade it. However, his home was so new and luxurious, she couldn't imagine changing anything.

Yet his question about how to change the place surprised her: he was focused on the outdoors. He pointed to an unused tennis court languishing off to the side of the property, vines inching up the side of the fence. He explained that his children had barely used it and ditto for the pool. And now that they had run off to college, nobody was using the tennis court. When she asked if his wife was using it, he skimmed over it, saying that his second wife had moved on. That led to a conversation about why he wanted to make any changes.

He explained that, although he owned several houses in other places, he loved Chester and the town's vibe. He was a successful businessman who traveled often, but he explained that the downside was that his social life had faltered. He liked meeting people and entertaining, but he couldn't find a way to bring people together at his home. Especially at his age; he was sixty. He acknowledged that his ex had orchestrated their social calendar in Chester, and he hadn't liked most of the people she brought over for weekly cocktails. The invitees all talked about the same thing; and slowly got tipsy, complaining about their lives, their kids, their aches and pains.

He told her he was more interested in a healthier lifestyle and had invited people to come over any time to play tennis, with lots of positive replies, but no uptake. He wondered if a renovated tennis court or pool would solve the problem. As the afternoon wore on, Halston and Jenn became more animated in their conversation, which had morphed into a consultation.

Jenn pointed out that there was nothing wrong with the outdoor facilities, which were top of the line, but they needed some landscaping love. She suggested a new pergola structure to link the outdoors with the indoors, improving traffic flow and making the space appear more inviting. Yet, she didn't believe the house and recreational facilities were the problem. After several hours of discussing his lifestyle, values, dreams, and wants, a crazy idea struck her.

When she asked how often he played tennis, he replied that he hardly played at all. He explained that it was too much running around the court, and few people his age were playing anymore—there were knee issues, tennis elbow, and the frantic bursts of running. That left younger players who ran him ragged on the court. He said he no longer enjoyed playing.

Jenn's brain was racing as he talked. When he finally took a breath, she blurted, "Have you considered a pickleball court instead of tennis?" He paused and said, "No, but go on." He said he played at his condo in Arizona.

She suggested that the tennis court could easily be converted into a pickleball court. They walked to the court with a tape measure. She said if they reconfigured it sideways, it could fit two courts. Suddenly, she could see wheels turning. Jenn suggested he poll his friends to ask if they'd be interested in playing pickleball instead of tennis.

When he reached out to them, his inbox was flooded with enthusiasm and questions about when the courts would be ready. In no time, contractors were retrofitting the tennis court into two pickleball courts, and he added an overhead mesh structure that shaded the court on hot days. Soon, Jenn was learning pickleball. She had played racket sports and badminton in her younger years, so she caught on pretty quickly. As the project neared completion and people were lining up to play with Halston and his friends, she was holding her own with locals in a league she called the Friday Afternoon Championships.

They formed a ragtag league of mixed teams and they came up with team names, like The Dill Pickles. The local bakery owner's team was The Bread and Butter Pickles. The musicians were the Pickled Beats, the Jewish group, the Kosher Pickles and the dog kennel owners were called the Chow Chows. The Spaniards in town were called the Pickled Jalapenos, and the French were known as the Cornichons. On and on it went. When they ran out of pickle names, the young lawyers called themselves Court in Session. It seemed like everybody in the village had joined the fun, and no wonder, Halston was so generous with his free courts, food and drink.

They shared endless moments at his place over pickleball, swimming and Friday night cookouts. Soon she was staying over on most weekends. At some point, it occurred to them that they were not only dating but now in a relationship.

By winter, he was begging her to join him in Arizona. She went for a couple of weeks, but reminded him she had a business to run back home. He was dismissive, telling her not to worry about her business or money. However, deep inside, she loved being an organizer and didn't want to give up her business. Yet she was still caught in a wave of fun. In the early summer, when they opened up the house in Chester, people showed up at Halston's place in droves. It felt like living in *The Great Gatsby*.

By the end of summer and the last tournament of the season, Halston had one more surprise for her. In front of a large group of people enjoying their cocktails, he grabbed the karaoke mic and proposed to her. She was shocked: it hadn't occurred to her that he would suggest getting married. And knowing he was on his third or fourth trip down the aisle, she was starting to think he was either a slow learner or that he was the problem.

A thought bubble hovered over her head, asking, *Are you sure about this?* She felt uneasy about the idea of a guy orchestrating a surprise proposal in front of a crowd. It put far too much pressure on her to say yes or risk being a buzz kill in front of an intoxicated crowd who only wanted a reason to cheer.

She knew better. Yet caught up in the excitement and feeling pressure from the chanting crowd, she conjured up a people pleaser smile and a nod, hoping that was enough to show interest without full commitment. Halston assumed it was a done deal. Suddenly, bottles of champagne flowed.

The next morning, as Jenn sipped her coffee on the chaise longue, she rehashed her concerns about how they might work as a couple. She felt uneasy, realizing that she didn't know him that well. Despite her attempts, they had never had a deep or soulful conversation about life, their dreams, or their worries. Not once. She figured that with his wealth, he either didn't have many worries or simply threw money at them to solve the problems.

They had never faced any obstacles as a couple, only light-hearted fun and sex. It reminded her of when she was dating in her twenties and didn't have a care in the world, thinking only of herself. While it felt fun at first, she realized things had changed in her fifties and the superficial dating thing had lost its charm. But Halston didn't. He thrived on whatever was in front of him and what was the most fun.

When he went on business trips, their calls and texts would often trail off. At first, Jenn brushed it off because they were both busy, but she felt a bit guilty that she didn't miss him, nor did she think about him when he was gone. The time in between calls grew longer and was mainly spent with him updating her on his business pursuits. He had only shown a sign of romance once—when he proposed. In her world, romance was about two people in love showing how much they cared about each other, offering little flourishes of love at unexpected times and places.

Many months later, she decided they either had to work harder on their relationship or call it off. She made a surprise visit to Arizona and got the shock of her life. Halston had met someone a lot younger and prettier than her, with plenty of time on her hands and a deep love of spending money. Jenn could hardly process what she saw. When she confronted him, he first denied it, then admitted it had started six months earlier—very innocently, he noted—as if to soften the blow.

Furious, she flew back home. On the airplane, she realized her earlier concerns were valid: she didn't know him at all. She didn't know much about his past, his marriages, his kids, his life—he was too focused on himself. And he was busy living in the moment, which translated to hanging out with friends, tending to his latest fling and making a fortune. Relieved they hadn't found time to marry, she vowed to have a good cry and move on. She didn't care about his money but felt crushed by the whole mess. And she vowed she wouldn't get hurt like that again.

Jenn heard a repeating sound and realized Maggie was snapping her fingers right in front of her face. "Jenn, are you still here? You're off in another world."

"Sorry. I was thinking back to that time with Halston—all for nothing. My track record is terrible. It's like I keep getting pickled in love."

"Translation for us non-pickleball players?" asked Maggie.

"In pickleball, when you beat somebody eleven to zero, you've pickled them. And that's what it feels like for me these days when it comes to love. Starts with a sizzle and ends with a fizzle. Eleven to zero."

"So, the prince turned out to be a frog. Or make that toad," shrugged Maggie.

"I should have listened to my Grandma. She said, 'Never let a fool kiss you, or a kiss fool you.'"

"Smart lady. Anyway, you had an adventure, and you became a good pickleball player."

"I suppose. Learning pickleball has been amazing and I've met a ton of nice people in Halifax," Jenn said, taking a slow drink.

Maggie set her mug down. "Okay, enough of the past. It's time to think about the future. I've got a very cool television project to tell you about."

Chapter 7
Mark

MARK HEARD A CAR horn honk twice. His brother Kevin always announced his arrival with an impatient double honk, even when he was early. Mark walked to the window and waved to him, then headed for the hallway to grab his coat and wallet.

Ten years older than his little brother, Kevin had teased Mark endlessly throughout their childhood. However, he had eased up since Annie's passing. To get Mark out of the house, a group of friends had created a bi-weekly pub outing and trivia night, finally convincing Mark to participate. Mark knew that Kevin had offered to pick him up, so he couldn't bail at the last minute. They'd been gathering weekly for a year, and now they were in the rhythm of it, all the guys enjoyed the outing. They talked, insulted each other, complained, shared sports scores and teased each other about stuff.

"Kev," said Mark, climbing into he truck.

"Hey, little brother," joked Kevin.

"Funny. I may be your little bro, but guess what, Kevin? I'm turning sixty this year, which means you are turning seventy. HA HA!"

Kevin gave him his usual punch to the arm and put the truck in reverse. "What's up with you seeing the doctor about that cough of yours and your lungs?"

Mark sighed. "How the hell did you know that?"

Kevin laughed. "C'mon, who do you think? Nicki always calls up Veronica and spills all the beans about you. Then Veronica tells me. Now, don't avoid the question. What gives?"

"No biggie," said Mark, dismissing the comment with a wave of his hand. "It's just to confirm what we all know: this cough is from a lingering cold."

Kevin pulled up to a four-way stop and looked over at Mark. "Well, Doc Singh isn't going to waste an X-ray on you for a cold. That guy is so frugal that he'd put both of us in an X-ray if he thought he could save a buck for the healthcare system."

"Well, he's the one who told me not to worry," replied Mark.

Kevin shrugged. "That's his job, right? Don't fret, he'll tell you. You and I both know there are lung problems on Dad's side."

"Of course. But there's nothing to be done until I get the results," he said, gazing out the window. Mark noticed Carl Baird on the sidewalk. Happy to find a way to change the subject, he rolled down the window and shouted, "Look what the cat dragged in!"

Carl gave him a nasty finger signal and laughed. Mark rolled his window back up and hoped that Kevin wouldn't keep pressing him about the X-ray. He was already worried enough and didn't need his brother rhyming off all the relatives who were sick or dying from lung problems. The two brothers didn't do well sharing emotions or fears.

By the time Kevin swung the truck into the pub's driveway, he had already started scanning the parking lot for the others. "Uh-huh. I see T-Bone's car, Lonny, Jeff and Tyrone. The gang's all here."

Mark was relieved that Kevin dropped the doctor conversation. They walked into the pub over by the pool table. It was the perfect spot for them to order dinner and play a game or two of pool before the trivia started. They were all good in certain subjects, but not brilliant in all. Mark had joked that, together, they added up to one brain.

In no time, they were insulting each other and Mark was fending off cheap shots about being pudgy. His recent weight gain was yet another health concern, but he pretended it didn't bother him at all. He knew the drill: return bigger insults than he received and they'd stop. They did pretty well in trivia that evening, placing third out of ten. And Mark did his best to focus on the friendly banter, but he worried about what was going on in his body.

Chapter 8
Jenn

"You say a television producer contacted you? Do tell," said Jenn, leaning in. The two friends had collaborated on productions in the past, and Jenn loved the excitement of a new project, especially for TV.

Maggie topped up her coffee and sat at the kitchen table. "Well," she said, stretching out the word as she scrolled the company's website. "This is Blue Tartan Media, an indie company based in Nova Scotia. They produce a variety of different shows. Their new series is called *Clutter Bye Homes*."

"I like it already," laughed Jenn. "And I'll bet it focuses on reorganizing homes that have too much stuff and are out of control."

"Nailed it. They're shooting six shows in Nova Scotia. And they are searching for different types of families—some with kids, a couple with pets, retirees, blended families and a student apartment shared by four or five students."

"I like the variety."

"Yes, and they'll all have one thing in common: chaos and clutter. They are good people doing their best, but due to their busy lives, maintaining their homes has taken a back seat. The producers don't want to shame these people; they want to bring peace to their lives by transforming their homes from a state of chaos to calm. In addition, they want viewers to learn tips to inspire them to make positive changes in their homes."

"I love the concept," said Jenn. "Very straightforward. What would we do?"

"Manage the home refresh. Our job is to work with a team including a handy person, a carpenter, a cleaner and a social media person. We would first review the house together, then prepare a plan for repairs, storage systems, new paint, different furniture or whatever."

"Okay, and then what?"

"We start by removing everything from the house and setting it up in a large storage space. And with gentle coaching, we will help the residents identify all the stuff they no longer need or want. With your background in psychology and years of experience supporting people who are downsizing or reorganizing, you'll help them navigate a big change. Once they select what they want to keep, we repack the goods and store everything for a week. We'll then hold a sale with the rest of the items they no longer want, and the owners will get some money in their pockets. Any unsold items are donated to charity."

"Sounds like a decent concept," said Jenn.

Maggie continued. "Here's the twist: whatever changes we propose as a team, we can't spend any additional money. We will rely on labor and recycling as much as possible from the contents of the house. We will have a social media page, and we can post updates, ask for items, sell and trade things. So, if we need paint, we don't go to the paint store, unless they are donating it. If we want to redo furniture, we can either use the existing furniture or trade online. Plus, many have families and friends who will want to help out."

"Wow... that sounds exciting and exhausting," laughed Jenn. "I love the emphasis on recycling and reusing. Halifax has a long history of curbside giveaways and donating to charity, so I think it will be an easy sell."

"Are we up for this?"

"Totally," said Jenn. "When would it happen? I have a few projects on the go and it's important that I meet my obligations."

"Of course, me too. It will be in a few months' time and the shooting will take place over eight weeks. We will be busy in spurts, with time in between to do other things."

"You in, Maggie?"

"One hundred per cent if you are. If yes, we have to send a proposal, a budget, bios for each of us and a professional photo. Piece of cake."

"Wait, Maggie. Do they know our ages? Well, I mean me. You're in your forties and look great, but I'm fifty-five. Not exactly star quality."

"This isn't *Housewives of Halifax*," laughed Maggie. "I already sent them footage of us working together. They want real people of all ages and backgrounds."

"That's a relief."

"You know what sold them on us as a team?" asked Maggie.

"What?"

"We work seamlessly together, but we also have lots of laughs. That will help to lighten the burden of people trying to face a major change in their lives. Since you're in, we can get started on the proposal. I'll keep you posted," said Maggie.

"Great," said Jenn. "What else is going on this week?"

"I'm working on a real estate staging in the west end. It's a great old home with some nice upgrades, but, as usual, it's a mess. I can whip that house into shape in no time. You?"

"I have an appointment with a guy whose daughters believe his life will improve with a little help from an organizer. He lost his wife a few years ago and sounds like he's having a hard time clearing out."

"Is he on for this change?"

Jenn smiled. "That's the burning question. His two daughters say yes, for sure, but we'll see. We both know that family members mean well, but sometimes they can get pushy when they believe they are helping."

"You're good at reading the room. I know you'll figure out if his daughters are pressuring him. And, if you do work with him, you'll do a fantastic job of making changes without steamrolling him."

"That's the plan," said Jenn. "And now I have to get ready for the meeting." She gave Maggie a big hug and left the house.

Chapter 9
Jenn

JENN DROVE AROUND THE North End of Halifax, taking in the lovely neighborhoods that had sprouted up over the past hundred years. Back when she was in a running group, they had run these streets many times, so she was familiar with the houses.

She drove up Isleville Street, crossing Duffus before turning into Drummond Court, an enclave of cozy homes built out of red brick, unlike most older homes in Halifax that were constructed out of wood. Drummond Court had thirty houses nestled around a square. Since it was quiet and had an old-fashioned setting, families tended to stay there for a long time.

She pulled into the driveway and turned off the car. She was ten minutes early, so she pulled out her notebook and reviewed the notes from her discussion with Charlotte. She remembered the keywords: *widower, rooms disorganized and filling up with crap, not functioning well*. She wondered if Charlotte meant that the house wasn't functioning well, or that her father wasn't.

A burst of activity in the living room window caught her eye: a small white and brown dog barking and jumping vertically on the top of the sofa, giving her the gears. She opened the glove box and grabbed a couple of dog treats, stashing them in her left pocket. Then, she added cat treats to her right pocket, in case there were multiple pets. She saw a man come to the window and glance out. His hair looked like the roots of a green onion sprouting randomly, possibly caused by a nap.

Jenn got out of the car and walked to the side door, which led to the kitchen. Traditionally, many Nova Scotians used the side door because the front door was saved for special guests, and nobody assumed they were special.

She knocked on the door and could hear the dog barking furiously right by the door. Nobody answered the door right away, so she stood quietly waiting another thirty seconds before knocking again. As she raised her hand to knock, the door edged opened. He had tamed his wild hair since looking out the window. He coaxed a smile to show he wasn't scary, but she sensed unease.

"Hi there, you must be Mark," Jenn beamed.

"Yes, and you are?" he asked in a pleasant yet cautious tone used by someone getting ready to say no to a salesperson.

"I'm Jenn Morrison, from Happy Space Organizing. Your daughter, Charlotte, asked me to come and have a look at your place."

He opened the door. "Sorry, I forgot you were coming today."

"No problem. Is this still a good time?"

He shrugged and waved her in, while the dog prepared for battle. "Jack," he clipped. "Stop barking." Jack looked annoyed by the command but stopped.

"And who is this cute little bruiser?" asked Jenn.

"This is Jack."

Jenn held out her hand for Jack to check out. "Is it okay if I give him a doggie treat?"

Mark half-smiled. "Sure, but he needs to earn it. Come in," he said, swinging the door open.

"I come prepared when visiting homes," laughed Jenn. "I have dog treats in my left pocket, and *c-a-t* treats in my right."

"In that case, give him a cat treat instead; he'll love the idea of stealing a snack from a cat," he said, bending over and petting Jack.

Jenn took off her boots and set them aside on the mat. Sensing a bit of reticence in his voice and seeing how he interacted with Jack, she wanted to build a friendly connection before launching into a conversation about his home organizing abilities.

"How old is he?" she asked as she held up the treat for Jack to grab.

"About two years old. I rescued him from the pound. Actually, he found me and wouldn't let me leave without him," Mark chuckled.

"What kind is he?" she said, slipping another treat to the dog to earn his trust.

"He's a Jack Russell terror."

Jenn tilted her head. "You mean *terrier?*"

"Nope, he's a terror, all right. I knew from day one."

"I see," Jenn laughed and then paused. "Wait a minute." She flipped through her notes. "Your last name is Russell. So... he's called Jack Russell?"

Mark burst out laughing. "You're quick. Yes, I couldn't resist."

Score, she thought. He looked so much better when he laughed. It seemed like that was his natural demeanor rather than the way Charlotte had described him: a formerly fit gym teacher and coach who now appeared uninterested and lethargic in life. He wasn't tall, well under six feet, but he looked strong when he stood up straight. While his hair was a bit messy, it was a rich walnut brown, with wisps of gray on the side that gave him street cred. And somewhere, deep in those blue eyes with strong creases, she sensed a funny guy who would laugh again given the chance. She wanted to keep the positive vibes going. "How did you get the idea to name him Jack—aside from the chance to crack up your home organizer with a once-in-a-lifetime canine pun?"

Mark picked up Jack and petted his head. "He was a young pup at the SPCA. They called him Pookie, and he refused to answer to it. I didn't blame him, so I renamed him. Worked like a charm."

They walked into the kitchen. He looked slightly awkward. "Do you want a cup of tea or something?"

Jenn waved her hand, "No thanks, I'm good." She saw a look of relief on his face as if boiling the kettle might have been too big an ask, or else he was out of tea. "This is a lovely home you have. Great bones, as we say."

His face turned red. "It's kind of a mess at the moment."

"I blame Jack," she joked.

He set the dog down. "Good one," he said. "So, I know nothing about this visit. My daughter organized everything. What are we supposed to be doing?"

Jenn took a breath, now ready to ease into the purpose of her visit. "First of all, Mark, I am so sorry for your loss. Charlotte told me about your wife's passing. I can't imagine how tough that must have been."

"Thanks," he muttered, staring at his shoes.

Jenn paused briefly because sometimes people wanted to talk about it, and once they got started, they couldn't stop. He didn't say anything else, so Jenn continued. "People ask me to come to their home for different reasons. Usually, when there's a change, such as people moving in or out, children leaving home, the home is out of control, or nothing functions well anymore. I look at the space to get a feel for the rooms, the storage systems and the functionality. Then we have a good conversation about how you use it daily, and for special occasions or entertaining."

"That's easy. I don't do any entertaining," he joked.

Jenn understood it was important to listen and not argue. "Okay, that's fine. Shall we have a walk-through and you tell me about each room?"

"Well, not much to say about the kitchen."

"Do you cook at all, Mark?"

He chuckled. "Hang on here, this will answer your question." He rustled in a drawer under a pile of flyers and pulled out a large envelope. "I recently finished a cooking class, 'Entrees for One.' Here's the certificate they gave me."

Mark passed the paper to her. She read it out loud, "Let's see. 'Least Likely to Succeed as Chef.'" She saw Mark smile as she handed it back. "I take it you were neither surprised nor insulted by this award."

"Nah, they were having fun. They're a great bunch. A few of them take pity on me and occasionally drop off a meal or a treat," he said, pointing to the leftover containers on the kitchen island.

Jenn moved them to the dining room, which had open doors to the living room and the hallway. The tablecloth was pushed to one end, and it was full of items. Around the walls, boxes were piling up on the floor, plus a buffet and a large china cabinet. "How often do you use this room for dining?"

"Not once since Annie died. My daughters do all the hosting now for birthdays, Christmas and holidays."

Jenn looked around. While she could guess the answer, she wanted to hear his description. "I see. So, how do you use this room?"

Mark drew in a breath. "It's a walk-through room and the dining room table threatens to spiral out of control with stuff. I call this table 'shipping and receiving' because my daughters are always dropping things off or picking them up."

Jenn laughed. "That's a great description." She liked his humor, and he was sounding more relaxed than when she arrived.

He continued. "There's a pile of mail here that needs attention, and projects, like my daughter's designer clothes for toddlers, as well as casseroles and dishes," he said, stacking them. "From well-meaning people who drop off food. And I know I should return the dishes at some point."

They walked into the living room, which had evolved from a formal room into a man cave. "This is mission control here, for me and Jack," he said, pointing to the center of the room, which included a recliner, an end table full of remotes and snacks, a dog bed near the chair, and a giant TV screen on the wall. On the other side of the room was a treadmill, with a towel and a t-shirt hanging from the handle.

"I see," said Jenn. "Looks like it works well for you." She noted his smile when she made that statement. She knew that people sometimes misunderstood the role of an organizer. She wanted him to see she didn't come to pass judgment on spaces; she went in to help people optimize their home for their needs.

They wandered upstairs and poked their heads in each room. One was his daughter's former bedroom, now a guest room, which Mark said hadn't had any visitors in years. The other was Annie's sewing and craft room, which Mark hadn't touched since her passing. And then there was the principal bedroom, which had some design elements, and a bed that looked like he had started to make it and lost interest halfway through the task.

"There's one more space I guess you should see," said Mark when they came back downstairs. "In the basement."

"Lead on," said Jenn, bracing herself for something weird or disgusting. Many homes with basements had become nightmare storage areas filled with kids' toys, broken appliances, cobwebs, and items that everybody thinks they'll use someday but never do.

When she got to the bottom of the stairs, she stopped. "Oh," she said.

"Surprised?"

"Clean and tidy. A rarity in my business." She scanned the area. There was a furnace in the corner, a laundry area with storage and a place to hang clothes to dry, a tidy workbench with all the tools stowed properly.

"I insist on law and order in the basement," he said.

"What's this separate area with a door?"

"That is a small apartment."

"Anybody live here?" she asked before walking in.

"Not for years," he said, showing her into the space. "We have an adopted son who came to us as an angry teenager. He'd been thrown out of the house by his father, who had some serious mental health issues. He didn't want to live upstairs or put the girls out of their bedrooms—long story," he added, in a matter-of-fact tone.

"It's not a bad space. At least there are windows and natural light."

"I insisted on that for safety reasons, and of course, having as much light as possible for somebody living in the basement."

"Have you thought of renting it out? There are so many people desperate for a place to live in Halifax."

Mark started to answer, which turned into a cough. He looked slightly irritated while catching his breath. "I don't have the energy right now."

"I totally understand, Mark," she said, turning toward the stairs. "Don't mind me. I'm always optimizing spaces in my head." She felt sorry for the guy. He looked tired and discouraged. She could see his energy racing up and down peaks and valleys, depending on the room they were in. She sensed he was still grieving, and she knew he needed to tackle reorganization one day at a time or he'd be overwhelmed. "Shall we go back upstairs?"

They returned to the kitchen and sat at the island discussing the use of his home. Topics pinged in every direction. Her phone buzzed, which was a reminder of her next meeting in an hour. She said she needed to wrap up her work. She stood up and stretched. "Okay, Mark, this has been great. If you are interested in continuing with this project, I will go back to my office and review my notes. I'll present a proposal and if you like it, I will do up a budget and send you a quote."

"A quote?" Mark bristled. "Charlotte assured me there would be no charge."

"Not for today, of course. That's complimentary. Only if you decide to continue. And, of course, there's no obligation."

Mark went to speak and then stopped.

"What?"

"That's not how Charlotte explained it. She said you'd do the whole thing for free." He folded his arms. "I should have known it was a scam."

This is awkward. Jenn noted the shift in his demeanor. "Oh dear, there must be a misunderstanding."

"Yup, somebody misunderstood all right, but not me." He shifted back and forth, running his hand through his hair. "Why would I pay somebody to come in, nose around and then charge me a big fee to tell me what I already know?"

"Look, Mark, I am so sorry for the mix-up. And I have a rule of never pushing someone into something they neither want nor are willing to pay for. I've worked hard for years to build my business through word-of-mouth, so it's not in my best interest to be dishonest in how I represent my business." She placed a card on the island and slid on her boots. "Please accept my apologies and I'll let Charlotte know." Feeling a flush of embarrassment, she rushed out the door and got into her car.

She glanced up and saw Mark in the window, looking forlorn, yet defiant. Usually, she sat in her car to make notes and check messages after a meeting, but not here. She backed out quickly, drove around the corner, and turned the car off. She pulled in several deep breaths, letting out a sigh. She felt terrible for the guy. Did she mess up? Did Charlotte misunderstand? As a business owner, Charlotte surely knew she couldn't work for free. If they were family, freebies would be expected, but they didn't have any connection.

After a few minutes, she'd regained her sense of calm. While she didn't enjoy confrontation, she preferred to tackle things head-on before they turned into something bigger. She dialed Charlotte's number, and Charlotte picked up right away, sounding delighted to hear from her.

"Hi Charlotte, it's Jenn. I just wrapped up with your father…"

"Yes," she jumped in. "How'd it go?"

Jenn wasn't sure where to start. "Well, I think there was a big misunderstanding."

"How so?"

"At first, he was confused by what I could do for him, but as we walked and talked, he warmed up."

"Good. Then what?"

"As a wrap-up, I explained the process. I said if he wished to continue, I'd send him a quote to do the work."

"Did he freak out?" she squeaked.

"He was surprised. And he was adamant that I shouldn't be charging him. I explained that the first visit is complimentary. If he wanted to go ahead, there would be a charge."

"Whoops," Charlotte said quietly.

"What?"

Charlotte sighed. "My fault. Nicki and I know Dad needs help badly, but he'd never spend money. Nicki and I agreed that we would split the cost as a gift to him, but I forgot to tell you."

Jenn sighed. "Well, that explains it."

"I'm so sorry, Jenn. Of course, we expect to pay you. It didn't occur to me that money would come up in the first meeting. Even that now sounds naïve."

Jenn sat up a little straighter. At least she hadn't messed up. "It's okay, Charlotte. Nothing to forgive. I'm not sure if he's ready anyway, so nothing ventured and all that."

"Oh, he needs it all right. He just doesn't know it yet," she giggled. "Nicki and I need to work on him. First, I need to tell him we messed up, not you. I will come clean about our plan to pay for it as a gift. Then he can't say no. Will you give us some time, Jenn?"

"Of course. Give me a call if anything changes. But please keep in mind, I will not work with someone if they are against it." Charlotte agreed and hung up. Jenn had no idea if she'd be invited back—it could go either way. Too bad, because the longer she talked, the more ideas she had for his place.

Despite his grumpiness when he thought she was going to ambush him with a big invoice for organizing, she found him to be a fun guy. And he was attractive. She hoped he'd get in touch.

Chapter 10
Mark

As he watched Jenn slip out the side door, Mark considered calling her back to talk about what had just happened. That's what he did as a coach, and most of the time it solved the problem. And, if he could get Jenn to come back, he'd make it clear there'd be no money exchanged.

So typical of people these days. It's always about the money. Worse, he felt like he was being duped with the most common bait-and-switch tactic of salespeople. He should have seen it coming. Funny, she didn't seem that way when she arrived. He was quite enjoying the conversation they had had in the kitchen—they were talking about everything.

Aside from his two daughters, nobody had visited his home in a long time and having a visitor had felt good. His wife Annie had kept a steady stream of friends flowing through the house, with accompanying snacks for everybody who came by. Now, it was an echo-filled house with no energy. He hadn't realized how quiet it felt until somebody new was in it, making it feel lively again.

He walked into the living room and headed to the sofa, where Jack was perched, looking out the window with his little eagle eyes focused on the departing intruder. For once, Jack wasn't barking like he usually did to warn strangers off the property. Mark sensed Jack had taken to Jenn. Mind you, she had bribed him well, even convincing Jack to perform tricks to get his treats (Jack was known to walk away from treats if he was being played). But she was genuine in her attempt to make friends with the dog. That was impressive. It was obvious she liked dogs.

Mark had to admit he had taken a shine to her. She had the energy of someone who stayed fit. Her petite yet sturdy frame looked ready to move furniture or lift boxes, which he imagined she did safely by bending her hips and using her knees. Her hair was blondish and she smiled easily, her hazel brown eyes full of interest everywhere she looked in the house. And she had sparkle—not everybody had sparkle.

When he looked out the window, Mark saw Jenn glance up from behind the steering wheel. Their eyes met and they both got awkward looks on their faces. Suddenly, she backed out of the driveway in an S shape, narrowly missing the hedge on one side and the tiny fence on the other. He turned to Jack and chuckled, "She might be organized in the house, but not so much behind the wheel." With the car out of the driveway and Jack's job done, he ran down the side of the sofa and headed for his cushion on the floor.

Mark returned to the kitchen to tidy up but soon lost interest. He saw Jenn's card on the counter and reread it, flipping it over and back as if it might yield further information. He was still stewing about their exchange, though he also wondered if he was being a little harsh with her. When he called her out, he saw the flush of embarrassment on her face. She didn't do much to counter his assertion or propose ways to make it work. Instead, she left as fast as she could.

He knew he'd felt a bit off when he woke up that morning. Aside from not sleeping well, he was worn down and sluggish. And the damn cough was driving him crazy. After revisiting his family history of lung issues, he figured that the X-ray would reveal something dire. Only a few of the men on his father's side had landed safely in their fifties without lung problems, mostly cancer. Of course, there were a couple of ancient uncles who drank and smoked daily, and never exercised, yet lived into their eighties.

Mark felt discouraged. He had dedicated his life to staying healthy and now he'd be one of those guys that everybody pointed to, saying, "See that? Mark Russell ate well, drank moderately and exercised all the time, and look what happened to him!" Of course, he knew that many factors influenced what would happen to his body over his lifetime. Yet he felt frustrated because he realized that sometimes you did all the right things, and you still got a medical condition you didn't deserve.

He had felt on edge ever since Dr. Singh had ordered the X-ray. He could see that he was a bit impatient with his dining buddies. Even his daughters, whom he loved dearly, would sometimes give him a hard time. Yes, they meant well, but they overwhelmed him with all of their ideas, improvements, and projects that they thought he should be embracing. Meanwhile, he could think of a few things they could be doing to improve themselves, but he kept them to himself. He wished everybody would leave him alone or at least stop nagging him.

He looked over at Jack, curled up happily on his cushion. That's why he loved the dog so much. Jack was straightforward with his needs: walking, eating, managing intruders and sleeping by Mark's feet. Jack offered unconditional love for truly little in return.

Mark walked to the kitchen and grabbed the crackers and a jar of peanut butter. He knew he should ease up on the peanut butter, but today wasn't the day. It was his comfort food. He told himself he would have a few crackers, then take Jack for a walk.

As he relaxed into the chair, the phone rang in the kitchen. He walked back to pick up his cell on the counter. A wave of sweat washed over his face when he saw it was the doctor's office. The receptionist had called to make an appointment. He asked if he could get the results over the phone. She said no, the doctor wanted to speak in person. She could squeeze him in two days later. That sounded serious and he couldn't wait to hang up the phone. Now he was in a super funk, expecting the worst.

Chapter 11
Jenn

Jenn lit up when she saw her son's name on her video app. Between her work and his teaching in Thailand, plus a twelve-hour time difference, they had a small timeframe when they could speak. They texted back and forth every day or two, but nothing compared with the thrill of hearing her son's voice and seeing his face.

"Kyle!" she squealed. She could see Achara behind him. "And hello, Achara!"

"Hi Jenn, how's she going?" said Achara. They laughed to hear her speak like a Nova Scotian.

"Great. And how's your family, Achara?" asked Jenn, keen to hear about her world.

"Fine. They want to know when you are going to visit Thailand."

"That's so sweet," said Jenn. "Right now, I've got quite a bit going on with work and my fitness activities. I'm running a pickleball league, which wraps up with a tournament. Once that's done, I'm open."

"Well, there's a bowl of Khao Soi here with your name on it," said Achara.

"Not fair! You know egg noodle curry is my favorite," she laughed.

Achara said she'd say hello to the family for her and disappeared from the phone to let Kyle talk to his Mom.

"Wow," said Jenn. "Her English is improving."

Kyle nodded. "Her family and neighbors are all keen to learn too. Now I have to push them to teach me Thai."

"How is your teaching going?"

Kyle beamed. "It's wonderful. At first, we were at an international school in Bangkok, which was okay, but the city is chaotic. Then we moved closer to her family, and I love Chang Mai. It's much smaller, the pace is slower and people are so nice here. I hope you'll visit."

"I'd love that, Kyle. But that's part of my news. I may be working on a TV series for a while." She explained the concept of cluttered houses to him, which made him laugh.

"Sounds right up your alley," he said. "What else is going on?"

She brought him up to date with the milestones with their family and friends. "Speaking of that, have you been in touch with your father lately?"

"No," said Kyle. "He's busy with his second family and three kids. I'm a low priority."

"I saw him at the hardware store a few weeks ago. He was asking about you and wanted your email address."

"Same email as always. And of course, he'd ask about me, what else would you two talk about? Sorry, but the last time I reached out to tell him I was going to Thailand, he didn't respond. I'm done."

Jenn flinched. Kyle was right and that made her sad. She and Ben had split up twenty years earlier, and Jenn had raised Kyle on her own since he was five. During the divorce, she found Ben curiously agreeable to her having full custody of Kyle—her lawyer had suggested it, and he didn't fight it.

Within six months, she understood why: he had met a woman before she and Ben split up, not that she cared anymore. They moved in together at a breakneck speed and had three kids in quick succession. While Ben always fulfilled his financial commitments to Kyle's upbringing, his role as a father became less involved. Kyle noticed and gradually stopped visiting his father. They had occasional awkward calls and emails, but otherwise, they didn't stay in touch. "I'm sorry it's like that, sweetie," said Jenn. "You know I love you more than anything, right?"

"Of course. I always felt your full love, Mom. I'm starting to realize how much you sacrificed for me when I was growing up."

"In what way?"

Kyle coughed lightly, his eyes softening. "I don't know. Be assured that I felt well-loved. You registered me for all the activities I wanted—and sometimes I didn't stick with them."

Jenn laughed. "Hello, summer camp, tai chi and competitive swimming."

"And I was always hitting you up for money for the next school trip."

"Yup, you were better traveled," she laughed.

"I know, I know. But let's say they all contributed to my character. Anyway, I see that parents give up so much, and as kids, we take and take."

Jenn saw his eyes look a bit sad. "It didn't feel like that to me. All I cared about was your well-being and happiness."

"Well, I'm forever grateful. So, tell me, what else are you up to?"

She jumped into the news about her book club and the list of books to read because they both loved discussing books. She covered her fitness circle and whatever else she could think of to keep him on the phone. She missed him terribly, yet she didn't want to make him feel bad for being halfway around the world—he wasn't responsible for her happiness.

And while it was lonely without him, he had a life to live. That's exactly what she did at his age. At twenty-six, she spent months traveling through Europe. She didn't exactly worry about her parents and whether they were missing her. What made her happiest was that Kyle sounded busy, excited, and in love. She wondered if that might lead to him settling there; she hoped not. She didn't want to ask him about that... yet. When they wrapped up, a lump grew in her throat—her baby was now grown up and he seemed so far away.

⟫⟫ ⟪⟪

When Jenn ended her call with Kyle, she felt at loose ends. She didn't have another client meeting that day, so she was free. She looked at the outstanding business paperwork piled neatly on her desk, which was labeled "Important, Not Urgent." It wasn't grabbing her.

She glanced at her watch and noted that a drop-in pickleball session was starting at the Halifax Games Center in half an hour.

She texted three friends and Kara replied instantly that she'd meet Jenn there. Staying busy and positive was Jenn's way of staying motivated in life. Without her son living nearby and no partner in her life, she had built a large network of friends to keep busy. Buoyed by Kara's response, Jenn grabbed her bag, paddle and ball and jumped on her bike.

As Jenn locked up her bike, her happy-faced friend pulled in. She loved playing with Kara. She was an excellent player, and Jenn always learned something from her. Together they made a good team for playing doubles and they shared many laughs.

"Thanks, you saved me," said Kara, giving her a big hug. "I was this close to starting some laundry," she said, holding up two fingers an inch apart.

Jenn lived for these moments at the pickleball court. Finally, she had found exercise that was so much fun, it didn't feel like exercise. She'd had many conversations at gatherings with people who didn't play and said they didn't get pickleball. They wanted to know why people were obsessed with it.

She would patiently explain her theories while trying not to bore them. First, for many people aged fifty and up, she said, pickleball felt nostalgic—it was like going back in time when life was simpler. All you needed was a paddle and a ball. Many people found it easy to learn if they played badminton, racquet sports or table tennis. It was fun to play, a great workout, and everybody loved the socializing.

Jenn would then rhyme off statistics about the number of players in North America and the sport's growth, concluding with, "No wonder this game is sweeping nations." At that point in the conversation, the people either rolled their eyes and excused themselves to get another drink or asked where they could play. Jenn always had a full rundown of available courts, gyms and leagues for people. That's how it grew.

Jenn and Kara placed their paddles on the bench which put them into the rotational system of play. While waiting for a court, they stood at the sidelines, stretching, talking, and making sure they were ready to go when someone shouted, "court," which meant that a court was now free and the next paddles in line could go play.

Everybody was friendly, introducing themselves to the other players in that game. Every game played out differently, and Jenn didn't worry if she won or lost. Sometimes she and her partner lost by a couple of points, while at other times they won in a battle with a score that bounced back and forth with exciting moments of victory. What she loved about pickleball is that you never knew how it would turn out. In a game that went only to eleven, anything could happen.

The courts were full of people. When pickleball started, it was played by people over fifty, but lately, a younger crowd had been showing up. Jenn loved their energy, but they were a challenge to play with. They were incredibly fit and full of energy, and they were willing to lunge sideways for the ball, run backwards to return a lob and drive forward to drop a quick shot over the net. Most people over fifty worked to avoid injury by doing the opposite. Jenn took a certain delight when she occasionally beat younger players. The last time she partnered with Phil, a guy in his seventies, they beat the younger pair. He turned to her and mumbled, "Isn't that great? I love beating those little shits."

Jenn laughed and reminded him that they were meant to be good sports in pickleball. He smiled with an evil eye and replied, "Yeah, whatever." She was trying to summon the courage to play in a doubles competition with Kara. But for now, a couple of hours of playing would take her mind off all the minor troubles in her life.

Chapter 12
Mark

Two days later, Mark made his way to the doctor's office as if dragging two heavy weights strapped around his ankles. All night he'd dreamt of the catastrophes and diagnoses he might face.

He thought about the devastating loss of Annie and the impact on their children. He worried they might be facing something dire with him, too. While his children were adults and out on their own, he knew they cherished him even more since their mother's passing. He couldn't bear the thought of bringing more bad news to them.

Mark gave his name at the reception, then trudged toward the packed room full of people seated, their faces like statues etched with concern and worry. Usually, he'd speak to people beside him to try to cheer them up or talk to little kids who were bored and getting into trouble with their siblings. This time, he felt worried and had nothing to say.

When the receptionist called his name, he took a deep breath to propel himself to a standing position. He reminded himself he'd have to deal with whatever the prognosis was. He was led to yet another waiting room where he stared at posters without reading anything, his mind far away. He jumped lightly when

Dr. Singh arrived; the doctor said hello, then sat to review the file.

"Well, Mark. I have good and bad news."

"Good news, first, Doc."

"There's no sign of cancer, tumors or big problems."

For the first time since the X-ray was taken, Mark let out a sigh. He still had the bad news to deal with, but at least it wasn't his biggest fear. "That's great," he said, shifting in his chair. "What's the bad news?"

"You have walking pneumonia."

"Oh," he said, puzzled, but relieved. "I've heard of it, but I don't know what it is."

"It's like a milder version of pneumonia, with less severe symptoms. You might think it's a cold or the flu, but you are still able to 'walk around,'" he said. "Let's try some antibiotics to see if we can clear it up quickly. But you have to promise me one thing..."

"I know what you are going to say; I have to finish the course."

"You do listen... sometimes," he joked. "One more thing." He pulled out his prescription pad and wrote a few notes on it, then passed it to Mark.

"Seriously, more drugs?" Mark couldn't believe it. He prided himself on not being on any meds, so taking two at the same time would ruin his track record. He studied the piece of paper and tilted his head slightly. "Does this say, 'exercise three times a week'?"

"Yes."

"And participate in more social activities?" Mark asked, looking back at him. "That's my second prescription?"

"Yes. You've always been healthy, so you have a solid foundation. But that won't last forever. You need to lose twelve to fifteen pounds and socialize more."

Mark stared at his hands. "I know, Doc, it's been a challenge since Annie passed away…"

Dr. Singh nodded. "Yes, Mark and I'm sorry. I also sense you are a little lonely."

Mark shrugged. He was right, but Mark had never acknowledged that to himself, let alone tell somebody else.

"Maybe you need to find love again."

"Well, let's not get carried away with that prescription pad, Doc. Shall we start with an exercise program?" said Mark, standing up, dusting off his black jeans even though there was no lint showing.

"What's this 'we' thing? I already exercise regularly because some pushy gym teacher in high school badgered me into the habit."

"*Touché*," laughed Mark.

"Keep me posted on the antibiotics for the pneumonia so we know they're working. And once you start to feel better with more energy, I want to see you drop some weight. Got it?"

"Yes, sir," he said, saluting, then turned and left the office. Suddenly, he wanted to click his heels in celebration. He made a beeline for the pharmacy to get started on the antibiotics and popped one as soon as he paid for them.

Outside the pharmacy, he pulled out his phone and texted a summary of the good news and a light description of the walking pneumonia that would be easily treated. First, he messaged his daughters, Nicki and Charlotte, then his brother Kevin. The girls sent heart emojis that filled the text box. Kevin sent back a fist-bump emoji and said he'd swing by later.

Mark felt a sensation of hope sweeping over him, like a light switch that had been stuck in the off position too long. He hadn't realized the level of sadness that simmered in the background for god knows how long. His body knew something wasn't right, yet his inability to deal with the potential outcome had prolonged the whole ordeal. And he'd been miserable, with himself, his children and his friends. This was not like him. He was the sports coach who had always faced uncertainty straight on and urged others to do the same. Also, he knew if Annie had been around, she would have nudged and cajoled him to get checked out with the doctor months earlier. But she wasn't here, and he needed to deal with it.

Once he was back home, he stood at the refrigerator and pasted up a chart that he had created on the computer. He called it "Operation Lard-Off." That was his tough love plan to shed fifteen pounds. He stepped on the scale and groaned but recorded his weight on Day One. He recalled all the motivational talks he'd given to others, saying things like, "It took a long time to gain that weight, so don't expect it to come off in a day."

Next, he went to the freezer and reviewed the many healthy meals his daughters had delivered and he had yet to eat. He pulled out a vegetarian lasagna that Charlotte had made, with hearts drawn on the label. She packed it with red peppers, mushrooms and a thick cheesy sauce made with a smooth cottage cheese that still tasted good for being so damned healthy.

On his next trip to the grocery store, he picked up a bag of pre-made salad because he knew if he'd bought the ingredients, he'd never get around to making a salad. Finally, he pulled out his beloved jar of peanut butter and put a sticky note on it to cut his consumption by half. That would be a killer for him, but he had to break the habit.

On Saturday morning, he weighed himself. He'd lost half a pound—hardly a reason to jump up and down after four days. But he'd take it.

He headed over to Nicki's home, which was not far away. This was his favorite day of the week, when he got to look after his livewire grandson, Augustus. For a few hours, he played court jester while Nicki and her husband ran errands. Augustus was four and a half and bursting with energy, which was perfect for Mark. He'd usually arrive around 9 a.m. and the adults would start with coffee. Whenever Charlotte was available, she'd drop by and soon they'd be sharing updates and news in the kitchen, which Mark loved. This was a new tradition since Annie's passing and it was clear they all enjoyed their time together.

Mark tapped on the front door and walked in, shouting hello to everybody. He said *hi* to Ethan, Nicki's husband, who was in the middle of a project in the basement and heading back downstairs. Augustus spotted his grandfather and burst out of his play area. He ran hard and wrapped his little sausage arms so tightly around Mark's legs that he could hardly move.

"Grand*papapa*, can we go to the playground?"

Mark laughed because Augustus never knew when to stop with the *pa*'s at the end. Mark swept him up, hugged him and swung him around before setting him down. "You bet, Gusto."

"I heard that!" shouted Nicki from the kitchen. He knew his daughter insisted on using his name in full, but he found it a bit pretentious for a child who was two-and-a-half feet tall. The kid was spring-loaded with energy, and Mark had once observed that the child was full of gusto, which made everybody laugh.

"Sorry," he said, arriving in the kitchen while hugging each daughter. "Augustus it is."

Nicki laughed. "Right, that's why he comes back from the playground telling me his name is Gusto."

"I'll do better," he said, walking over and kissing his tiny granddaughter Katarina on the forehead. She was bouncing lightly in her little jumper chair and looking happy. He loved to make her smile and couldn't wait until she was mobile and able to play at the park with her brother. "Speaking of doing better, I've lost almost a pound this week."

Nicki and Charlotte clinked their mugs in celebration. Augustus arrived, dragging his favorite toys to show his grandfather, as if it were the first time he was showing them. Nicki kissed him on the head and asked him to play by himself for a bit while they talked to Grandpa, and they'd take him out to the playground afterward.

In no time, the three of them were exchanging news and stories. When Annie was alive, she did most of this socializing with the kids, but Mark realized he'd been missing out. While some of Nicki's stories about her latest followers on social media didn't exactly grab his attention, he listened patiently.

When the two daughters finally slowed down the conversation long enough to take a breath, Mark jumped in. "So, the organizer, Jenn, came by earlier in the week. It started well but went sideways." He noticed the two of them swap a look that meant something, but he didn't have the code. After describing his experience for five minutes, Charlotte finally cut in.

"Uhm, Dad, we have something to tell you about that," said Charlotte in a wispy tone.

"Oh? Do tell."

"That whole money issue was a misunderstanding. We were worried that if we left it up to you, you wouldn't do it. Nicki and I decided we would pay for the project as a surprise for you. We would cover Jenn's consulting and organizing fees."

"Hmmm," said Mark. "What happened?"

"We forgot to tell Jenn about the plan. So, it wasn't her fault that she raised the topic of money. That's what a consultant does."

Shit. Mark was now reflecting on the conversation when he had been cross with her. "How did you find out about the meeting?"

Charlotte squirmed. "Jenn called me after the appointment and was quite embarrassed by the whole thing. She knew how upset you were. I explained the misunderstanding."

"And you're only telling me now?" Mark's agitation was now shifting from Jenn to his daughters.

"I'm so sorry, Daddy," offered Nicki. "We were both crazy busy this week and didn't get around to calling you."

"Now I feel like a jerk for the way I responded. While I'm still not convinced that the house needs a reorg, she was doing her job." His expression shifted into coach mode, which he knew made the girls feel they were about to be chided. "You two crossed the line. First, you should have been honest with me about your plans. And more importantly, you should have told Jenn."

"Sorry," they chimed together.

"I did talk to her, Dad," said Charlotte. "She wasn't angry; she was more relieved because she didn't want people to think she was dishonest."

"That's understandable. I will apologize to her next week." He shot a stern look at the two of them. "No more secret plans, okay?"

They nodded. "Do you still want to spend time with Augustus and Katarina this morning?" Nicki squeaked. "I'll understand if you don't."

Mark was still annoyed, but he had said what he needed to. "Of course I do. But please stop doing weird things on my behalf, okay?"

They both agreed. Nicki helped dress the two kids for the outdoors and set up the carriage that was so sophisticated and complicated that Mark felt like he needed to watch a video every time he used it.

Now that he was relieved not to be dying from a slow and painful lung disease, he was feeling buoyant and suddenly interested in everything.

The whole time he was playing with Gusto and pushing him on the swing at the playground, he was recalling how rude he was to Jenn. The longer it had been since their meeting, the more attractive he found her. Now she was becoming like a tiny obsession bouncing around his head. He couldn't stop thinking about her.

Although he was embarrassed, he wondered if he could patch things up with her. He had to try at the very least. And bumping into her needed to look like a happy coincidence.

Chapter 13
Jenn

JENN SAT IN HER compact office, willing herself to do one of the many dull tasks required by a self-employed person. In her world, she was the chief executive officer, sales rep, admin, tech support and finance manager all in one wobbly package. Some things she was good at, like organizing, of course. The rest was the price she paid for the freedom to run a business the way she wanted.

Yet she recognized that life as a sole proprietor could be a lonely one. There were no people to chat with in the lunchroom, and nobody to call when it was a bad tech day. There were no colleagues to bounce crazy ideas off of or reel her in when she got carried away. That's why she teamed up with another business owner, Maggie. They were in a similar business and could solve problems together, vent a little, then get back to work.

Jenn was reviewing the accounts when she noted a man who looked like Mark Russell strolling by her office. It wasn't surprising to see him; they were located in the same general area. Although Halifax was growing into a larger city, it remained a small collection of distinct neighborhoods. They didn't have fancy names like *arrondissements* in Paris or boroughs in London, but they still served the same function.

She loved Halifax's North End and its link to the past: the Hydrostone houses built over a hundred years ago after the Halifax Explosion devastated the area. The focal point of the North End was a stretch of boutiques, coffee shops, a bakery and local businesses that included a boulevard park in the middle. Neighbors stopped to chat while their kids ran around the mini-park, and older folks sat on the benches chatting over a cup of tea. Other than people wearing contemporary clothes, Jenn could picture the same style of socializing a hundred years earlier.

Jenn returned to her paperwork and noticed the man strolling by again. He glanced through the window but kept walking. This time, she was sure it was Mark. Why was he in the area? Was he strolling or searching for a nearby store? Should she speak to him or let him pass? The last time she saw him, he seemed peeved, and she didn't want to upset him further. In her business, she understood that reorganizing a person's home could be traumatic for some, especially if they'd experienced a loss. She never judged people who had a hard time downsizing or reorganizing their homes.

On his third stroll by, she walked to the door, opening it gently. By then, he'd passed by with his back to her. "Mark?" she asked.

He turned toward her, looking surprised. "Oh, hi, Jenn. Is this your office?"

She nodded. "I had a call from security that there was a suspicious character pacing outside of my office. Thought I'd check it out."

He chuckled. "I suppose it might have looked a bit odd."

"Are you looking for an office?"

He glanced down at her business card in his hand. "Okay, busted. I was coming to see you."

She opened the door. "Come on in. I was about to make a coffee. Would you like one?"

"Sure."

"Coming right up," she said, walking over to her machine. Whatever motivated him to come here, she needed to let him reveal it when he was ready. She noticed him looking around the tiny space. She sensed he was trying to figure out who she was. Each wall was full of multiple styles of shelves and storage solutions that might inspire clients.

He raised his eyebrows. "Wow. You are super organized. Look at you. The shelves and files on your desk are color-coded and stacked neatly. Even your pen holder is in order. A little OCD, are you?"

She handed him a mug. "I prefer CDO. Then it's alphabetized."

He paused, then chuckled. "Good one," he said, taking a sip. "You are probably wondering why I'm here today."

She offered a neutral smile and said nothing, indicating that whatever he said was not going to shock her.

"I came to apologize for being a bit rude last week."

"A bit?" she joked. "Kidding. Don't worry—"

"Turns out there was a miscommunication. My daughters had conspired to hire you and pay you to help me get my home organized. But they didn't tell me."

"Yes, I heard from Charlotte," she said.

"I gave them a rollicking for doing that." He shifted his weight and sighed. "Even so, I shouldn't have been so cranky. You were doing your job."

She noticed him wince. "No problem, Mark. I've seen way worse. I know that lots of people have a hard time making changes in their homes, especially when it's loved ones trying to force the changes."

"Thanks," he said, his body relaxing. "Aside from the concern that I could be the target of a scam by an attractive and smooth-talking lady, I was also worried she'd tell me my house was a damn mess."

Attractive. She heard only that word in his sentence; all the other words dropped away as if they didn't matter. It surprised her and it took a second to process the rest of what he had said. Was he flirting with her? He looked so damn nerdy and nervous; he reminded her of someone stuffed into a time machine, emerging as an awkward teenager trying to signal his interest in her without her noticing. "Well, it's not every day I get compliments like a 'smooth-talking lady,'" she joked. "Or was that meant to be an insult?"

"The thing is, you are kind of right. No, you *are* right. I need to make some changes in my home, but I wasn't ready to face that last week."

"It's fine, Mark. I get that." She saw him take a breath and pick right up where he left off.

"The other thing is that I wasn't feeling well for quite a while; I had this damn cough that wouldn't go away. I was awaiting X-ray results and fearing the absolute worst, so I was grumpy."

"I'm sorry," she said, wondering if he might suddenly be ready to reveal something that she didn't care to hear.

"But it's all good. You know what it turned out to be?"

"A man cold?"

"Zing!" he laughed. "It was walking pneumonia. But you got me. It's like you had a breakaway in hockey, racing toward the net and scoring a goal with a wicked wrist shot before I knew what hit me."

"I was messing with you to see if you could take a joke."

"We okay, then?" said Mark, holding out his hand to shake hers.

"Of course."

"Great, because the other reason I came here today is to see if you would come back and help me organize my house. Maybe not on a grand scale, but—"

"What made you change your mind?"

"After you left, I wandered around and realized it would benefit from a spruce up, or 'make-over' as my daughter Nicki would say," he said, using quotation marks.

"Yes, Nicki's a going concern, isn't she? I read about her in the paper. Her custom-designed clothing line for kids is getting a lot of attention on social media."

"She reminds me all the time," he said, waving his hand like a royal person. "Apparently, she's got fifty thousand followers on Instapot."

"You mean *Instagram*?" she laughed.

"Whatever. I follow her, but I don't get it."

Jenn's phone dinged; she checked her phone.

"Look, I'll get going. Sorry, I didn't even have an appointment."

"No problem, my next meeting is half an hour from now. Would you like to set a meeting at your home? The consultation is still free at this point," she laughed.

He nodded. "Sounds great."

She scrolled through her calendar. "What's a good day and time for you?"

"Well, I've got next to no social life, so you pick what works for you."

That sounds sad. She wondered if he was trying to sound pathetic or being honest. "Let's see. I've got a project that will take a few weeks. How about Thursday, the fifteenth at 10 a.m.?"

"Perfect."

She grabbed a business card and a pen. "Here, let me write this appointment on the back. You don't want to forget."

"No chance of that. See you then," he said, turning to leave. Then he stopped and pointed to her overstuffed gym bag by the door. "Is that pickleball gear?"

"Yes, do you play?"

"No, but I've been thinking about it for a while. I hear it's lots of fun."

"It is a riot," she said. "You were a gym teacher, right?" She saw him look a bit puzzled. "Charlotte told me," she said. "She was trying to paint a picture of who you are."

"Yup, that was me."

"I imagine you've played some racket sports in your day."

"Oh yes. Jack of all sports, master of none."

"That's not what I heard," Jenn teased. "Charlotte said in the reorg, you'll need a place for all your trophies."

Mark stared at his running shoes. "Pickleball is sweeping the nation, so I think it's time to learn."

Jenn said, "Well, I run a fun league and there's a drop-in at the Halifax Games Center, so feel free to come and check it out."

"Maybe I will," he said. "I think I'll learn the basics first. I mean, there's a net, a paddle and a lightweight plastic ball with holes in it. How hard could it be?"

Jenn laughed. "Watch your trash-talking there, Buddy. You can come by anytime and get pickled."

"What's that?"

"In a game that goes to eleven, I beat you eleven to zero. That means you got 'pickled'."

"Oh, you think so?" he chirped with a sly tone as he walked toward the door.

"I know so, mister."

"We'll see you in court!" he said, looking mighty pleased with his pun. And with that, he turned and smacked squarely into the door jamb. Shaking his head and laughing at the same time, he scuttled out of the office.

"Smooth move!" she taunted. As she watched him walk away, she noted that he had a little bounce in his step.

Chapter 14
Mark

A CAR HORN BLASTED in the driveway. Mark closed the side door and ran down the steps toward his brother's truck.

"Hey, Kevin," he said, climbing in.

Kevin looked at him, one eyebrow raised. "What's with you?"

"What?"

"I haven't seen you run down those steps in a long time. Today, you look... almost energetic."

Mark nodded. "Well, two things. The pneumonia is clearing up."

"And you're going to live to see another day?" Kevin joked.

"Something like that."

"I knew you'd be fine," Kevin said, punching him in the arm and easing the truck into reverse.

"Well, *I* didn't. Now I feel like I have a new lease on life."

Kevin smiled. "Way to go, little bro. Anything else?"

"Nope," Mark said. "Just keen to exchange some insults with the guys this afternoon."

When they arrived at the Tiger's Paw Pub, they headed to the pool table room and chatted for a minute before playing. The waiter, Frankie, swung by with a tray full of beer. "Well, boys," he said, passing a draft to each person, "Enjoy playing pool while you can; the table is coming out soon."

"What? This is our favorite place," said T-Bone. "Why would they do that?"

Frankie shrugged and passed him the credit card tap. "They can make more by taking out the pool table and adding tables and chairs."

"That sucks," said Jeff, looking at everyone. "Where will we play after the table is gone?"

"Don't know," said Mark, standing up. "I guess we'd better fit in some games while we can."

They took a drink and walked over to the pool table. They laughed and poked fun at each other while they played. After a few games, the guys sat down and ordered food. "So, how's it going, Captain Pudge?" said Jeff, looking at Mark.

"I'll have you know I lost almost two pounds in the last two weeks."

"Wow, maybe you should start a weight loss blog," joked Jeff.

"C'mon, we all know gradual weight loss works better than yo-yo dieting," said Mark, slipping into gym teacher mode. "But now that I'm getting over pneumonia, I'm keen to do exercise that makes me sweat."

"You mean like running?" asked T-Bone.

"Sadly, that pounding is too hard on my knees," Mark said, staring at his plate with a burger and poking at a salad that he swapped for French fries. "I'm thinking about pickleball."

"Great," said Lonny. "I'm in a league and we're always trying to recruit substitutes."

"I might want to learn to play first," Mark said, sipping his beer.

"C'mon, you were a gym teacher, Mark—" said Lonny.

Kevin chimed in. "And a good racquet player. You'll pick it up in no time."

"Maybe, but I was kind of trash-talking this lady who sounds like a good player, so I don't want to arrive and look like a jerk."

"Well, you are one, so just be yourself," laughed T-Bone, high-fiving Kevin.

"Is that why you are trying to get back in shape?" said Kevin.

Mark shook his head. "I told you, I'm feeling better." But he couldn't stop himself smiling.

"Yeah, right!" said Lonny. "So, what's this plan to take on this lady... oops, I mean learn how to play pickleball."

"I've been watching a bunch of YouTube videos, so I know the rules and now I want to give it a go. Do you want to help or not?" asked Mark.

Lonny laughed. "Okay. How about early Friday at the North End Park? I'll bring a couple of buddies and we'll give you a crash course on playing doubles. If any of you guys want to come, I've got spare paddles."

⟫ ⟪

On Friday morning, after stretching for twenty minutes, Mark concluded he needed to work on his flexibility. Hell, everything needed work. He could feel the effects from a few years of haphazard commitment to fitness. Not only had he gained weight, but he'd also lost strength and stamina. He was determined to return to his happy fitness place.

Mark held out the leash for Jack, who jumped like an acrobat to show his enthusiasm. They slow-jogged to the park, and Mark felt a little breathless when he arrived, but knew he had to get his fitness levels back.

Lonny pulled out his paddle and talked about the basics: the court size, scoring, the serving areas and the non-volley zone, known as "the kitchen," where players would lightly tap or "dink" the ball over the net.

Mark was soon hitting decent serves, but like a newbie who played other racquet sports, he walloped the ball too hard and it went flying. In no time, he was sweating, panting and mopping his face and neck with a towel. He tried to teach Jack to fetch the ball when it flew far away, but Jack scampered off to a corner with the ball in his mouth and chewed on it, so he was fired from his role.

After an hour, he said it was time to stop before he had a freakin' heart attack. He was out of shape yet exhilarated. He sat with Jack and watched the others play, learning something from each player. When he and Jack left and walked back home, he couldn't remember the last time he felt like he had truly exerted himself.

* * *

Within a couple of weeks, Mark had mastered the basics, according to Lonny. He found another newbie, Phil, who wanted to try playing a real game at the Games Center. And after some careful sleuthing, he figured out the days of the week when Jenn might be there. He had lost a few pounds—enough to encourage him to keep going. He loved the sensation of pickleball and running hard to whack the ball. Even during a game of doubles, he still had to move quickly and ended up quite sweaty.

When Mark and Phil walked through the front door of the center, they could hear the sounds of pickleball in the distance—it sounded like a giant popcorn maker was in full swing. He loved the constant crack, snap and thwack of hollow plastic balls full of holes bouncing around the court, followed by laughter erupting over funny moments. With such a lightweight ball, it tended to do crazy things when it was hit, like crawl along the top of the net without revealing which side it would land on.

Since the drop-in sessions were held during the day, most of the players were over fifty and either retired or working on a reduced schedule to fit in a session. As one of his still-working friends joked, "This work business is getting in the way of my three-times-a-week pickleball habit."

Even though six courts were going full tilt with mixed doubles, there were still lots of keen players waiting on the sidelines. This crowd didn't waste time creating a system to ensure everyone took their turn.

Mark spied Jenn off to the side, chatting and laughing with a group awaiting their turn. He tried not to stare, but he was reminded of the details that had caught his attention the day she came to the house. She was small, with cropped sandy hair cut into a style that was perfect for pickleball, as it wouldn't fall into her eyes. There were little wisps of silver on her temples, which he liked. More importantly, she looked energetic, moving with ease around the court. She wore safety glasses with the lens popped out, which was popular because the pickleball could not go past the frame to injure the eye, and there was no lens to fog up.

While she was talking, her head turned his way and he noticed she had stopped talking. She smiled and walked across the room toward him, spinning the paddle in her hand. His heart sped up and sweat beads formed on his brow. He hadn't even played yet, so he figured his body was preparing for a good workout.

"Hey, Mark. Welcome to the pickleball court."

"Thanks," he mumbled. "Ah, this is my friend, Phil. Phil, this is Jenn, who organizes the league." He watched as they shook hands.

"So... it looks like you've learned to play in the last few weeks," said Jenn. "If I recall, you suggested it wouldn't be hard to learn."

"I've learned that it's more complicated than I thought," said Mark.

"That so? Do you still plan to clean my clock?"

"Absolutely!" he blurted, wondering why on earth he would say such a thing. As he watched the crowd, he could see that there were many levels of play, including lots of excellent players.

"Okay, but we'll need to take turns. And it's all luck of the draw who you play with, until late in the session. Lots of people leave after ninety minutes, so we can find a court and play." Jenn explained that on one bench, there was a pile of four paddles for the winners of the previous game, with an orange marker on top to show they were up next. On the other bench, the losers of the last game stacked four paddles awaiting another play. When a group finished their game, they'd shout "court," and the next four paddles in line would head to the empty court.

Mark and Phil placed their paddles on the loser side of the bench, which matched them with players who were new or learning skills. Mark and Phil did okay with the group, especially when paired with players who had some experience. They even won a couple of games, mostly thanks to their teammates' skills. During the game, Mark noticed he needed to ease up on his hits. His body responded as if he were playing with a tennis ball, when in fact he was whacking a much lighter ball. He sent it flying high on numerous shots, which meant his opponents would smash it back. Plus, he was a little distracted keeping an eye on Jenn, who was skilled at the game.

Finally, around 3:30 p.m., Jenn came over to Mark and Phil, who were watching another game. "Want to play? I've got Michele over here who is a newbie too." He liked the camaraderie of the pickleball court. Everybody introduced themselves whenever they started a game. They were good sports, complimenting everybody when they made a good play.

"Let's do it," said Mark. "But don't play down to us because we're newbies."

"Don't worry," laughed Jenn, tapping the top of her partner's paddle. They took their place in the court, preparing for the first server, who was Mark. Jenn's energy filled their side of the court. She stood lightly, her feet moving side to side, getting ready to respond to the serve.

"Zero, zero, start," Mark shouted to show he knew how to keep score. He'd watched umpteen videos until he got the hang of it. Jenn smiled at him. He bounced the ball in front of him a couple of times to calm his nerves and focus on his serve.

Suddenly, he didn't feel as confident as he had a few weeks earlier. On his first serve, he surprised himself with a firm hit that whipped across the net, clearing it by inches and landing close to Jenn's feet at the back of the court. Focused entirely on the afterglow of his impressive debut serve, he missed her quick return drop shot that landed in the kitchen barely over the net—and he didn't have time to run fast enough to tap it back. They lost the serve and sent it over to the opposing team.

He watched Jenn tee up her serve. "Zero, zero, one," she called out, followed by bouncing the ball several times. And with a full-on sidearm serve, she gave it a serious whack and it raced across the net, dropping at the back of the court. Surprisingly, Mark was able to return it, but he and Phil quickly caused errors. The points for the other team began to mount.

Anticipating where each ball might land, Mark raced around the court, valiantly lunging at shots and returning the odd one. When he got a good return and the ball landed right, Jenn and Michele would shout out compliments. But Mark and the others were no match for Jenn. In ten minutes flat, her team had won eleven to nothing, which meant Mark was 'pickled.' She whooped but didn't gloat. He was glad nobody had their smartphone out capturing the game. She was excellent in the court and way better than she had let on when they discussed it. When he thought back to the conversation, he realized that she hadn't bragged about her skills—he had started all the trash talk.

At the end of the game, they all walked to the net and tapped their paddles. "I guess I asked for that one, didn't I?" laughed Mark.

"You got some good shots, Mark. You've spent some time learning the game and strategy. And you've even got a decent spin on the ball that most beginners can't do. How'd you learn that?"

"I suppose being a racket and table tennis player helped. Plus, I spent hours watching videos on how to play pickleball and competitive pickleball. It was time well wasted."

They laughed and walked toward the benches as people wrapped up for the day. Mark was sorry it was over; he felt like he had just started. He wasn't even embarrassed over the fact that she had trounced him.

"Well, you have potential," she said, wiping her face with a little towel. "But never forget that I pickled you in the first game!"

"As if I could forget—you'll always remind me." His face reddened. *Did he really say that?* He made it sound like they'd be spending time together in the future. That wasn't his intention, though it was his secret hope. But the adrenaline pumping through his body caused his mouth to jump in without a filter. Would she notice? If yes, might she be insulted? Or worse, would she think he was being totally presumptuous? *What a dork.*

She pushed her paddle and orange ball into the bag. "Does that mean you'll come back?" she said. "Hope so. I predict you will liven up this league in no time."

"You mean that?" *Damn.* All she did was encourage him to come out to the league, and he was flustered. He realized his best line of defence was to pull his large foot out of his mouth and stop talking.

"Gotta run," said Jenn, packing her paddle into her knapsack. "Nice to see everybody," Jenn waved to the crowd as she departed. As she walked past Mark, she said, "And I'll see you in a few days at your home to talk about my favorite topic, organizing!"

"You bet!" said Mark, waving to her on her way out. By the end of the session, Mark learned something that day that was too incredible to process: that it's possible to fall in love twice in one day. First, there was playing pickleball. After a couple of hours of running hard, sweating and adrenaline pulsing in all directions, his body was now flooded with endorphins and dopamine. He felt great. This is what he'd known he needed and had craved for some time but couldn't motivate himself to get started. Now he'd finally broken the tired grip of grief and opened the door to a sport that motivated him. He loved it because it didn't require the same strength needed from his tennis days, and he didn't have to run rampant over a large court that threatened his knees. Everything in pickleball was like an easier and even more fun version of tennis, yet it still required skill, strategy, balance, quick reflexes and a decent level of fitness. He was hooked.

Secondly, and more importantly, he felt an incredible connection to Jenn. It wasn't easy to fathom, but it was a persistent sensation. He wondered if Jenn had any of the same feelings for him. His feelings were strong enough that they might even override his fear of rejection if he asked her out. *Maybe.* He realized he'd need to work his way up to that stage.

He didn't feel sure of himself. Not yet. At the pickleball sessions, Jenn was the center attraction among players and it was obvious why. Who wouldn't love someone like that? He watched Jenn stride off the court, looking confident and strong enough to play another ten games. While he hadn't thought about what he found attractive in a woman, it occurred to him that confidence and mastery of skills were up there. She had all of that in her consulting work and her pickleball hobby. He also loved her looks—healthy and athletic, not a supermodel. And while her hair was cut and styled, she didn't seem to worry when it sprang in every direction during the games.

Mark was now counting the days to their appointment, even though he didn't give two hoots about organizing his home.

Chapter 15
Jenn

"A GYM TEACHER, EH?" said Maggie, stretching her arms lengthwise on the yoga mat, with Jenn on a mat beside her. They were waiting for the class to start and they usually got caught up on the events that had happened since the last time they saw each other.

"Yes. He asked me about pickleball a few weeks ago and I told him about the league that I organize. For someone who had never played before, he was impressive—of course, I didn't tell him that."

"No?"

"Well, I still beat him—pickled him actually, but he had some wicked shots. Once he learns to control the ball, he'll do well."

Maggie turned her head sideways, "It's going to take some time; you're an excellent pickleball player. But you had a head start with your prince... I mean toad."

"At least something good came out of it. This guy, Mark, seems less slick and more grounded."

"Sounds like he's interested in you to go to all that work of learning pickleball."

"Maybe," said Jenn, lowering her knees and stretching her arms out front. "But I'm nervous. I've had too many one-off dates that went nowhere."

"That's normal; you are just figuring things out. They might be a good person, but not right for you."

"Exactly, I get that," said Jenn. "But there were also guys that I liked who seemed to like me. Things heated up, and it felt exciting, then they stopped suddenly. I've been ghosted so many times I could be a keynote speaker at a paranormal conference."

Maggie laughed and shook her head. "We know people ghost for many reasons: they prefer the chase to the catch, they are trying to prove they are still attractive or they've got baggage that causes them to panic when things are going well."

"I guess." Jenn sat up and took a sip from her water bottle. "It seems to get harder to date, especially after fifty."

"Why is that?"

"Who knows? As we age, our bodies change. I work out and eat well. But look at my skin starting to wrinkle when I'm in downward dog. And it's only going to get worse. Gravity is cruel."

"You still have muscle tone."

"Yes," said Jenn, "But I also have a few extra pounds and my hair is turning grey."

"Yikes, I don't recall getting an invitation to your pity party."

"Sorry, but I'm on a roll here. And aside from looks, by our fifties, we've all faced life challenges, like loss, separation or divorce. Then, when we finally get the courage to date, we get burned by a jerk—"

"And then you view the next person with too much suspicion," blurted Maggie, adjusting her tank top.

Jenn nodded. "I guess we feel vulnerable."

"Which isn't fair to the next guy, who might be perfectly nice."

"I know, I know," said Jenn, waving her hand like she knew what was coming, but couldn't stop herself. "And sometimes we get stuck on our idea of the perfect relationship. And when they don't meet our expectations, we get freaked out. Plus, we can be a little stubborn about change and compromise."

"You know what I think?" whispered Maggie, as they watched the yoga instructor close the door to the studio and walk to the front.

"What?"

"You might want to give this guy a chance before you make assumptions or write him off. Maybe he's different and he'll be the one to love you for who you are, not what you look like. Although, for the record, you look amazing."

"Thanks, Mags."

"And don't forget, it cuts both ways. You have to accept him for who he is, not what you think he should be. Seems like people get into a relationship, then start trying to change their partner."

She's right. Jenn looked at Maggie. She seemed wise for someone who hadn't dated in decades and was happily married. Jenn put her hands together in front of her face and bowed deeply to her wise friend, then took her place on the mat.

⊱ ⊰

When Jenn got home from yoga after a stop at the grocery store, she noticed Kyle had pinged her on a chat app. She was keen to talk to him because the last time they had a chat, she felt like he was holding something back. She was his mother and she could feel things, especially since he had moved to Thailand.

They had a long talk, and while it felt great to talk to him, he asked different questions from the usual ones, such as her plans for Thanksgiving and Christmas. When she asked him about it, he reminded her that this was the first year he'd be away from her and he felt guilty because she was on her own.

Jenn told him that he was sweet, but there was no need to worry about her. She had many friends, including some single women she could invite over for a shared dinner. She told him that while she loved having him around for holidays, living his life was the most important thing. He sounded relieved.

She asked if there was anything else he wanted to discuss. She heard him halt for a microsecond before he said no. Knowing the conversation wasn't going any further on this call, she said she needed to wrap up for a meeting. They shouted "love you" umpteen times at each other, laughing, as if neither of them wanted to hang up.

Ten minutes after the call, she got a message from Kyle. He apologized for sounding odd, saying a lot was going on. While work was going well, Achara's Mom had a health problem that hadn't been identified yet. Not surprisingly, Kyle was worried, and Achara was stressed. Her father had died years ago, so Achara and Kyle, along with some of her cousins were looking after her Mom. Kyle said it made him think about her, and he worried about what might happen to her while he was away.

Jenn loved that her son was thinking and caring that much about her, but she didn't want him fretting. She texted back and said, "Who me? Don't worry, I'm as healthy as an..." Then she found an emoji that looked like an ox. Kyle pinged back lots of laughs and then said he'd be in touch soon.

Feeling better that she understood more about her son's situation, she turned her thoughts to her next appointment tomorrow morning at Mark Russell's. *This ought to be interesting,* she thought.

Chapter 16
Mark

A FEW MINUTES BEFORE 9 a.m., Mark heard a car turn into the driveway. From the upstairs window, he could see Jenn arriving. He took one last look in the mirror and ran his hands through his short hair, trying to get it to lie flat.

He could tell by the sound from the living room that Jack had bolted to the sofa and had started a series of minor woofs that would soon grow into a full-blown bark. But suddenly the woofing stopped. He walked downstairs and noted that Jack was wagging his little tail while galloping off to the side door.

Mark felt a little nervous, but he reminded himself that she was here on a professional visit. He didn't know what they'd do today, but he dressed in jeans in case he was put to work.

"Hi Jenn," he said as he opened the door and invited her in. Her smile disarmed him, filling the kitchen with warmth that went beyond a simple smile to appear professional. She wore a light blazer with a t-shirt underneath, along with navy cords. A light frisson rippled through his body.

Jack pushed past Mark to greet Jenn and leapt in the air when she offered him a little treat. "Well, hello to you, too, Jack," she laughed and patted his head. Then she turned to Mark and said, "Sorry, I didn't bring you anything."

"It's fine, I never cared for Milk Bones," he joked, waving her in. "Don't worry about taking your boots off, it's dry outside."

"That's okay," said Jenn, opening her backpack and tossing her slippers on the floor. "It's a habit, in case my boots picked up something from the yard." She stepped inside and looked around. "Wow, somebody's been cleaning."

"Yup, scrubbed this place to within an inch of its life this morning. I figure once every couple of years will do it."

"Looks great." She set her bag on the island counter and started pulling out her notebook and a pen.

"I'm not sure how this is supposed to work."

"No problem," she said, opening her notebook and clicking her pen. "We are going to start with a little conversation about your home, your lifestyle and how you use the space."

"How about over a coffee? I made a pot a few minutes ago."

"Sure." She placed one foot on the bottom of a bar stool, while he brought over the mug, and offered the spoon holder and sugar on the counter. He then went to the fridge to fetch a carton of milk.

"Thanks, but I drink it black," she said, raising herself onto the barstool at the end of the island.

"Jeez, I don't know if I'd sit there..."

"Oh?" she stepped down.

"Technically, it's Jack's," he grinned.

"Jack's?" She placed her feet on the floor. "A bar stool is a bit of a stretch for a dog that's only twelve inches high. How does he get up there?"

"Watch this." He looked at the dog, snapped his fingers and said, "Jack, Happy Hour." In a vertical swoop so quick and effortless it deserved an instant replay, Jack was standing on the barstool.

"Don't tell me you two share Happy Hour at your kitchen counter."

"Only on Fridays."

"I've seen a lot in my work, but that's a first," said Jenn.

"It's a little party trick I taught him, so I don't have to drink alone."

"And what, pray tell, do you talk about during this Happy Hour?" she asked in mock seriousness.

"I tell him all about my day."

"I'm more interested in what Jack says."

"Mostly he whines."

Jenn laughed and raised her pen over the notebook. "Okay, we should get to work. How about we go through each room and you can describe how you use it and what you like or don't like about it. My goal is to optimize the space you have and reorganize things to function better, not spend your money on a big renovation—unless that's what you want."

"Hell no!" said Mark.

"So noted," said Jenn, underlining his words in her notebook.

"I agree it could work better, but I don't want to spend more than I have to. I walked through the other day and I realized that we used this house differently when Annie was around. She baked, entertained and did crafts, and had the family over quite often. But I haven't found my rhythm since she's been gone."

"Before you go too far, I feel I should ask: Any chance you might want to move?"

"Not at all. It's still my home."

"Good to know," said Jenn, scribbling. "Okay, let's have a nose around the kitchen while you tell me how you use it."

Mark gave a brief tour, pointing out cupboards that held cooking appliances he didn't know how to operate. There was one section jammed with leftover containers and duplicates of pots and frying pans of every size. He admitted he didn't cook much.

At the far end of the counter was an old landline with an answering machine and a blinking red light alerting him to messages. However, Mark said he never answered it because the only calls were from telemarketers and scammers. There was a laptop, papers, files and envelopes. Underneath the counter, a stack of bankers' boxes with crooked lids teetered slightly. To the side was an old office chair with a back piece that flipped and flopped when he tried to sit and was too low for the counter. Mark explained it was like an office, but not really. He'd always meant to set something up but never got around to it, so it was getting worse by the day. "And what would you call that in your biz?" he asked.

"Chronic disorganization," she said. "But don't worry, this is an easy fix with a rethink, some serious containerizing and a better functioning space."

Jenn turned and wandered over to the fridge. "May I?" she asked, pointing to the fridge. "It's helpful to know someone's lifestyle for prepping meals."

He nodded. "I developed a bad habit of heating food in the microwave after my wife died. Something has to change."

"Don't be hard on yourself. You've been through a lot." As she closed the fridge door, a plastic-coated calendar on the front caught her eye. "What do we have here? 'Dad's Social Calendar?'"

"Yup, my daughter Nicki's attempt to shame me into doing things by posting a near-empty social calendar."

It was a month-at-a-glance with one lonely entry. She leaned in to read aloud, "R.O.M.E.O. on Wednesdays? I'm intrigued."

"Don't get too excited," he said. "That's short for 'Retired Old Men Eating Out'."

"In twenty words or less, how would you describe a typical member?"

Mark paused. "I don't know. Just your average retired guy with a heart of mold."

Jenn chuckled. "Who's in the club?"

"Me, my way older brother Kevin and some friends we both grew up with. We get together every couple of weeks at the Tiger's Paw Pub for a beer, a bite and some pool. That's about it for my social life," he stated matter-of-factly.

"I see," she said, without making notes.

"Even that's in jeopardy," he said. "The waiter, Frankie, said they were taking the pool table out. That was the whole point of going there."

"That's too bad. Where will you play?"

Mark threw up his hands. "Dunno. The pool halls are too loud with their blasting music, which we don't like. Anyway, enough complaining."

As they wrapped up the kitchen, Jenn stopped and gazed at the fancy kitchen chalkboard with a long list of entries. Some were underlined. "Wow, that's a big To Do list."

"That was Annie's running list of things for me to do, which used to drive me crazy. I know I should erase it. But I still can't—"

"Mark, there's no timeline. If it still brings you comfort, leave it there."

Mark turned his back to the board. "Should we head to the dining room?"

They stepped into the dining room, which had open doorways between the kitchen on one side and the living room on the other. Mark commented that there was nothing to say about this room because he had only walked through it to get to other rooms. He didn't dine there; he only ate in the kitchen.

"Understood," said Jenn. "And, what about this china cabinet, dining table and buffet?"

Mark shrugged. "I have no idea. That was Annie's. I guess it's full of dishes and silverware."

"Have you thought about what you would like to do with the items?" she asked.

"Jeez, no. I walk by and no longer notice anything."

"I see. So, you don't think you'll use them?"

"A hundred percent no. My daughters now host family events at their places."

"Hmm. I see some possibilities for what we call flex space in this room."

"You mean use it for something other than a dining room?"

Jenn nodded. "But first, we have to clear out what isn't being used. Have you thought of asking your daughters if they'd like the furniture?"

"No, but they'd be welcome to it. I'm betting they won't want it; it's too old-fashioned for Nicki's perfect home that looks like a magazine and Charlotte seems to live in small apartments."

"We'll park that for now. Let's keep going."

Each room they visited had bits and pieces of Annie and strong memories that Mark didn't know how to process. He watched as Jenn took notes, without commenting positively or negatively. Everywhere, there were boxes stowed or stacked along the wall. Mark had attempted to clear out things and got stalled at every box. By the time they got upstairs in the arts and crafts room, Mark let out a big sigh.

"What?" asked Jenn.

"This craft room overwhelms me. Annie had so much stuff in the room, and there is even more in the boxes everywhere. She knew where everything was… but it's all a jumble to me."

"Don't fret. There are numerous easy solutions. It's not a big issue. How about we stop for today and grab a cup of tea?"

"Sold," he said, bolting down the stairs.

They returned to the kitchen island and talked nonstop for an hour. They talked about life, travel, dreams, fitness, dogs and more. Mark picked up Jack and kept him in his arms, while petting his head. Jack's head turned back and forth as Jenn and Mark chatted and laughed about things. Mark hadn't noticed the time until her meeting reminder pinged from her purse.

She looked at her watch. "Oh wow, where did the afternoon go?"

"Beats me," he said. "Usually, the afternoons drag for me."

"Unfortunately, I have another meeting. But let's take the next ten minutes to wrap up today's meeting."

"Okay, tell me what to do."

"If you feel like you want to get started, my suggestion would be to invite your children over and ask them to identify any items or boxes they'd like to take. Also, you can ask them to clear out their childhood bedrooms, so you can start thinking about repurposing the rooms and spaces."

"Will do," he said. "I remember Annie tried that once. They came over and left with a few items in a small grocery bag."

"Not a problem. But if they don't want anything, it allows you to sell or donate items you no longer want. Then we can make things happen."

Jenn gathered everything at the door and leaned over to put on her boots. Jack was making her laugh by attempting to lick her face while she buckled her boots. Mark pulled out her jacket from the closet and opened it to let her slip her arms in easily. "Thank you," she mumbled and turned the door handle. "I'll be back in touch when I've got a plan. And I've got an intriguing idea for your dining room."

"Really? What's that?"

"Nah, I'll wait until I've reviewed everything to make sure it works before I suggest it."

"Perfect," said Mark, not focused on what she was saying. Her sparkling brown eyes sidetracked him.

"Uhm...Mark?"

"Yeah?"

"I can't leave. You're blocking the doorway."

Mark twitched as if he'd suddenly woken up. "Of course, that makes it tricky, doesn't it?" Even Jack looked at him with an impish *what-the-hell?* look on his face. Mark stepped back.

"See you, Mark. And don't forget to drop by the pickleball league when the mood strikes you."

"How about tomorrow?" *Damn, too enthusiastic. Get a grip on yourself.*

"Sure," said Jenn with a smile as she walked out the door.

Chapter 17
Jenn

As Jenn drove off to her next meeting, she felt a light-heartedness that made the day happy. As she settled in at the café with her afternoon herbal tea, her thoughts drifted back to Mark.

She thought about all the funny moments they'd shared while she was there. She found it amusing how hesitant he was about changing anything in his own home, as if he needed approval from his daughters. Jenn noted that Nicki stuck her oar in the water pretty heavily when it came to decisions, and Mark seemed okay with that. Jenn figured it came from a place of love, as his children were trying to work through their mother's passing as well. Charlotte seemed more interested in supporting whatever Mark wanted. Jenn knew she had to find a balance between helping Mark set up his home the way he wanted it and not upsetting Nicki.

The more time she spent around Mark, the more she liked the guy, even though it was clear he was still working through his grief and had been going in circles for several years. She sensed he wanted to move forward in life but didn't know how.

She didn't know what to make of the situation because if someone had described Mark on paper, she would have given him a polite pass. Meanwhile, friends who were setting her up with "vetted" dates were missing things by a wide margin.

Jenn was trying to figure out what it was about him that made her smile and want to beat him again in pickleball. He had a sense of humor, which she liked. She found his comments amusing, as well as the antics with his dog. It seemed like Jack had arrived in his life at the right time and had helped him through some lonely moments.

Jenn also liked that he was really into fitness activities, unlike some of the men she dated. They often said they planned to become more active but hadn't done anything about it.

She sensed he was still interested in engaging with life, even though he had the stuffing knocked out of him. It looked like he needed someone's help to get back up on that horse. She figured pickleball would help. If he stuck with it, he'd meet lots of people.

Jenn was excited that she had an excuse to return to his home. She had many fun ideas up her sleeve.

Chapter 18
Mark

MARK HEARD AN EXPLOSION of excitement at the door. Nicki knocked and walked in with Katarina in her arms and Augustus hollering, "Hi Grandpa! Where's Jack? Jack, come here!"

"Make yourself at home," joked Mark as he watched Augustus charge into the living room to join Jack and the ruckus on the carpet. He adored his little grandson, a rough-and-tumble little kid who thrived on antics.

Nicki walked to the doorway of the living room, checking on Augustus. She turned to her father, "Dad, there's a three-foot radius of crushed crumbs and general grime around your recliner. When was the last time you had the carpets cleaned?"

Whoops. "Sorry, dear. Your Mom did that, but I'm not sure when she last did it. But don't worry, I will add it to the reorganization list," he said, scrambling to sound mildly interested in cleanliness. "In the meantime, it's helping Augustus to build his defences against germs," he joked.

She shot him the playful stink-eye. "Nice try," she said, rocking Katarina in her arms.

Mark's grandson reminded him of when he was four and ripping into everything with his older brother. Kevin had ten years on him, so he took the opportunity to toughen Mark up at a young age. Kevin and his buddies thought up endless ways to torture his little brother. Remarkably, Mark escaped with only minor injuries to his body, given how robust Kevin's activities were.

They had a middle sister, Gabrielle, who learned to hold her own with the boys. And she found the perfect way to keep her brothers at bay: excessive talking. They nicknamed her Gabby and she did her best to live up to it. They loved her and protected her if any guy in high school misbehaved, but at home, it was non-stop teasing. Gabby now lived with her family in Wolfville in the Annapolis Valley, and fortunately, close to their Mom in a local nursing home. She visited their Mom several times a week, and Mark knew she'd report any problems to them.

Charlotte arrived and walked into the kitchen. She and Nicki poured coffee and immediately got into a conversation about Nicki's business. Mark returned to the kitchen and poured a cup of coffee, dumping a spoonful of sugar into his mug, and the rest flew over the counter. Nicki went and picked out the dishcloth under the sink and held it up to show that it was stiff. She scrunched her nose and dug through the tea towel drawer to pull out a clean one. She wetted it and wiped the counter.

"Dad, how did your session go with Jenn?"

"Great," he said, launching into a lengthy summary of everything they worked on in the house, and ending with a near play-by-play description of their first pickleball game—including Jenn's triumphant win. Mark saw his two daughters exchanging glances like code that only they understood. He realized he had barely taken a breath, so he stopped.

"Wow," Charlotte said, "I'm so happy that she's so helpful in the house and on the pickleball court. I heard you mention you might start playing, and suddenly you're having games. Good for you, Dad."

"Jeez, it sounds like she's going way beyond helping with the house," said Nicki.

Mark wasn't sure what Nicki had implied with the comment, but he chose to believe it was positive. He beamed and tickled Katarina under the chin as she rocked back and forth in her baby carrier. "Yes, and I finally get why you wanted me to tackle the house. I didn't know how to get started."

"It's a nice home, Dad, so we want you to settle into the next phase of your life," said Nicki.

Mark heard Augustus shriek in the distance, which meant that he and Jack were having a riotously good time. "I'm glad you both feel that way because that's why I asked you over here today. I want to clear out a bunch of stuff and I need your help."

"How?" the two girls asked in unison.

"I'd like you to walk through the house and pick out anything that you want to keep. Any furniture, dishes, whatever—"

Nicki waved her hands. "Thanks, but I don't need anything. You keep it."

"Hang on, I'm not finished yet," he said, turning the spoon in his mug. "And I'd like you to clear out your bedrooms."

"Why?" asked Nicki.

"Well, I'd like a proper office, for one," said Mark, pointing to the corner. "This is a makeshift office in the kitchen and I need it to be better organized."

"Fair enough," said Charlotte. "Anything else?"

He decided to rip off the household bandage. "I need to clear out your mother's craft room. And I want to clear out the dining room too."

"But, Daddy," said Nicki in her little girl voice. "Those are all the best memories of Mom."

Mark sighed. He knew that it wasn't a good idea to start arguing, but he also didn't want to let things drag on further. "That's why I want to offer you anything you want, my dear. Please take the dining table, the china cabinet, the dishes—you two can work it out."

There was a long silence. "What?" he said in his semi-serious father tone. "If there's an issue, I'd like us to discuss it right away. No sense in letting stress build up."

"Why can't we keep everything as is?" asked Nicki. "I mean, I love coming here and looking at Mom's stuff... and yours, of course."

Now Mark was feeling antsy. It was hard enough for him to get on board with Jenn's suggested changes initially. Now he had finally tackled the job, and Nicki was pushing back. "So, Nick, when was the last time you were upstairs in your old bedroom or your mother's craft room?" He saw tears welling in Nicki's eyes. "I'm sorry," he said, hugging Nicki. The last thing he wanted to do was hurt his children. He looked at Charlotte. "Honey, how do you feel?"

Mark knew Charlotte didn't like conflict, especially with her older sister, who was used to making pronouncements and pushing for things she wanted in the household, even when Annie was alive. She got her way nine times out of ten.

"Char?" Mark asked quietly.

"Well, they're only material things. While I might want an item to remember Mom, I don't need a roomful of things. I appreciate that you are trying to move on with your life. And if you don't think you need a fancy cabinet or a room full of yarn and crafts, I support you."

"While I agreed to you having an organizer, I didn't expect her to encourage you to dump everything sacred to the family," said Nicki.

Here we go, Mark thought. Nicki had a flair for the dramatic and wheeled it out as needed. "Okay, let's take a breather here. We are a family, and I don't want things to get complicated."

"Does that mean you'll keep everything?" Nicki said, beaming and suddenly full of sweetness.

"Sorry, sweetie. It is time for items to go. However, I'm willing to extend the deadline for a few weeks to figure this out. Nick, if you want some things for your cottage or your friends, please take them now. But I need to finish this. Okay, girls?"

"Fine by me," said Charlotte, taking her mug to the dishwasher and placing it in the rack.

Nicki didn't answer, and within fifteen minutes had invented an excuse to depart.

"Do you still want me to take Augustus to the park?" asked Mark.

"That's okay, thanks. I'm squeezed for time. Augustus, time to go!" she shouted to the living room.

Augustus ran out with Jack behind him. "Are we going to the park, Grandpa?"

"No, Mommy has some errands," said Nicki.

"You promised!" Augustus sulked and squirmed while Nicki put a jacket on him.

"Sorry, buddy." Mark sighed and gave Augustus a big hug. He felt like Nicki was punishing him. But enough tension had already flared up and he didn't want to have an exchange in front of Augustus. "Next week. Okay?"

Augustus nodded, but he wasn't happy. "Where's Jack? I want to say goodbye." As soon as Jack heard his name, he raced into the kitchen and straight to Augustus.

Mark reached into his pocket and got out a dog treat, handing it to Augustus. "Here—you can give Jack a treat but make him do a trick for it." Augustus held it, taunting Jack while he twirled in circles, impatiently waiting for his treat. Soon, the boy was giggling and leaving the house in a better frame of mind.

Charlotte waved her sister and the kids out the door. She turned to her father and hugged him. "I'm sorry, Dad. This was meant to be a positive change for you."

"It is a positive change," he said, hugging her back.

"Nicki didn't need to respond like that. It's not like she would keep anything in her house that she didn't want."

"And it's not your fault, darling. That's who Nicki is. Despite all the constant activity in her life, she doesn't always accept change."

"Yeah, like when you and Mom helped out Andrew. She was rude to him on occasion, when the poor guy was just trying to cope with a terrible family situation," said Charlotte.

Mark winced when he pictured the night Andrew had landed on their family's doorstep more than a decade ago. He was the least motivated student in Mark's class who detested gym and fought participating in any physical activity. While he sensed the teenager had troubles at home, Mark still applied his tough-love style and insisted that Andrew find some physical activity that he enjoyed. He told him he wasn't going to sit on the sidelines in class.

Begrudgingly, Andrew agreed to join the walking group as a way to escape class. It was a motley crew of five disgruntled teenagers who had only one thing in common: they hated gym class. At first, they walked to the park, taking turns complaining about life and school. Then a funny thing happened: one day, someone threw a snowball at Andrew and he shot one right back. Soon they were chasing each other and laughing. They spent so long on the snowball fight that they had to run back to class. Nobody was more surprised than Mark to see them arrive at the end of gym class, puffing and panting with smiles on their faces. It morphed into a jogging group and Andrew turned into a runner, then a track and field athlete. Mark encouraged him while still pushing him hard. One day, Andrew blasted him, "Why are you never happy with my performance? I've worked so hard with my running and track meets, yet you still push me. Why?"

"Because I believe in you," replied Mark. Choked up, Andrew ran out of the gym and Mark turned back to resume the class. He'd try to find him later to explain more about what he meant. Andrew was an extremely sensitive kid, and Mark wondered if the lad was still angry with him.

That fateful rainy, cold Sunday evening, when the Russell family was watching *Jeopardy* on TV, the doorbell rang quite insistently. Glancing at Annie with a question mark on his face, he jumped up to answer it. Andrew stood outside on the mat, soaking wet and tears streaming down his face. Mark gasped. "Andrew. Come in out of the rain."

"Sorry, Mr. Russell," he whispered. "I had nowhere else to go." Mark brought Annie to the door and introduced her to Andrew. In between gulps and sobs, he explained that his father was drunk and had kicked him out of the house.

Right away, Annie hugged him and said, "My dear, you are safe here." Mark loved that about Annie—her sense of humanity and outpouring of care for a person in distress she barely knew. Mark cared too but found it difficult to express those feelings in the same way. They brought Andrew in and got him into a change of clothes, followed by a dinner of leftover shepherd's pie, which he inhaled. During gym class, Mark had sensed that his home life wasn't happy, but this made it all the clearer.

Nicki and Charlotte knew him from school and watched as their parents took him under their wings. Mark contacted social services the next day and learned that he'd have to go into the system. Andrew flatly refused, stating he'd run away before he did that. Mark and Annie offered to look after him temporarily until something was sorted out.

Weeks later, Mark and Annie called a family meeting while Andrew was out. Since Andrew had turned sixteen, they suggested taking care of him until he graduated from high school. While it was hardly Andrew's priority, Mark and Annie knew it was important for him to finish high school. Nicki asked if that meant she and Charlotte would have to share a room. They said they'd have to figure things out. Nicki went into a big sulk and showed her dislike of the situation by behaving passive-aggressively toward Andrew.

Andrew understood her feelings right away. He told Mark and Annie he'd leave rather than disrupt the family. And he certainly wasn't going to force the two girls to share a bedroom. Annie wasn't happy with Nicki's attitude at all. Finally, she suggested they fix up the basement, which gave Andrew his own space and the girls would keep their rooms. They all agreed, even though it was clear that not having him at all was Nicki's preference. He was a hurting and sometimes angry young man, but everybody understood why. Mark and Annie treated him like a son and supported him with his schoolwork to keep his marks up.

It was a Christmas gift that changed things. They had given Andrew a bunch of art supplies to try out. He discovered he had a deep love of drawing and painting. They enrolled him in different classes and the teachers said he was a natural. Plus, they noticed Andrew seemed to find it helpful to process the "unhappy years," as he referred to his family situation. Andrew once commented that he didn't know his father drank until one day when he saw him sober. While it was meant as a joke, Mark could see the pain and sorrow on the young man's face.

Andrew stayed with the Russell family for two years, long enough to apply for and attend Ontario College of Art and Design in Toronto. When he found out he was accepted, he danced around the kitchen—it was the most excited he'd been. Annie made a cake to celebrate.

When he went to Toronto, Andrew never looked back. He thrived in the design program and channeled his energy into becoming an illustrator. At college, he met Kimmiwan Menard, also known as Kim, who worked part-time in the registrar's office. She helped him find scholarships. An alumnus of OCAD, she was Métis from northern Ontario and was gaining recognition for a range of projects in painting, sculpture and music. She had recently won a Constellation award for her powerful meditative album called *Rhythm and Breath*. She had persuaded ten percussionists from around the world to contribute a solo track, to which she added soulful and restorative vocals.

Andrew told Mark that they bonded over tough childhoods. Soon, they were a couple, and as Andrew embraced his new life, his anger began to ease. While Mark and Annie cared for him deeply, they knew he wanted to leave his terrible childhood behind in Nova Scotia. They wished him well and told him he always had a home to come back to. Andrew flew back when Annie passed away, and he occasionally texted or called Mark, but mainly focused on his life in Toronto.

"Yes, I remember Nicki's response to Andrew coming to stay with us. She gradually accepted him, but when he left for TO, it was clear she was happy," said Mark.

"I don't get it, Dad. You and Mom never behaved like Nicki did. Where does it come from?"

Mark put his arm around his daughter, who had a heart the size of Halifax. "You didn't know your grandfather. My Dad had a nasty little streak to him when he didn't get his way. Nicki is nowhere near that bad because she still has love in her heart."

Charlotte nodded. "Well, I have to take off. So, you are doing the big reorg with Jenn next week, right?"

Mark nodded. "You bet. I am clearing out the garage so I can stow items in there to let you two have one more chance to take some of your Mom's things—especially jewelry."

"Don't worry about me," she said from the door. "I got a couple of things that I love a few years ago, and some of her rings and necklaces. I'm good." She waved and headed out of the house onto her bike.

Mark looked at Jack. "Well, two daughters visited and didn't take a single thing away." Jack trotted over to his dish and stared back at Mark. He grumbled, accusing Jack of being a mooch, but still tossed him a little cracker with a light dab of peanut butter.

Now he knew exactly what he needed to do to clear out the house, even if it upset the girls. He needed a little help from Jenn. It's funny how her name kept coming up in so many different situations.

Suddenly, things were getting interesting.

Chapter 19
Jenn

JENN REVIEWED HER CALENDAR for the week and her two ongoing projects. The first was preparing a client's home for sale. Once it was cleared out and ready to put up for sale, she'd call Maggie to help with the staging.

The second project, which excited her way more, was the work at Mark's place. They'd gotten to know each other further because he was coming out to pickleball and improving each week. She could see that his career as a gym teacher and former racquet player served him well in pickleball. And even when he wasn't playing, she noticed him on the bench, perched like a hawk, eyeing every player's move and shouting compliments when they made nice shots. At this pace, she figured he'd be beating her at the game in no time.

In the past month, they had played together in mixed doubles and even won a few games, which Mark always said was due to her skills. They smiled and tapped paddles with their opponents at the net after the game. Then he and Jenn would move to the bench to discuss what worked well and what didn't. He even gave her a few pointers to improve her game. At first, she teased him about it, asking when he became an expert on a sport he barely knew.

"I'm in coaching mode," he said. "Remember, Ted Lasso didn't know a thing about soccer before he moved to England."

"You do know he's a fictional character, right?"

He chuckled. "Of course I do, but the writers understood his value as a leader and a coach," he said, placing his paddle in a bag. He turned to her and said, "Want to continue this debate over a refreshment?"

She nodded and they headed next door, where many of the pickleball players had gathered after the session. The crowd in the café noted the two of them together and a few smiled and waved as Jenn and Mark took a seat off to the side.

⚘ ⚘

On project day, Jenn pulled into Mark's driveway and groaned as the rain pelted down. It was a typical soggy spring day in Nova Scotia, as if the weather gods couldn't choose between snow, rain, shine, or sun, so they opted for all of the above. It didn't matter since most of the work was indoors, except for taking some items to the garage. In the worst-case scenario, she figured they could move the boxes and furniture another day. However, Jenn was a "get'er done" kind of person, so she hoped the rain would lift enough so that they could clear out the house. As a professional box checker, she liked the sensation of finishing a job on the day that she had planned.

Mark looked enthusiastic as she walked into the house and tried to keep Jack calm, even though he knew something was up. He flitted up and down in anticipation. Mark and Jenn mapped out the rooms in the house that they would each tackle.

Knowing he didn't want any items from the dining room, Jenn suggested that she start there so that she could pack everything into boxes.

"What should I do?" asked Mark.

"I thought you could start with your bedroom. Do you feel okay about packing up Annie's clothes?"

"Yes," he said, tapping a pen against his left palm. "It's time. More than time. The girls have all the jewelry and items they want, so the rest is mostly clothes and everything can go to charity."

"Great. When you finish with her clothes, I suggest you purge your closet."

"*Moi*? What on earth would I get rid of?"

"As a guideline, anything you haven't worn in two years should be eyed suspiciously."

"C'mon, I would never part with my collector's item—a pair of gym pants that have seen me through four decades!"

Jenn giggled. "Because you never know when velour pants might make a comeback."

"My sentiments exactly."

"Mark, I'm not here to tell you what you can and can't save. Here's my suggestion: take each item out of the dresser or the closet. Think about the last time you wore it. Ask yourself if it feels important to keep that piece. And if it's worth the effort to fold it up and put it back, then keep it." She handed him a bunch of clear plastic bags for collecting his clothes.

"Deal," he said, looking pleased as if he had won that round. He started towards the stairs and turned back to her. "If I'm not sure about something, can I ask your opinion?"

"Sure, whatever," she said. Jenn didn't care, but she knew people sometimes needed a push to take the next step.

Jenn assembled a bunch of boxes, a tape dispenser and a bundle of paper for wrapping the dishes. The china cabinet had a set of twelve Royal Albert dishes with yellow roses. They needed the right person to love them, but Mark made it clear it wasn't him. She always believed that it was far better to donate unused items to charity and let the proceeds help others in need.

Upstairs, she heard Mark humming and rustling around with purpose, pulling out drawers and walking back and forth. He shouted down the stairs, "Mind if I play a little music?"

"Great idea," she responded. Soon, Al Green, The Temptations and Chaka Khan were filling the house with soulful sounds. About twenty minutes later, as she taped and marked a box of dishes, she heard Mark hollering that he wanted her to check out an outfit. She stood up and stretched her back from bending for too long.

With a soundtrack of Barry White accompanying him, Mark shouted proudly, "This outfit is twenty-five years old and it almost still fits!"

Jenn looked up to see Mark in a Boy Scout leader's uniform, the shirt and pants one size too small, with buttons working overtime to prevent everything from bursting open. Even the hat was a smidge tight, and it sat more on top of his head than on his head. She wanted to laugh, but wondered if he was being serious.

He drew in a breath and assumed a mock stand-at-attention posture. "Well, what do you think?"

"I love a man in uniform," she drawled.

"Darn, I thought I could give up my uniform, but with that response, maybe not." He turned around and tramped up the stairs with Jack hot on his heels.

She laughed and turned back to her packing. Later, he came down the stairs with four bags full of clothing.

She looked up. "Wow, you did well."

"They're mostly Annie's clothes. However, I filled one bag of my own. Let me tell you, it wasn't easy parting with my worn-out yellow polyester golf shirt and stone-washed denims."

"I can imagine," teased Jenn. "I think this calls for a break from all that stress."

Mark nodded, carrying the bags toward the back door. "I'll stow these in the back porch. And when the rain lets up, we'll take them to the garage."

As they stood in the dining area that now started to look empty, Mark asked, "So, what's this big idea you had about how to use this room?"

"I measured this room, and it got me thinking. Since you and your buddies enjoy getting together to chat and play pool, what about installing a pool table? Plus, you could also get a table tennis converter for the top."

Mark looked around the room. Silence. Jenn worried that he had second thoughts about dismantling his late wife's dining room and she had taken her idea too far. She waited a bit; he looked deep in thought. Finally, he looked at her, his expression laced with surprise. "I can do that?"

"Sure. If you don't think it works as a dining room anymore, you can do whatever you want."

"I love it," he said, taking in a big breath. "I had always hoped to put one in the basement, but Annie didn't like the idea."

"That tells me you've wanted one for a long time."

His expression looked like a mix of childlike wonder and worry. "What will the girls think?"

"It's your home, Mark."

He shoved his hands in his pockets. "I know, but I don't want to let them down. This is their home too."

"I get it, Mark. And that's something only you can decide."

"Honestly, I'd love it so much." Suddenly, he started chatting about where he'd place the pool table, the rack for the pool cues, and an end table for their refreshments.

Jenn could see the whole idea tickling his imagination. "By the way, I have a client moving from a house to an apartment in Calgary. He has a premium pool table that he's keen to sell. He's only asking a fraction of what he paid."

"Seriously?"

"Yup. Of course, you'd need to pay to have it moved, too."

Mark nodded. "Can you let me think about it a bit?"

"No problem. Okay, let's get back to work," said Jenn, turning toward the boxes.

"Wait. On second thought, tell him I'll buy it."

"You sure? That's fast to decide."

"Not really. I've wanted one for many years."

"I'll tell him right now. And I know a good mover. Want me to organize it?"

"Yes," said Mark, clapping his hands, spinning like a soul singer. He turned toward the stairs, whistling along with Barry White, who was crooning, "Oh Baby."

During lunch, they sat at the small round table in the corner, which Mark cleared by pushing all the mail to one side. They discussed their favorite soul singers from the seventies, trying to outdo each other and then moved on to rock and pop songs. Jenn could tell Mark's brother had a big influence on him, being ten years older. Finally, Jenn's eye caught the time on the kitchen clock and she announced they should be getting back to work. She noted that the two of them were having more fun than expected every time they got into chats.

They tackled the craft room together and found a way to work efficiently. She assigned Mark wrapping and boxing duties, which allowed her to inventory the goods going into each box. Annie had belonged to a local church and had actively donated her time and goods to every fundraiser. Jenn suggested donating everything to that group. Mark agreed but said he didn't want to call them because they always tried to invite him into the fold and he didn't care for the sermons. Jenn offered to call as the professional organizer and got out her phone. Within ten minutes, she had arranged the donation and announced they were thrilled.

"We're a great team!" Mark said, hi-fiving her.

Jenn gushed back, "Yes, we are!" Then they both blushed, and Jenn could see they were having a moment. Even though she didn't know him well, she felt like he had livened up a lot more than the first time they'd met. She wondered if it was because he had recovered from his pneumonia and was feeling better, or if he was finding her attractive. Maybe both. She had learned not to make assumptions about men, especially after they began dating.

That's because in her experience, a pattern had emerged: first, there would be several fun dates with lots of laughs and shared moments, sometimes followed by fireworks as they revealed that they cared for each other. In Jenn's observation, it was always the turning point. She wouldn't hear from the guy again. She'd call a couple of times, leaving an upbeat and friendly voicemail, and then she'd summon the nerve to send a few texts, with no response. That's when she knew the guy had opened the escape hatch and disappeared without a trace.

Lessons learned. She decided to play it cool this time and let things unfold naturally. She turned her attention back to the tasks at hand. Once the craft room was packed up and the boxes wrestled downstairs, they moved the makeshift office from the kitchen to the upstairs. The rain had eased up briefly, so they opened the garage and stacked the craft room boxes on one side for donation. This whole thing was going so well, Jenn felt proud of their achievements. That wasn't always the case with her clients. Some became increasingly agitated or sad as progress was made; others became stuck and couldn't do a thing. Mark's burden seemed to lighten with each box piled up in the give-away area.

By late afternoon, they had set up the office upstairs and Mark hollered he had found more items in the attic that he wanted to remove. Jenn heard him whistle a merry tune, as if he were enjoying himself. Finally, they carried the last boxes downstairs and Mark cheered. Heavy mist was coming down outside, so they set the boxes by the door, waiting for the rain to stop.

"Wow, wow, wow," he shouted. "We are done cleaning and clearing! I'm exhausted but happy."

"Me too."

"I'm starving," he said, swinging open the fridge, and frowning at the paltry offering of butter, jam, bread and condiments—and a case of beer at the bottom. He walked to the cupboard and opened a bag of nuts, putting them in a dish on the counter. Jack sniffed the air and leapt up to his chair. "No, Jack, these aren't for you." He pointed to Jenn to help herself, which she did. He asked, "Are you hungry?"

"I am." Jenn was super hungry, as well as sweaty and tired with a few aches from moving boxes. They had worked hard all afternoon. "And I am so looking forward to an Epsom salt bath in my soaker tub at home, and a glass of wine." She noted a look of disappointment on his face. "What?"

"I was hoping you'd stay for a bite," he blurted out. "I could order a pizza from Ciro's in the Hydrostone to celebrate today's victory. My treat, of course."

"Oh," Jenn said, sighing inside. Her energy was running low. But then again, she thought about eating alone every night of the week without much joy. She'd have an occasional glass of wine, but she was more of a social drinker and she didn't enjoy it on her own. Hell, Jenn didn't even have a dog to share Happy Hour with, like Mark did. Only weeks earlier, she'd complained to her book club friends about how dull it was to eat alone. And here she was ready to turn down the company of somebody that she was enjoying more by the minute just to go home to her bath. She scooped up some nuts and said, "Know what? That sounds like a great idea, Mark."

She'd barely uttered the words when he hustled to the junk drawer in the kitchen to grab the flyer for the pizza shop. He started to dial, then hung up. He turned back to her and said, "Whoops, I've been on my own too long. I forgot to consult about toppings. What would you like?"

"I'm pretty flexible."

"Come on, everybody has opinions about pizza toppings."

"I don't like a ton of meat, but other than that, I'm good. Well, one other item, but no biggie. How about you?"

Mark smiled, "There's one item I can't stand, but I can pick them off."

"I'd say there's only one way to deal with this. Let's do rock, paper, scissors, and on the count of three, shout out the word."

They faced each other and each shook their right hand up and down. On the third, they both yelled "pineapple" and then laughed.

"That's a relief," he said.

"What did you think I was going to say?"

"Bacon!" A grin swept his face as he picked up the phone again and ordered the pizza. When he hung up, he said, "It's going to be forty-five minutes. Is that okay?"

Jenn nodded and watched him go back to the fridge.

"Would you like a drink while we're waiting? I've got some local beer and wine."

"Beer sounds good after all that hard work." She glanced at the packed boxes by the door. They were the last thing to be moved to the garage and she knew it would irritate her if they didn't complete the day's task. "Would you mind if we took the last three boxes to the garage? Sorry, but my need to complete a task has kicked in," she joked.

"No probs," he said, opening the side door and carrying two boxes. "I can do this."

She was used to doing a lot of lifting. "This box is light, I can carry it," she said, slipping on her rain boots. She picked up the box and walked down the steps.

"Okay, but be careful because those stepping stones covered in moss get very slippery in wet weather—"

"Shit," she called out, as she felt herself sliding on the stone, dropping the box and landing butt first in the sludgy lawn that had turned into a marsh. Mark set boxes down in the garage and raced back, extending his hands to help her up. "Hurt anything?"

"Just my pride," she said, as she stood up with his help and surveyed the damage. Her jeans were soaked with mud from the waist down. She tried to push away the mud and water, but it was embedded in her jeans.

"Well, aren't you a mucky pup."

"And the day was going so well. Now I'm asking myself: why was it so important to get those boxes out?" she sighed.

"Beats me, I was all ready to sip on a beer and dream of pizza."

"Sorry..."

He waved his hand. "Don't worry about it. You can have a quick shower and I'll pop your clothes in the washer and dryer. You'll have them back after dinner."

Jenn usually had extra items in her SUV trunk, including extra sporting gear she could wear, but she'd taken everything out for this job to make more space. Bad luck. "Okay, but I need something to change into."

They walked back to the house and she stood on the rubber mat, dripping.

"Let's see. My clothes would be way too big for you."

"Yeah. But I don't feel comfortable wearing Annie's clothes."

"Course not." He stood staring ahead, deep in thought. Then snapped his fingers. "I know, you can wear the girls' clothes from high school. Funny, last weekend I asked them to clear everything out of their rooms and they didn't do a damn thing. You're similar in size to them back then. How would you feel about wearing fashions from the early two thousands?"

Jenn sighed. "Why not? I'll wait here for the clothes, so that you can take the muddy items right down to the laundry room."

Mark hustled upstairs and returned with towels and a stack of folded clothes. She surveyed them quickly. There was a pair of low-waisted track pants, tank tops and other pieces that would offer little help in covering her body. *Whatever.* She'd have to make it work.

She went into the bathroom and removed her muddy clothes, then cracked open the door and called to Mark, who whisked the clothes off to the laundry. She stepped into the shower, feeling the warm, sudsy water washing away all the work of the day, as well as the damp mud caked on her legs. In minutes, she felt renewed as she stepped out of the shower. She dried herself vigorously, then examined the clothes. Jenn shimmied into the shiny black track pants that were meant to be worn low, but she unrolled the low waistband and hitched them up a bit, which barely helped. They were snug, but to her relief, stretchy. Then she found a tank top that was at least long enough to tuck into her pants, and she put the tracksuit jacket over it. She glanced in the mirror and felt like a fifty-something woman trapped in a Y2K outfit.

Jenn stepped into the kitchen, feeling a little shy. "Let's do the time warp, yeah?"

Mark did a double-take. "Whoa. I didn't know those would fit you so—"

"Snugly?" she quipped.

"I was thinking, perfectly," he mumbled.

"I forgot, you do love a good tracksuit, eh?" Jenn appreciated that he wasn't making her feel self-conscious for wearing something that looked so revealing.

Mark chuckled. The doorbell rang and he grabbed his wallet off the counter, looking relieved to close down that topic. He returned with a box of steaming pizza and soon they were tearing into slices and chatting about the success of the day.

When they finished, they moved into the living room, each with another beer. Gradually, Jenn was feeling more relaxed and even let him razz her a little about her outfit. He got up, plugged his phone into the speakers, and selected a random playlist.

A few songs in, Jenn heard the memorable guitar riff and bongo drumbeats of a mega hit from the seventies. "Hot Chocolate," she announced. "'You Sexy Thing.'"

"Why, thank you," he said, exaggeratedly moving his body. "One of my favorites. Kevin played this a lot when he had friends over," said Mark, starting to groove to the music. He moved in a jerky way that looked like he was trying to catch up with the rhythm instead of moving with it.

"Is someone going back to the Disco Inferno era?"

"Oh yeah. Hang on here...wait. I feel something coming on." His pace picked up a bit, the moves grew more disjointed, while the smile on his face grew bigger.

Jenn could tell a few beers had helped him relax. "Oh dear, is that a Dad Dance coming on?" she shouted over the music. She saw him wave to join him as the music swelled.

He took her hand and pulled her gently into the dance. "Am I that bad?" He feigned hurt as he swung his arms and hips almost in time to the beat.

"Yes." She was laughing so hard she could hardly move. Undaunted, he extended his hand and spun her in a way that looked like disco and jive moves that had collided. Aside from Jack, who looked bemused, she reminded herself that it was just them being goofballs. *What the hell.* She mimicked his style of dance moves, which lacked self-consciousness, and they both laughed. Soon, she was exaggerating her own over-sexy moves in the black shiny pants that were perfect for the song. "All I'm missing," she leaned over and hollered to him, "Is a pink sequinned jacket."

He slapped his thigh and kept dancing. When the song ended, they came together breathless and laughing. "That was fun! Now be honest: Did I move like Jagger or was it more Prince?"

"Hmm..." she mused, as if she were a serious judge for the world's most important TV talent show. "I'd say more like... if Homer Simpson and Elaine Benes had a love child who liked to dance, that would be you."

"Ouch. As George Costanza said after watching Elaine dance, 'Holy, sweet Moses.'"

"Now you get your revenge. Who did I most resemble?"

"Hmmm... Madonna or JLo."

Expecting an insult, she raised her eyebrows when she heard his compliment. "Well, thanks."

"Cheers," he said, clinking their beer glasses as they both took a long drink.

Suddenly, the mood switched when the next song came on. It was April Wine's "I'm on Fire For You Baby," and he held out his hand to her, and they started slow dancing. It reminded her of high school dances when nobody knew how to dance to a ballad, so they clamped onto each other and swayed to the song. Halfway through, he released her but kept her close to him. He pointed to his massive chair in the corner, "Care to join me on my magic recliner?"

"Sounds promising," she whispered, half joking, half acquiescing as they moved there.

"I've never invited anyone to join me here before," he said, his voice cracking slightly. Jack woofed lightly from the floor and Mark looked at him and smiled. "Sorry, correction. Jack has visited. But that's it." He waved his chair remote and said, "Shall we?"

Feeling heady from the drinks, the pizza and the dancing, Jenn faced him and eased onto his lap. A tiny bolt of excitement surprised her. Jenn wasn't sure where this was going and her brain conjured up different scenarios that might transpire—some more thrilling than others. The background song, sung by Miles Goodwin, was a poignant reminder of a lonely young man aching for a woman he's in love with and is missing.

In the recliner, she leaned over him as he eased back. Then he stopped midway and kissed her. Suddenly, she felt her body floating with a sensation of desire she hadn't felt in years. They kissed, looked in each other's eyes and kissed again. The movement was slow and languorous, as if they had all the time in the world. Then she felt an increasing urgency as energy flowed through her body in a figure eight, like a race car tearing up the track. She leaned in a bit closer, hoping that it wouldn't stop—it was such an intoxicating feeling.

Her heart fluttered like a hummingbird's wings at a hundred beats per second. She felt so young and carefree, as if she were in her twenties again, doing something that seemed so normal. The only difference was that time now slowed down to a crawl instead of unfolding at the frenzied pace of her youth. She smiled, thinking that if they'd been in their twenties, by now they would have had enough time to tear off each other's clothes, finish several rounds of passionate sex, and return to an upright position with time left over to share a smoke.

The April Wine song faded out and there was a quiet moment while they waited for the next song to come on. Their kiss continued. It was so peaceful, Jenn thought she heard some rustling and a light cough in the distance. *Nah, just my imagination.* Until she heard a throat clearing and the terrible screech of an angry female voice.

"Daddy?"

Chapter 20
Mark

Startled, Mark pulled back from Jenn. At a forty-five-degree angle, they both saw Nicki standing there looking like a stern chaperone who'd nodded off on the job and was jolted awake five minutes too late to stop the offending party. Wearing a super scowl, she accentuated her displeasure by anchoring her hands on her hips and standing with her feet apart.

"Sweet Jesus, Nick," he barked. He knew he sounded angry, but she had ruined the breathtaking moment with Jenn. Humiliated, Mark grabbed the remote and pressed insistently to return the chair to an upward position. With the two of them facing each other and leaning way forward with little chance to move, the motor belched and moved at an eye-wateringly slow pace. The chair creaked and the gears ground as if angry about having to raise two people at once, and taking its good old time. Cursing to himself, Mark realized it was designed for old geezers who needed a lot of time to reach an upright position. As it crawled upward, Mark surveyed the mess they'd created: beer cans on the table, abandoned pieces of pizza and balled up napkins in the box.

"What the hell is going on?" Nicki demanded.

He and Jenn finally managed to get into an upright position. The chair lurched forward in a final gasp, as if to turf them out of the chair. As the two of them scrambled to regain their balance and dignity, their heads collided. Jenn suppressed a laugh.

"What?" he said, now only a few inches from Jenn's face. He could see her lips and chin quivering.

"Sorry," she snorted. "I think we just had a seniors' moment in the recliner."

He chuckled until Nicki barked, "OMG, you two!"

Mark turned and glared at Nicki. "And you? Don't you ever knock?"

"*Well, excuse me for caring*," Nicki said in her perfected sorry-not-sorry tone. "I was headed to the grocery store and wondered how your 'organizing day' went," she said with air quotes. "Looks like it went a little too well."

Mark sighed and ran his hands through his hair. There was nothing to be done but get out of this situation as soon as possible. "Nicki, this is Jenn. Jenn, Nicki."

Jenn turned toward her. "Yes, uhm, nice to meet you, Nicki."

Mark noticed Nicki eyeing Jenn up and down, then halting mid-stare. "Is that my tracksuit?" she gasped in a shocked and nasty tone that she might use for someone kidnapping her children.

Jenn looked down, her face a rush of beet red. "It's not what you think—"

"No, it isn't, because I haven't a clue what to think. Why the hell are you wearing my clothes?" she demanded.

Mark's collar suddenly starched. "Now hang on, Nicki. We were moving boxes out to the garage and Jenn slipped into the mud. We had to wash her clothes, so I borrowed things from the dresser upstairs. Nothing to see here, folks."

Nicki turned toward the dining room. "And what's this? Where's my mother's china cabinet?" She glared at Jenn. "I thought you were supposed to be a professional and help Daddy, not take advantage of him."

"Nicki!" Mark spoke in his sternest Dad voice. Heated words screeched to a halt.

Nicki pointed her manicured finger at Jenn, then the door. "You need to leave. Right now!"

Surprise rippled across Jenn's face. "Um, Mark, I'll let myself out," she whispered as she gathered everything and headed to the door.

Mark's hot moment with Jenn had imploded in a millisecond. There were so many things he wanted to say, but no words came out. Worse, his daughter had just treated him like a child in front of someone he found incredibly attractive. He watched Jenn leave and heard the car squeal like a getaway car in a movie. And Jenn's clothes were still tumbling in the dryer. He wondered what else could suck at this moment.

~≫≫ ≪≪~

"How dare you?" Nicki said, turning back to him once the car pulled away.

"I was about to say the same thing to you," Mark replied. He knew that Nicki had always been a drama queen and, if left unchecked, her bossy attitude could become a terror. "Why would you behave like that? You came far enough into the living room to notice something was happening. Why wouldn't you leave discreetly? You could have asked me about it later."

Nicki paused. "You are a vulnerable widower and we have to be careful."

"News flash, I was putting the moves on her. You know why?"

Nicki's pinched face looked like a boiled ham squished in a vise grip. "No."

"Because it's the first time since your mother died that I've felt attracted to a woman."

"What about all the nice women from Mom's church group? Many widows have shown great interest in you. You didn't even respond."

He raised an eyebrow. "Oh, you mean the Casserole Brigade? Yes, they all dutifully showed up after Annie died with their home-cooked meals."

"Not nice."

Mark tapped the remote nervously. "Of course, they are all lovely and well-meaning women, but frankly, dull as dishwater."

"But... " sputtered Nicki.

He held up his hand in a *stop* gesture. "I'm not finished." He'd let Nicki have her say, but he was just getting started. "I got this little shiver the first time I met Jenn, even on her first visit when I told her to leave the house. And it's grown since then. She even cleaned my clock in pickleball."

"What? She beat the finest all-around athletic gym teacher. Why was that good?"

"She's a very experienced player. I love that she didn't lose the game to protect my ego. And we can talk about anything..." he said but decided to stop there.

"She crossed the line at our home," said Nicki. "You were working together."

"Oh, jeez," he rolled his eyes. "It's not like I was her employer. Besides, we finished the contract. I got swept up in the moment and showed my interest."

"I guess," Nicki shrugged.

He felt a slight shift in her tone and he needed to win her over. "Do you know how hard it is to meet somebody in your later years, Nick? People our age become skittish. We carry around a sack of scars filled with painful wounds, tough lessons, and rejections from the past. Add to that the new array of scary dating challenges: the fear of showing interest in somebody, only to be rejected. The terror of finally committing to someone, then they abandon you, or worse, die. Not to mention all the stupid habits you develop from living too long on your own and expecting others to behave exactly like you do: You load the dishwasher like a Swiss watchmaker, and she tosses everything in like an obnoxious raccoon rooting around your composter. And then, no matter how good it seems between two people, at the first sign of a single tiny issue, you're both telling yourselves, 'It will never work.' I could go on—"

"No need. Got it." Nicki waved her hand to dismiss the conversation. "Now what?"

"Don't know. All I know is that you and Charlotte have harangued me to socialize for the past two years. I finally summoned up the courage to ask her out and now you're damning it. What's with that?" Mark looked at her; Nicki didn't say anything. But he could see the wheels turning in her head, which meant she had taken in what he said but was neither ready to explain herself nor apologize.

"Uhm, Dad. I have to go. They're waiting for me at home."

He knew they wouldn't solve all the problems tonight, but it was a start. "Okay." He stood patiently, arms folded, waiting for her to leave. She had a look of regret woven tightly on her face. "Anything else?" he asked.

"Can I have a hug?"

"Of course," he said, walking over and throwing his arms around her, rocking back and forth. He might have been angry with her intrusion, but he would never hold a grudge against his children. "Love you, Nick."

"Love you too, Daddy," she said, tears teetering at the bottom of her eyelids. She picked up her keys on the counter and walked out.

As she closed the door, the tumble dryer stopped. His mind rewound to the evening that had been going so well. He could only imagine what might have transpired if Nicki hadn't barged in. He wondered if Jenn would speak to him again. He reflected on the number of times they'd clicked and told stories that cracked each other up. He realized he hadn't been laughing a lot in the past few years. Other than with his brother Kevin and the guys, but that was about it.... until he met Jenn.

Of course, he hadn't dated in decades and didn't know how to handle this. Should he call her, or should he wait for her to call? He didn't feel confident calling her up right after his adult daughter had thrown a hissy fit.

He decided he'd wait for everything to settle before reaching out to her. Better yet, he hoped she'd call. But as he thought about it, why would she? She was so youthful and lively for her age; he was sure she would have men lining up to date her. He noticed how some of the single men responded to her at pickleball. Besides, on paper, he wasn't much of a catch: a maudlin widower spinning his wheels and going in circles in life. It was enough to make anybody dizzy. Worse, he didn't have a plan. Funny, all the years as a coach, helping people to pull up their bootstraps and move forward, and now he was stuck. He couldn't dig himself out of a hole, and it totally bummed him out.

His only hope was to find a way to reconnect with Jenn. All he needed now was a bucket of courage.

Chapter 21
Jenn

As Jenn pulled out of Mark's driveway, she saw a silhouette of him and Nicki in the living room in an animated conversation. Jack was perched on top of the sofa, where his attention shot back and forth between the conversation indoors and her departure from the outdoors. That little twelve-inch canine soldier took his role very seriously.

She backed into the middle of the quiet street and put it in drive, taking a deep breath before pressing the accelerator. Calming down, she eased forward and turned the corner onto Leaman Street, pulling over to the curb. She had had a few beers at Mark's, and while she had eaten plenty of pizza, she wondered if she was okay to drive. Given she was still fuming and lived only twenty minutes away on foot, she figured a brisk walk was the best option. Parking a street away from Mark's home would ensure that she could return the next morning to pick up the SUV—and with any luck, not bump into him.

She locked up the car, zipped up her waterproof jacket, and tucked the cursed track pants into her rainboots. God forbid she might sully these ugly but treasured vintage pants. A soft veil of mist settling over the street made for a peaceful walk down

Isleville Street. She checked her watch and laughed when she noted it was only a little after eight o'clock.

When Jenn reflected on her day, she realized she had fit in a lot of things since eight this morning. She felt excited that they had cleared out the house and prepared the dining room for the pool table delivery in a few days. Mark had sounded so pumped about having a pool table so that he could invite his brother and their friends over to play. Why not? It seemed like all the work they had done to change and rearrange everything in the house helped him transition to move on in life without Annie.

She wondered if Mark would contact her to talk about what had happened that evening with Nicki. She recalled how much fun they'd had all day, working on the house. Then afterward, they'd had a lively, spontaneous time hanging out and dancing together. She realized how much her feelings for him had snuck up on her over the past few weeks, especially today. She wondered if she should call him or wait for him to call her. She needed to wash the tracksuit and return it, so it could be a good excuse to chat, or he might want to drop off her laundry, and they could talk. But then again, maybe not. Why was this so damn hard?

She didn't know what kind of influence Nicki might have on him. By the sounds of things, she was pretty strong-willed about what she thought was best for her father. Based on Jenn's observations of her behavior, it was clear Nicki was conflicted. According to Mark, one minute she was bugging him to get out there and start a new life, but at the same time, she was having a hard time letting go of her Mom's memory. It was like she wanted her Dad frozen in place and time, as if sealed in a family bubble. Charlotte, on the other hand, seemed comfortable with everything. It sounded like she wanted her Dad to move on.

And that's what Jenn found so discouraging. She wanted to give it a try with Mark, a guy she might not have felt excited about if she had read his dating profile only. She realized that's why dates with other men had not worked in the first place or started and then fizzled in no time—she was attracted to characteristics that would eventually cause her grief. Mark was different. He had a great sense of humor and a fun way of looking at life.

In her mind's eye, she could picture them sitting outdoors near an ocean campground, sharing a beer and laughing over something inconsequential or a constellation in the sky. She liked the idea of spending more time with him and his family (hopefully, if Nicki could get past her angst). Jenn's parents had passed away years ago, and she had no siblings, so she felt like she had to work so hard to stay connected with others. While she was happy for Kyle's exciting new life with Achara in Chang Mai, she missed him terribly. As she was getting teary-eyed, her phone pinged. She pulled it out and saw that Kyle was sending her a message asking if it was a good time to call. Excited, she replied that she'd be home in ten minutes and would call him.

～∞∞ ∞∞～

When she got home, she made a beeline for her dresser and changed into jeans with a high waistband. Relief! She made a cup of chamomile tea and settled into her reading chair for a chat with Kyle. It would be morning in Thailand, so he'd be starting his day. From the minute he answered on the video app, she sensed something. They jumped into a quick exchange of family news and friend updates. She wanted to get past that so she could find out what was going on. But she felt she should allow him to tell her when the moment was right.

Five minutes later, when they finally both paused for a breath, he said, "Mom, I have some exciting news."

Her heart fluttered as she sipped her tea. Maybe they were coming back to Nova Scotia. She knew Achara loved it here, and with her language skills improving daily, she'd find a job within a reasonable time. Jenn immediately started picturing how she could reorganize the second bedroom at her place, so they'd have somewhere to live in the short term. Of course, they'd want their own home eventually, but this could be a no-cost option to get started. She had everything nearly settled, but then she reminded herself to find out the news first before making big plans.

Kyle pulled in a breath; from his tone, it was clear that he was bursting with joy. "Mom, Achara and I are going to have a baby."

"OMG, Kyle," she cried out, trying to sound happy for him. This news was never on her radar, so it threw her for a loop. "What, when? Tell me everything!"

"You sound like you're in shock."

"I'm fine, Kyle. I'm... surprised. It's not what I was thinking. Funny how we get our own ideas about the news we're expecting."

"What were you thinking the news would be?"

Anything but that. Kyle was only twenty-six. "I wondered if you two were coming back to Nova Scotia. You know... your Mama can always dream, right?"

He chuckled. "Yes, it's in your job description. But we have some complicating factors. As you know, Achara's Mom is not well, which is why we came back here in the first place. It seems..." he said, drifting and pausing.

While Jenn loved video apps so they could see each other's faces, moments like this were awkward. "Is her condition getting worse, Kyle?" she asked gently, even though she knew what was coming.

He nodded. "She may have a year at the most," he whispered. "Everybody is pitching in to help look after her. There's an incredible sense of community here."

"Oh, Kyle, I am so sorry. This must be so hard for everyone, particularly Achara and her Mom. I know they are close."

Kyle coughed. "Exactly... which leads to the second part of my news."

"Oh?" Jenn placed her left hand on the armchair rest, bracing herself.

"It's her Mom's dream to see the baby before... you know. And she *really, really* wants us to be married. Those are her two wishes."

Holy moly. Suddenly, her son's life was taking so many turns she was getting whiplash.

"Mom? Say something. And please, be honest about what's on your mind. Don't tell me what I want to hear."

"Well, my initial thought is that you seem so... young."

Kyle smiled. "We're the same age as when you and Dad got married."

Remember how that turned out? She knew she would only alienate him by expressing that concern. Besides, Kyle was a very grounded and smart young man who took his responsibilities seriously. "Well, I guess *touché* would be the appropriate response, wouldn't it?"

"Exactly," laughed Kyle. "I'm glad you get the irony."

She took a second to organize her thoughts. And then, she wondered, what exactly were her thoughts? "Kyle, I guess for me, this news is massive. One minute, my son is a carefree twenty-something pursuing career dreams and traveling the world. Next, he's moving into a huge responsibility as a father in another country and getting married. Suddenly, you seem so far away from me. I know you're grown up, but you'll always be my baby!"

"I get it, Mom."

"I'm excited for you and Achara, but please give me a little time to process this, okay? You two have probably been discussing these things for some time."

"Fair enough."

"I sensed something was up the last few times when we talked."

"We wanted to sort out a few details before we sprung it on you."

Consider it well and truly sprung. She felt thunderstruck by it all, but she needed to support him and Achara. "And if I may ask one more question, since this is such a major step in your life: Do you absolutely love her?"

"More than anything. That's why it's such a happy occasion for us—the baby and the wedding. We want to grant her mother this special wish." He stopped for a second. "And, Mom, this is between us: It's also practical for us to be married with a child coming. You never know when we might want to move back to Canada."

"Really?" She sat up.

"Easy, Mom," he said, raising his hand in a slow-down gesture. "I'm not making promises."

She jumped up from the chair and turned the phone so he could see her doing a happy dance. "I know anything could happen, Kyle. But I'm so excited to hang onto that tiny thread of hope." When she finished, she plonked back into the chair. "So, when is the wedding?"

"We still have some things to sort out. We don't want to wait too long, but we also have to find the perfect lucky date—that's important to Achara's family. So, it may be in a few months. And Mom, we sure hope you'll come."

Her mind raced with a mix of excitement and worry. Most of her traveling had been in North America and Europe; she had never been to Asia. She had no idea what to expect because it felt quite different to her.

"So, what happens at a Thai wedding?"

"That's for another call, and a long one," he joked. "Seriously, there are traditional Thai weddings that involve blessings, ceremonies, a procession and receptions for starters. However, young people tend to pick traditions they like and leave out the others. We are still working it out. I will keep you posted."

"Wow, sounds amazing. I can't wait to hear more."

"Does that mean you'll come? It would mean the world to me."

The look of love on his face filled her heart. "Of course, darling. I'll make it work." She couldn't believe she had blurted that out before getting her life organized.

"I can't tell you how happy it makes me to hear that, and I know Achara's family will be thrilled." He glanced at his watch and said, "Whoops, I have to run off to work."

"Send my love to the family, Kyle. We'll be in touch soon."

As soon as the call ended, Jenn burst into tears. She had already been through an embarrassing showdown at Mark's place. Now she had all of Kyle's news to figure out. She immediately turned her thoughts back to her initial worries. What if they grew attached to living in Thailand? Yes, he dangled the advantages they'd have as a married couple if they decided to come back to Canada. Who knew? They might make a plan, but anything could happen.

She also had to figure out how to travel to Thailand for the wedding. She didn't like the idea of traveling alone. She hoped to convince one of her girlfriends to join her because she was truly out of her comfort zone. Her friend Maya might go; she was always traveling to Asia. Somehow, she'd figure this out if she wanted to be with her child and the love of his life.

She also thought about the TV series she and Maggie might be working on. They'd been planning it for some time and she hoped the timing wouldn't interfere with her trip. She hadn't signed a contract yet, and if it came down to it, she'd choose her son over the contract. Maggie might not be happy, but she'd understand. They both knew other organizers and she'd find someone to take her place.

It was all a bit much, and she grabbed a wad of tissues as she thought about things. Since she was on a roll, she started a small pity party with only herself invited and wondered: Why do our children herd us onto an emotional roller coaster, then press the big green Go button before we've even had a chance to take it all in?

Jenn sighed with an exhausted sputter. She knew she couldn't solve all her challenges in one go. Then something important struck her: she was going to be a grandmother. Imagine that! She gave her head a shake and asked herself: Wasn't that the most important and exciting news of all? A precious newborn was coming into her life! That's all that mattered.

Why on earth was she focusing on all the stressful details like where they were going to live? Those were logistics that she'd need to navigate and decisions that Kyle and Achara would make, not her. But she could be there to help her son, and the rest of the details, like traveling to Thailand, were simply items for her to organize.

She realized she was shocked because she had never asked Kyle if and when he wanted a child—she had no idea he would embrace this new life phase with such excitement. While she had always dreamed of having a grandchild, she never wanted to pry. And more importantly, she knew he wouldn't like being nagged about it.

This news was too amazing and suddenly she had the urge to run out and buy adorable baby clothes in bulk. Were onesies cheaper by the dozen? She took a couple of deep breaths but couldn't slow down her racing thoughts. She headed down the hall to the spare room to daydream about endless scenarios that might involve hosting Kyle, Achara and an adorable new baby.

She eased open the door and her heart pounded. She looked at the cat and muttered, "What a mess!" Over in one corner, the cat glanced at her, then strolled back to its luxury velvet sleeping cushion and chose a pile of winter clothes to curl up on instead. She shook her head and walked over to it. "Typical cat," she said scolding lightly, petting its head while it purred sweetly for her.

Jenn turned her attention back to the array of boxes and oddball pieces of furniture, filling in the space. As a professional organizer, this was Jenn's very own dirty little secret: The kind of room that she wouldn't want clients to know about because she was breaking her own rules. When she and her husband split up, they sold their home, and she decided to buy a condo while she figured out her next move. Apparently, that *was* her next move, but she still wasn't sure if it was the endgame.

It was one of those part-guest, part-storage rooms that had never been properly set up. The truth was that her place had never really come together. She had no excuse; she'd lived there for years. When she moved in, she had plans to paint and decorate but felt uninspired—she knew quickly it wasn't her forever home. Truth be told, this was a holding pattern living space. It mostly felt a bit sad and lonely because it lacked the energy of love and people around her. When she ate meals on her own, she mostly read a book or listened to podcasts.

Early on, she had invited many friends over for brunch or dinner, which would have motivated her to spruce up the place. And while friends had every intention of dropping by, those with families, busy lives and endless school activities couldn't manage it. Jenn understood why but had gradually given up on trying to organize regular visits.

Since Kyle had left on his travels, Jenn decided to organize holiday potlucks for those on their own. She invited singletons who didn't have families to get together with on holidays like Canada Day celebrations, Thanksgiving and Christmas. She knew Halifax could be a lonely place because most people had family to gather with on holidays, and those who were alone often found long weekends could drag.

It was always a ragtag group of people who showed up, yet they managed to share excellent food, wine, and lots of laughter, especially while playing "Lost in Translation" charades with guests whose second language was English. However, when she glanced around the dining table, everybody was smiling, but deep inside she sensed a longing to be with their own families and loved ones in other provinces and far-flung countries.

Between holidays, she kept her life super busy so that she'd only have to eat, shower, and sleep there. The rest of the time, she immersed herself in activities that connected her to people and made her happy, which included work, fitness activities, and socializing with friends.

One year after she had moved in, she complained often to Maggie that she still hadn't done much with the place. Finally, during a slow business week in the winter, Maggie arrived at her door with paint gear and brushes to help Jenn tackle re-decorating. When she walked in, she looked around the room, beamed at Jenn, hugged her and shouted, "Yay!" When Jenn asked her why she was cheering, she said she realized Jenn wasn't perfect—and what a relief, because her home was always in a frenzy. Jenn reminded Maggie that she had four children and a husband at home, while Jenn had nobody but herself and a highly independent cat in her condo.

With Maggie's help, they'd painted and decorated enough of the place so that visitors would at least get a decent impression. And it worked for her book club and other guests: they thought it looked good. But gradually, when there was nowhere else to stow things, Jenn stashed them in the guest room, and chaos was building in the room. This had to stop.

She grabbed her laptop and fired up her design software to enter the room's dimensions and begin designing it. All she could think about was convincing her son and daughter-in-law to move to Halifax and providing them with a delightful nursery. Now she was motivated. She needed a plan, and a good one to whip her home into something more interesting.

Her phone rang and she answered with a laugh. "Hi, Mags. Your ears must be ringing. I was thinking about the guest room at my place and what you and I would do with it."

"Ha," she laughed. "What's this 'we' thing? I already got you started. Besides, I can't find time to do *my* place. You're on your own."

Jenn feigned hurt. "Well, I'm shocked." Jenn could sense excitement in her friend's voice. "What's up?"

"Manny Schuyler liked our proposal for the TV series."

"Really?" Jenn couldn't believe how life was improving by the moment.

"Yes. He says there are a few details to iron out, budgets to tweak and timing to confirm, but it's looking good."

"Woot, woot!" Jenn shouted.

"And one more thing. He's in Halifax this week to deal with another series they may be shooting on the South Shore. He wants to meet. Fingers crossed! By chance are you available on Wednesday morning?"

"Let me check my calendar," she said, toggling to her phone calendar. "Oh dear—"

"What?" asked Maggie, her voice dropping an octave.

"I've got pickleball on Wednesday morning." Jenn waited a few seconds, then laughed. "Kidding!"

Maggie blew a raspberry. "You'd better be, girl. What's with you pickleball players? Always got to be playing. Or maybe you want to bump into Mark."

"A little of both," she sighed. "Actually, I think he's been lured over to the Halifax Games Center to their drop-in sessions."

"Maybe you should wander over there yourself."

There was so much news about Mark that she hadn't told Maggie yet. This wasn't the time to start. "We'll see. Anyway, where do we meet Manny?"

"How about The Jumping Bean at 4 p.m. on Wednesday?"

"You got it. Can you believe it, Maggie? This could be so much fun!"

"Yes! Gotta scoot. There's a three-way food fight unfolding in the kitchen. Bye!"

Jenn buzzed with excitement. She grabbed her paper and markers and settled in for some serious planning before the meeting.

Chapter 22
Mark

LATER, MARK WAS STANDING at the kitchen counter studying a crossword puzzle. He hadn't slept well, and it was one of those days when the clues weren't ringing any bells. For the life of him, he couldn't conjure up a seven-letter word for a feeling of annoyance, irritation or hostility. Mark tried to remind himself why he did the crossword when he was tired, because today he felt useless.

Jack barked and wagged his tail as he rushed to the kitchen, which, for the pup, meant that "a friendly" was visiting. From the kitchen window, he saw Charlotte cycle up the driveway in her usual way: jumping off her bike without coming to a full stop and stowing it behind the house. She bounded up the steps, gave a well-pronounced knock and walked in. Checking the bottom of her shoes, she wiped them half-heartedly and walked to the island.

"Hey, Dad," she said, smiling. She pressed a light peck on his cheek, followed by tossing Jack a little dog treat. "Sounds like this place is action central at the moment."

"News sure travels fast in this family," he said, knowing Nicki would have called her straight away last night after her visit.

That would have been followed by a lengthy analysis of what the two of them should do about it.

"Yeah," she blushed. "Nicki kind of told me, but not all the details... " She paused, awash in an awkward expression, as if searching for the right way to present her thoughts.

Mark knew her thought process, but he felt a bit cranky and wasn't going to make it easy for her. "Why don't you ask me what you want to ask?"

"Uhm, were you and Jenn really, you know... uhm... doing it on the recliner?"

What the hell had Nicki told her? "Are you kidding me? That chair is covered in sticky vinyl material—what do you girls call it? Pleather?"

"OMG, Dad," she said, waving her hands. "Too much information!"

Score one for me. It shut down that conversation in a hurry. "Listen, Char, I don't ask about your after-hours life, so you should show some respect for mine."

Charlotte's shoulders heaved up and down in a sigh. "You're right, Dad. I'm sorry."

He calmed himself. "Seriously, we'd been dancing and took a horizontal break, is all. Your sister took umbrage and started behaving rudely." He took the pen resting on his ear and filled in the crossword. "That's it. 'Umbrage' is the word I was trying to think of. Nice one, Nick."

Charlotte grinned, "Yup, that's what Nicki does." She walked to the cupboard and grabbed a mug. She pulled the carafe from the coffee machine and filled the mug, then waved it back and forth at Mark with a question mark on her face.

"No, thanks, I've got plenty here," he said, showing her his large mug.

She sat on the stool. "For the record, I like Jenn. I don't know her well, but she seems very smart, grounded and—"

"Cute," Mark interjected. "And peppy, very peppy. Trounced me at pickleball. Although I am improving," he chuckled.

Charlotte's blue eyes lit up. "That's cool; I haven't heard you talk that way about any woman since Mom passed away."

"That's because I haven't felt that way." Out of the corner of his eye, he caught tiny lines of sympathy on her face. "Tell me. When you suggested that Jenn should organize my home, were you secretly plotting to bring us together?"

She shrugged. "Nah, I was being a dutiful but annoying daughter trying to get your home functioning better."

"That's my girl," he said, hugging her. A text on his phone caught his attention. "Oh geez, it's from Andrew and Kim, saying, 'Go Tiger!'" He turned the phone so she could see a photo of them laughing, alongside a major wink emoji. "For Pete's sake, why don't I start a newsletter so everybody can find out my business?"

"Sorry, Dad. It's just that we love you so much. What's next with Jenn?"

Mark's foot jiggled on the chair rung. "I don't know. It didn't end on a good note, even though it started well."

Charlotte leaned in. "Tell me more," she said.

Mark felt more relaxed around Char because she didn't judge. "The day had gone so well. We worked hard, we played music, and we blasted through so much work that I didn't even know needed addressing. When we were done, we were both starving. So, I ordered a pizza. We even agreed on what should go on it," he recalled fondly.

"That's always a good sign, Dad," said Charlotte. "Then what?"

"While we were waiting for the pizza, Jenn suggested taking the boxes to the garage to finish the day's work," he said with a chuckle. "She's a get-things-done gal. On the way to the garage, Jenn slipped into a mudslide. I offered to wash Jenn's jeans while we waited for dinner. So, I loaned her Nicki's track pants from high school. Who knew it would trigger an international incident?"

Charlotte shook her head as she stirred her coffee. "They're twenty years old! She wouldn't be caught dead in them now."

"Tell me about it. Anyway, Nicki was Miss Bossy Pants and aggressive, so Jenn left in a hurry. Then I was peeved with Nicki. And the whole evening imploded."

Charlotte sighed. "Jenn is a good person. I'm sure you'll work it out. Yes, it was awkward, but someday you'll laugh about it."

Fat chance. Mark wished he knew what to do about Jenn. He didn't want to ask his daughters for advice, for fear they'd try to solve his love problems for him. He heard loud talking and laughing outside, and Jack raced to the door. His woofs increased as they drew closer. "Sounds like Kevin and the boys. They're here to play pool."

Charlotte pulled her cycling jacket over her head. "How's that going, Dad? Do you like the pool table?"

"Love it," Mark beamed. "We are having a great time. Jenn also suggested a set of speakers for this room and we can play music we like. And there's no restriction on how long we can play. All good!" The door burst open. Kevin and the guys walked in, saying *hi* to Charlotte, while she stood on the mat and rocked each foot, trying to put on her cycling shoes hands-free. As she hugged him and started out the door, she said to the guys, "And Uncle Kevin, whatever you do, don't ask Dad about his time on the recliner with Jenn."

"You're grounded, young lady!" Mark shouted as she giggled and closed the door.

"What's up?" asked Kevin with a big grin, followed by a chorus of others joining in as they moved into the games room. "Is this your cutie from pickleball?"

"None of your business," he said, handing a pool cue to each guy.

"You're right. But that won't stop us," said Kevin, the others laughing. Kevin stared at him, "Dude, you know we aren't going to start playing until we get details."

Mark sighed. It hadn't even been twenty-four hours and he felt like the topic already had too much discussion. But he knew his brother would stop at nothing short of giving him a noogie like he did when they were kids, if he didn't get the details he requested. He quickly gave the highlights, while the guys laughed and inserted jokes about trying to move from horizontal to vertical in under sixty seconds. The responses ranged from teasing him to expressing a bit of envy for his chutzpah and spontaneity in seizing the moment.

He corralled the pool balls into the triangle at the end of the table, then lifted it off. "Aww right, aww right," he barked, going into coach mode like he did to teenage boys in the locker rooms when they were getting silly. "You've had your fun. Now let's play pool."

Deep inside, Mark was pleased. All his life, he'd played the responsible adult role, the guy everyone could count on who never did anything wrong. In other words, boring as all get out. Suddenly, he was the talk of the family with comments that ranged from frivolous to envious.

This was new territory for him, and he liked it. Maybe he wasn't such a dullard after all.

Chapter 23
Jenn

A FEW DAYS LATER, Jenn removed the tracksuit that had been on the drying rack for too long because she didn't know what to do with it. She had hoped Mark might drop by with her clothes, not that she needed the items or even cared. The mismatched pieces were her official work uniform on the days when she was dealing with messes in people's homes. While he didn't know where she lived, he knew her office in the Hydrostone area. She wondered if the exchange with Nicki was too much and it would be too embarrassing for both of them to sort through.

Mark hadn't shown up for any pickleball games at the fitness center, which disappointed her. In fact, it made her downright grumpy, especially when her friend Kathleen said she'd played against him at a drop-in at the rec center. In no time, he'd become the fun player who liked winning but who also laughed his way through bad shots and losing games. He was also one of those rare amateur athletes who drew on his lifetime dedication to team sports, which meant that his skills improved with every game.

Kathleen gushed over how much people liked him and there were even a couple of players asking him to compete in a mixed doubles tournament for charity. Jenn bristled at the thought.

She'd pictured the two of them playing and progressing together and now he might be moving to a different rec center to play. Jenn asked about the sessions. She could casually drop by and bump into him. Kathleen replied with three open-play sessions a week; it was random. If Jenn were serious about 'bumping into him,' she'd practically have to stalk the guy. Not her style.

She stuffed Nicki's clothes in a bag and wondered if she should write a note. If so, what was the tone? Should she sound serious? *"Thanks for the loan of the outfit. Hope all is well."* She was falling asleep rereading it. How about jokey? *"I'd like to return these items for a full refund; they didn't fulfill their promise,"* *"Well, that was almost fun,"* or *"Care for an instant replay?"* She smiled at her wicked thoughts.

Could they start over, or was this all over before they even got started? Sadly, her track record of connecting with a guy was following its usual course: quick excitement at the meeting phase and dreams of what could be, followed closely by silly circumstances, misunderstandings and extreme disappointment. Sometimes it was her fault and other times it was the guy's. Who knew why all of this happened? But then she thought about Mark and the idea of another woman at pickleball vying for his attention, when Jenn believed they had found the perfect fit. It rankled her. And if that was the case, she reminded herself, this was no time to give up.

She stood for ten minutes leaning over the notepad on the kitchen table. After trying to write something clever, in the style of banter they'd enjoyed so far, she filled the wastebasket with a pile of little sticky notes. And each time, she was saying the same thing. It was like a battle between her sensible brain and the cheeky pen in her hand. What if he didn't feel the same way? She returned to the first idea, which was boring but would not offend.

Why was this so hard? Rehashing things in her head reminded her of how she used to agonize over every little thing in high school, a tendency which, in hindsight, now seemed like a complete waste of time.

She drove over to Mark's place and saw a few cars in the driveway and on the street. Plagued by insecurity and a gloomy sense of self-worth, she imagined him hosting a bunch of people and having a great time... without her. She parked the car on the street and grabbed the bag from the seat. In sneaky stealth mode, she glanced up and was relieved that Jack wasn't on guard on the sofa—he was likely herding visitors in another room. She gently climbed the side steps, relieved that her running shoes didn't make any sound. Off in the distance she heard chatting and laughter. She looped the bag over the doorknob and eased back down the steps, striding quickly to the car. Relieved yet disappointed she had delivered the clothes without bumping into Mark or his friends, tears welled up.

While she had many great things happening in her life—a grandchild on the way!—and wonderful friends and loved ones in her life whom she loved dearly, she felt like she was missing the one relationship she had always dreamed of.

Somehow, she had to find a way to give it another whirl. But for now, she was needed on the TV show planning and plunged in headfirst, as she always did with work.

Chapter 24
Mark

When the guys left Mark's house after an afternoon of pool, T-Bone found the bag hanging on the door handle outside. Grinning, he passed it to Mark and said, "Special delivery?"

Mark noted the tracksuit in the bag and a folded note from Jenn on top. "Nothing special," he said, tossing the bag on the counter in the kitchen. "Looks like one of the girls' outfits is coming back to the house." He was sorry to have missed Jenn knocking on the door. He figured there was too much noise inside.

When the guys said goodbye and Mark was left on his own, he opened the bag and fished out the note. He scanned it, then crumpled it. The tone was neutral, distant even. He sighed. This note had all the charm of a bag of hammers. This was her returning to their professional relationship—like the first day she came to his house for a consultation. He went to the basement and picked up her folded clothes; it was time to return them.

He needed to reply to her note. He pulled out a piece of paper and tapped the pen on his workbench, waiting for inspiration to strike. While he'd spent the last week dreaming up all kinds of funny and/or cheeky things to say, he now knew that was off the table. He wrote, "Here you go. Mark," then put his pen in his shirt pocket. He didn't want to go to her office during business hours in case she was there.

He went back upstairs and sat in the living room. He found himself sitting and staring into space, wondering what to do with himself. Reading wasn't an option; he was too distracted. Yet he couldn't sit there doing nothing—he needed a serious distraction.

He walked to the closet, picked up Jack's leash and rattled it, saying, "Wanna go for a walk, buddy?" Jack jumped straight up in the air and practically did backward hoops in celebration. Mark wished he were that easily pleased. At least he had a dog who adored him, which was helpful at this moment. He put on his running shoes and scooped up Jack, who was ready to rocket out the door.

Forty minutes later, they returned to the house, and Jack trotted happily to his water dish. Mark checked the clock. He couldn't believe it was only two in the afternoon. Even though he was more active these days, when he didn't have something planned, the days dragged. His body still felt programmed to be an active and busy gym teacher. He didn't ever think about what he'd do in a day; it was always scheduled and he happily moved from one item to the next. He didn't realize how much he defined himself by his work and coaching.

From the corner of his eye, he noted the large kitchen chalkboard with Annie's final list of To Do items. He picked up the eraser and held it mid-air, scanning the list. The items were nearly tattooed into his brain, they'd been there so long. There was the broken window handle that never quite made it to the top of the list. Given that it was in the guest room, he didn't feel it was urgent.

Annie had also wanted a set of shelves in her sewing room, which he had bought in a box at a yard sale but never got around to setting up. One of the few points of contention between them was the household chores. He was good at it and it was his domain. And by any objective measure, Annie had no talent for assembling or fixing things, yet had strong opinions about how it should be done. And he could never convince her to do something else so that he could work without her hovering. For a joke, he gave her a white construction helmet that he found at a yard sale—then had to explain that supervisors wore white hats on site. They had a running joke about putting the shelves up, but their respective jokes had a tinge of annoyance around the edges. That's why the shelves were still in a box somewhere in the basement.

Now that the room was cleared out, the shelves were no longer needed and could be donated to Habitat for Humanity. He erased that off the list and felt relief. He wondered why he couldn't bring himself to clear the remaining list off the board and write in something fun instead. Habit, he figured. This was the last step he needed to take to move on, and yet he still couldn't do it. While he'd been doing quite well for the past months, this certainly wasn't the day to let go. He was caught in a cycle of restlessness and needed to break it.

He glanced at the calendar and saw there was a pickleball drop-in at the fitness center starting in fifteen minutes. That was the fun distraction he needed. Mark changed into his fitness gear and crated Jack, who, despite his recent big walk, looked disappointed that he wasn't heading out on another adventure. "Your need to run is insatiable, my little pooch," he said, petting Jack's head. He filled a few play toys with peanut butter, grabbed the bag of clothes off the counter and walked out to the car. He tossed the bag in the car in case he got the courage to drive by Jenn's office.

He wondered if she might be playing pickleball. It would be so much easier if he could bump into her to gauge how she behaved around him. The note she wrote left him scratching his head, but in person, it would be easier to tell.

At the drop-in courts, he placed his paddle in the system for a turn to play. He walked to the back and started stretching. In no time, people who knew he was a gym teacher joined him and asked what they should do to stretch before playing. Soon they were joking and laughing, and then it was time to play. He played on and off for two hours and felt great when he finished. His former fitness level was returning, and he had peeled off most of his pudge from the last two years. His energy had vastly improved, and he enjoyed chatting with everyone waiting to play.

But even as he laughed and joked, he kept looking around in case Jenn had arrived while he was playing. It would have been much better with her there.

Chapter 25
Jenn

MAGGIE AND JENN SAT down in the café with their lattés and notebooks, ready for their meeting with the TV producer, Manny Schuyler. The place buzzed with conversation—everybody was in a good mood.

They discussed all their ideas and reviewed plans so that they were on the same page with the project. Jenn told her about Kyle's wedding with no specific date, only the month. But they knew the TV series would be shot by then and in post-production, which wasn't their responsibility. The rest of the project would be mostly paperwork, so they agreed that Jenn could do the job and still attend the wedding in Thailand. Jenn felt relieved to know the logistics were working out in her favor. She needed a big distraction.

They chatted excitedly for fifteen minutes, then stopped and looked around. "Hmm, I wonder where Manny is," said Maggie. "Let me check my phone in case he's running late." There were no messages, so they kept talking. After another round of discussions, Maggie checked again. "He may have been delayed at the shoot on the South Shore. I'll text him," she said, talking with her fingers clicking wildly.

"You okay for time?" asked Jenn.

"Yes, as long as he arrives in the next twenty minutes. Brendon is away and I have to pick the kids up at daycare. You know what sticklers they are about being late."

"Is there anybody else authorized to pick them up... besides me, of course."

Maggie shook her head. "Nope. I have no family or dear aunties waiting in the wings."

"Tell you what. You've been doing the upfront negotiations with Manny. If need be, I'll pick up the kids and take them home for snacks and entertainment while you talk to Manny."

"Okay, I appreciate that, Jenn. Sorry, I really wanted you to meet him."

"Me too, but don't worry. There's lots of time."

Maggie's phone pinged with a text. "Hmm, this is quite cryptic. I'm guessing he dictated it in the car. If I have my decoding skills down pat, I think he'll be here in half an hour. And he's got a flight back to Toronto tonight, so we need to keep the pace going when he arrives."

"We will," said Jenn.

Maggie's phone rang. She pulled out the phone, looked at the screen and said, "It's the daycare. I'm not late yet; what's going on?"

Jenn watched Maggie as she spoke to them in clipped phrases, sounding like a journalist asking who, what, when, where and why. She knew by Maggie's face that something was up. "What?" she asked when Maggie hung up.

"Talia started vomiting about ten minutes ago, and she wants her Mommy. I need to go right now. Can you do the meeting with Manny, assuming he shows up?"

"Of course. Go," she said, her hands waving her out the door. "I'll call you afterward. I can easily swing by your place if you need help with the kids."

"You're a lifesaver, Jenn," said Maggie giving her a quick hug. "Please give my apologies to Manny, but he can be a bulldog, so remind him it's his fault for being late," she said, rushing off.

"Will do," said Jenn to nobody. She went to the counter and ordered a decaf; she didn't need any more energy for the meeting.

When Manny finally walked through the door, she knew it was him without even guessing; he had an air of confidence and the look of a big-city guy. To start, his hair had been recently cut, dyed and styled. Plus, he was dressed in the most expensive designer clothes, which were meant to look informal and casual yet cost a fortune. His clothes were well-ironed and new, with crisp collars that looked like he'd only wear them for a week, then give them away.

Jenn stood up and gave a little wave. He walked to her with purpose and said, "Well, that was quite a day. Think I could get a beer instead?" No apology, no explanation or "Nice to meet you." Jenn flinched. "Sure. You order at the counter."

Manny got a local brew and a sandwich, returning to the table. He sat down and said, "Where's Maggie?" Jenn decided this was a good time to set some boundaries and show they weren't desperate to work with a big producer from away. "Maggie had to leave. We waited an hour, and then the daycare called with a sick child issue, and she had to leave."

"Hmm. I hope that if we work together, this won't be an issue."

"Not at all," said Jenn in a calm tone. "We'll know our schedule and we'll plan. Now, I know you're running late and you have a flight to catch in a few hours. Shall we get down to business?"

Manny nodded. "Let's dive in," he said, pulling out his tablet and bringing up his stylus to make notes.

Soon they were in a deep discussion and it was clear from his body language that she and Maggie had done a good job preparing for the meeting. As she talked through the proposal, he would nod and mumble "great idea," "good plan," and other signs of agreement. He cut in constantly, asking questions, but Jenn was ready for everything—or if she wasn't, she promised to look into the issue and get back to him.

She saw him lean back a little, as if he were feeling pleased about how it was going. And as he was doing that, he started telling little anecdotes about his other shoots, in which Jenn was only mildly interested, but she feigned light interest. At one point, they discussed managing people and expectations, particularly on a reality show, where people often try to steer the direction.

Since she had plenty of experience and felt it was relevant to their project, she began sharing some of her successes in home organizing with him. Suddenly, he launched into one of his film war stories about trying to shoot a romance series at a heritage hotel, The Fairview Inn in Bridgewater. He had booked the restaurant for the shoot at 5 p.m. He tried to get an elderly couple to wrap up their late afternoon meal, but they were having none of it.

First, they bristled at having to move their car out in the lot, where the crew was trying to set up for an outdoor location—but reluctantly agreed when he offered them a glass of wine. When he tried to get them to pick up the tempo with their dining, the woman replied politely but with a steely stare, saying it was their big night out and she wasn't going to be cowed into eating quickly.

When it was clear they wouldn't budge from the restaurant until they were finished, he offered to pay for their meal if they could wrap up in ten minutes. They finally agreed, although the woman snuck in a new demand: dessert, for both of them. He told the woman he liked her, even though she was annoying the hell out of him, which only made her laugh. He shot back that he would throw in two desserts, hell, he'd buy them the whole cake, but only if it was takeout. "Deal," said the woman, shaking his hand.

He leaned to Jenn and said, "I nearly offered her a job on the spot as a production assistant. She was far more effective than my twenty-year-old assistants." Jenn threw her head back and laughed from her belly. As she did, her eye caught the outline of a man, who was pausing at the window. She nudged her head sideways and saw Mark. Their eyes met. Then his eyes flicked back and forth between her and Manny. Judging by the disappointment on his face, she guessed what he was thinking: she was on a date. She lifted her hand to wave, but he had shot out of sight. She couldn't jump up and run out to the street; she was in the middle of a meeting. There wasn't much to be done.

"Somebody special?" Manny said, noticing her gesture.

Jenn nodded. "I'm working on it."

By the time they had wrapped up and Manny had finished a refreshing beer, and a bite, his mood improved. He told her that he felt confident with her and Maggie at the helm, and he would send the contract once they had made a few more tweaks. He stood up and shook her hand, saying how enthusiastic he was about the project. By then, it was near rush hour, and he had to race to the airport.

As soon as he left, she called Maggie. Talia's tummy had settled down once she told her Mom what she'd eaten earlier. Maggie laughed as she provided an update. "We discussed the importance of not eating slimy plastic toy bugs and worms from a jar even if they were pretty colors. Lord knows what she ate!"

Maggie insisted she didn't need her help, so Jenn decided to go back to the office to do some paperwork.

Chapter 26
Mark

WHEN THE SUN POKED through the large clouds, revealing a bright blue sky, Mark decided to walk to Agricola Street to meet Charlotte at the deli for a bite. He put on his knapsack and added the bag with Jenn's clothes, in case he got the courage to swing by her office later.

Whenever the sun came out, happy people appeared on the sidewalks of Agricola Street. It was a neighbourhood where people strolled and shopped but also stopped to chat with someone they knew.

Mark whistled a merry tune as he walked along. He loved that Charlotte worked non-standard hours, which meant she could meet him for a quick meal. It was the opposite of Nicki, who logged far too many work hours, along with the responsibilities of two children, a husband, and endless family activities. She looked perpetually tired and undernourished, yet on the few occasions he raised his concerns with her, she told him she had no choice. Nicki reminded him of Annie—they were both thrill-seekers who got swept up in the excitement of new work, projects and volunteer activities.

Annie would take on far too many requests, then stress about getting them done. Even church activities, such as small fundraisers, turned into pressure-filled days leading up to the event. Mark encouraged her to enjoy herself or not do it. She would nod while he talked, but continued doing the same thing and always ended up exhausted.

Charlotte was the opposite—she was more of a chill seeker. She'd encourage Nicki to come to yoga class, but Nicki would claim she was too busy and stressed, which, Charlotte would reply, was why she needed yoga. Even Mark had to book an appointment with Nicki to see his grandchildren, and sessions were often postponed or cancelled at the last minute. He didn't mind when it was due to family matters, but he resented taking a back seat to her social media demands and postings. While he was proud of her business success, he wished she would hire someone to manage some of the administrative tasks, giving her more time to relax and enjoy her family.

At the deli, Mark and Charlotte had a wonderful time as she described her latest phase of yoga teaching. She was training to lead prenatal yoga classes and was excited about it. He loved how much fun she was having in life. She mentioned that she had started dating a nice guy but wanted to wait a bit to make sure it "took" before she brought him to meet the family. They had a quick chat about how hard it was to date, along with a few laughs. He joked that he never thought her hassles with dating would be a topic they had in common. After listening to stories about her and her friends on some zesty dating apps, Mark was relieved that he didn't have to deal with that nonsense. He assured her that he was old school and no dating apps for him!

When they left the deli feeling full of good food, they shared a big hug before she jumped on her bike and scooted in the other direction. He was walking up Agricola by The Jumping Bean café when he caught a glimpse of Jenn at a table. She was seated with a well-dressed man, using massive hand gestures as if he were playing charades. He could see Jenn laughing and taking in every word. His body tightened as he glanced momentarily. While he had no right to be upset—after all, they weren't really dating—he was still peeved. At that moment, Jenn looked out the window and their eyes met. He turned his head and shot out of her view, pretending he hadn't seen any of it. Lame behavior, yes, but he couldn't help it.

Mark stewed as he walked. He reminded himself she had every right to meet with a guy, but he felt it wasn't fair. That should have been him, not some slick dude who was busy charming her with his overblown stories of how important he was. Jealousy was not something he had felt since his youth. Now, it bubbled inside him and he didn't like it one bit.

Still steaming, he went for a long walk up to Needham Park with an elevated view of Halifax Harbor. He sat for ages and leaned back on his knapsack, staring at the boats chugging back and forth in the harbor. Usually, he would find it relaxing to watch maritime activities and quite enjoy himself, but not to-day. Nothing felt right.

After half an hour, he told himself to stop this nonsense. He'd drop the bag off at Jenn's office and be done with her. She had moved on, and he needed to do the same.

He stopped at the store for some produce, then swung by Jenn's office. It looked closed for the day, which, for him, was perfect. He wouldn't have to face her. He slipped the handle of the bag on the door and then heard a voice in the distance.

"Mark!" called Jenn from the entrance to the café down the street.

Damn. His heart revved, but then he looked like a statue, as if he'd been caught doing something illegal when all he was doing was delivering a bag. She waved to him with a big smile. He tried to act casual. "Hey. How's it going?"

"Great," she said as she arrived at the door and put the key in. "Come on in."

His throat was dry and his head was empty. He was lacking small-talk options. "You look busy."

"I'm trying to get caught up on paperwork. And I like to torture myself by doing it at the end of the day when I'm good and tired. By the way, I saw you walking by The Jumping Bean earlier. I was about to wave when you took off."

"I didn't want to interrupt you," he said with a light edge to his voice. *And the guy who looked like an overconfident jerk,* he wanted to say, but held back.

"Yes, I was in a meeting with a guy from Toronto, trying to appear interested and tuned into his story that went on and on."

Business meeting. His shoulders eased. He realized how much he'd been assuming all afternoon. He was grateful he hadn't said what he was thinking earlier. Suddenly, he was feeling better. "Good meeting?"

"Yes. He's a reality show producer and he wants my friend Maggie and me to do a series about reorganizing homes that appear hopeless."

"You could have used my house," he joked.

"Sorry, your home wasn't messy enough, nor are you a hoarder."

"You're kidding, right?"

Jenn shook her head. "Your project was more like minor surgery in the world of home organizing."

"I'll take that as a compliment." He pulled his knapsack off to the side and dug in with his hand. "Oh, before I forget, here are your clothes." He pulled out the bag. "Sorry it took so long. I had to relearn my laundry skills."

Jenn stared into the bag as if she were half expecting to find a mud-filled mess.

"I know you fill the washer, add a bottle of detergent, and press the start button. Easy peasy." He saw her shoot him an "aren't-you-just-a-goofball" look. "So, how've you been?"

"Still great, from five minutes ago," she joked.

"Oh yeah. How about, what's keeping you busy these days?"

She shrugged. "Aside from work, pickleball. We've missed you at our court. People are asking about you."

Mark's eyebrows raised. "Oh?" He needed to level with her. "I'm still playing, but I found it easier to go to the rec center." By easier, he meant that he didn't have to worry about bumping into her.

"Sure, I understand. But remember, you are always welcome in our group. I'll bet you are improving quickly."

"I'm still learning." He turned and headed for the door, mumbling, "I guess I should get going."

"Mark?" she said softly.

Her voice was like a siren call. Mark turned back. She looked as beautiful as he remembered. He had to stop himself from staring at her and making her uncomfortable, so he focused on his running shoes. "Yes?"

"I'm sorry that Nicki walked in on us, but I'm not sorry that we had a moment that evening."

Hope wafted in the air and he wanted to wrap himself in it before it vaporized. He looked up and scuffed the floor with his toe. "Me too. Although I got heaps of abuse from my family and the pool players."

"Really?" Jenn giggled and signaled for him to sit on the reception sofa. "Tell me more."

Mark perched on the sofa. In no time, they were snickering as Mark described the conversations with Nicki and Charlotte, as well as the endless teasing from Kevin and the boys. He said a few of the boys sounded a bit envious about his adventure. He added that he even got a text from his adopted son, Andrew, in Toronto, who razzed him.

"Well, I'm glad everybody was entertained at our expense," said Jenn. "And seriously, I had fun. Did you?"

Duh! I was totally on fire that night. He nodded and said slyly, "*Oh yeah*, I had fun."

Jenn grabbed a tissue and wiped the dust off the decorative dish on the coffee table. "It sounds like we both had a good time."

"One hundred percent."

Jenn balled up the tissue and tossed it in the bin. "If that's the case, help me to understand why we've both been avoiding each other for the past few weeks."

"No idea," he sighed. "I blame the curse of people over fifty trying to date. We recall our younger dating years, the angst we felt and how bad we were at it. Whoops, I should only speak for myself. How bad *I* was at it."

"Me too," Jenn chirped. "Still am."

"We should have gone right back to that recliner and started over."

"Until we got it right," she chuckled. "However, that ship has sailed, I think."

He picked up a small cushion on the sofa, tossing it back and forth in his hands.

"What's up?" she asked.

What the hell, let 'er rip. "Jenn, would you be interested in going on a real date?"

She tilted her head. "What'd you have in mind?"

His mind raced, but came up empty. "Look, I'm terrible at picking out fancy restaurants... So, if you could suggest somewhere, I'd be happy with whatever you pick."

Mark saw a deep thought process taking over her expression. Either he had offended her, or she was running rapidly through a database of restaurants in her head. Halifax had grown exponentially in the last few years and there were many great restaurants. She'd be more familiar with them than him. Mark went out with his daughters a few times a year but always felt intimidated by the hyped-up menus and dishes with fancy, descriptive names that left him none the wiser about what he would be eating.

Nicki and Charlotte offered running commentary, but by the time he stumbled through ordering a meal and wine, he'd feel like a hick. Especially the time at a trendy restaurant where they had the dinner packages with endless "courses," every one of them paltry. One course had a side plate with a shred of lettuce and one lonely mung bean on top. Mark was in a deep conversation with the girls, so when the server came by, Mark handed him the plate and joked, "I couldn't quite finish it." The server missed his attempt at humor and reminded him he had just set the plate down.

It didn't help when Nicki spent most of their dining time taking photos of the dish for her social media feed instead of eating. By the end of the meal, he was relieved to go home and have a sandwich. Mark preferred it when she brought the grandkids so that they could go to a family restaurant with cushy booths, highchairs, laminated menus, and real descriptions of the food.

"I have a suggestion," said Jenn.

"Sure."

"Instead of a restaurant, how about a beach walk and a picnic? Let's say Martinique. It's a bit of a drive to the Eastern Shore, but it has fewer people. It's got miles of beautiful sandy walking. And we can have a picnic after that."

"Really?" Mark couldn't believe what he was hearing. She was officially his dream date. "Well, let me bring the picnic."

Her foot tapped the side of the table. "Uhm, okay. But I have a question: are you making the picnic items?"

"Hell no, I'll go to the Blueberry Bakery and Café. They've got great sandwiches and pastries. I'll bring some sparkling fruit drinks as well."

"Phew," she mimed wiping her brow. "I mean, weren't you voted most likely to *not* succeed in your cooking class?"

"Good memory," he said. "So, how about Thursday? It's supposed to be sunny."

She checked her phone calendar. "No meetings that day. Sounds perfect."

"Awesome. I can pick you up," he said as they stood up together and he faced the door. "Well, I must dash."

"Mark?"

"Yep," he said, turning back, hoping she hadn't changed her mind.

"Bring your little Jack rabbit."

Mark beamed. "You sure?"

"Absolutely. Imagine if you came home from the walk and Jack smelled seaweed on you. He'd figure out you'd been to the ocean without him!"

"Well, he does enjoy chasing birds that he'll never catch and plunging into little waves at the shoreline. He's been doing that since I got him."

When they faced each other at the door, he felt swept up with excitement and hope. He leaned over and kissed her on the cheek, and then, he shifted to touch her lips. He didn't know if that was a smart move until he opened his eyes. Jenn smiled. He paused before exiting to make sure he didn't run into a door, like the first time they connected at her office.

Back on the sidewalk, he floated along like a hovercraft on a cushion of air. He stopped at the bakery and ordered the picnic for Thursday morning.

Mark had found the woman of his dreams; now all he had to do was convince her that he was worthy of her love.

Chapter 27
Jenn

JENN WOKE UP FULL of excitement. The sun's rays nudged through the cracks in the bedroom curtains and she rose quickly to pull them open and welcome the sun. She was going on a picnic to the beach with Mark.

Martinique: Not the exotic French island in the Caribbean with its bath-warm turquoise waters, gently waving palm trees and endless sunshine. This was Martinique Nova Scotia style—a sandy beach perfect for walking, tough-as-nails sea grass swaying in the wind, marine blue water only warm enough for swimming two months of the year, and cold winds whipping up fast and furious waves from the Atlantic Ocean. A magnet for surfers who gathered there year-round in their wetsuits, looking like dark polka dots bobbing up and down on their surfboards, waiting patiently for the elusive perfect wave to ride to shore.

For Jenn, Martinique Beach was all about the light. She was dazzled by its ever-changing glow and colors, the sunrise beaming with rays of sunflower yellows, coral streaks and a golden ball of glory rising in the eastern sky. By late afternoon, the sun's rays shifted into a soft, silvery palette across the sky, and blinking lights bounced on the waves like an open treasure chest filled with jewels. Jenn had heard filmmakers describe the soft evening light as the "magic hour," and no wonder, because everybody looked perfect on camera at sunset.

She was excited to be heading out on a real adventure with Mark that they'd both agreed on. Martinique was her favorite of all the beaches in Nova Scotia, and not just because it was the longest sandy beach in the province. Even on the hottest days of summer, there was endless space to accommodate everybody once you got past the car park gridlock. And before summer and tourist season, it was a vast space speckled with only a few hearty people walking their dogs that larked about without a care in the world, digging up abandoned sandwiches and rolling in smelly seaweed. Walkers strolling by would say hello or nod to each other; everybody was in a great mood as they wandered by the ocean.

She couldn't wait for Mark to arrive. She beetled around her condo in search of the right running shoes for sand, a pair of sunglasses, a hat and layers of clothes, because temperatures at the beach could run hot or cold in any season. At the last minute, she tossed in a big bag of trail mix, in case they got marooned (a gal could dream) and her larger and fancier camera—a bulky pain to carry, but it took the best pictures of this dream-like beach.

She closed the door and went downstairs to wait for Mark, who was already parked in the driveway with Jack, doing acrobatic flips in the front seat. "Hey," she smiled as she opened the door and tossed her knapsack in the back. Before doing anything else, she pulled a doggie treat out of her pocket and handed it to Jack, who looked even more pleased to see her.

"Hey, you, too," he replied. "Come on in." He turned to the dog. "Let's go, Jack," he said in a firm tone, pointing for him to get into the back seat. Jack retreated under protest, but as soon as Jenn was buckled in, he tried to insert himself into the action in the front.

Jenn petted him while he stood on a perch between the two front seats. Mark looked at him again. "Okay, buddy, you've got a choice. You can go back to a seat and settle down or go to the dog crate in the back. What's it going to be?" Jack glanced at the crate, then returned to the seat and curled up.

"Smart little fella, isn't he?" said Jenn.

Mark nodded. "Sometimes a little too smart if you ask me. But when I say c-r-a-t-e, he knows when to settle down." Mark put the vehicle in drive and pulled out. "Oh, by the way, I picked up coffee for us. Hope that's okay."

"Are you kidding? I've only had one so far, so I have not reached my official daily limit." She reached for the cup. "Thank you."

"You drink it black, right?"

Jenn nodded as she sipped. She was surprised that he'd remember that detail. She and her husband had been married for years, and he still asked her what she wanted every time they went to a coffee shop.

He glanced at Jenn, "How are you doing today?"

"Great!" she said. "The sun's out, we've got a walk to do and a picnic. It will be a grand day."

"Day?" said Mark, looking at her bulging knapsack. "Looks like you're ready to camp for a week."

Jenn giggled. "Well, I brought my big camera and it takes up a lot of space."

"Sure," he joked. "I don't have half as much."

"Did you remember the picnic?"

He feigned hurt. "Of course I did! We have sandwiches, a shareable salad and some tasty cookies. I tried one already and it works for me." He leaned over and pushed a button, starting up a music stream. "How about a little seventies soul?"

"Perfect!"

"Any requests?"

Jenn thought briefly. "Bill Withers?"

"Good one. Any song?"

She scrolled through her music database in her head. Hmm, "Ain't No Sunshine" was a little too lamenting. "Use Me", no thanks, it reminded her of a few relationships. And while she loved "Just the Two of Us", it sounded like she was scheming ahead with ideas about Mark. She was overthinking things. She looked out the window and loved how the sun was making her feel so good. "How about 'Lovely Day'?"

"Now you're talking," he said. "I'm amazed you know some of these sixties and seventies musicians. Kevin listened to this kind of music back then and it still holds up in my mind. How'd you get into it?"

"I'm not sure. You hear something that moves you. Before you know it, you're headed down a rabbit hole of wonderful music."

They settled in, and Jenn told him about her son Kyle and his situation in Thailand, with a grandchild on the way. As she spoke, she felt more excited about Kyle's and Achara's news.

She then asked about his grandchildren, and he talked about how much he loved spending time with them and wished he could see them more often. Before long, they'd reached that remarkably high hill and curve in the road in Cole Harbour where the ocean is first revealed.

"Look at that beautiful ocean," he said, spreading his hand across the vista. After taking it in, they turned their conversation to the world of pickleball. When they arrived in Martinique, they were both comfortable with the rhythm of their conversation, with no awkward spaces to fill. They organized their backpacks for the walk, including Jack's items, water, and picnic provisions, because they'd be gone for a couple of hours.

As soon as the door opened, the dog burst into a gallop. "Jack!" snapped Mark, which brought the dog to a screeching halt. "Easy," he added.

"Is Jack okay off leash?"

"Yes, because he always returns to me when I use that command. I'll let him run rampant for the first half, in hopes of running down his batteries," he laughed. "Then I'll leash him when we get close to the piping plover nesting area."

Jenn drew in a big breath of salty fresh air. It was a heavenly scent for her, on a beach, near the ocean. That was her happy place. In minutes, they both decided to roll up their pant legs, take off their running shoes, and tie them to the back of their knapsacks so they could walk along the shore. They continued their chatting, as well as quiet moments when it was clear each of them was enjoying their time by the water. At one point, while Jenn was avoiding a sharp clam shell in her path, her hand brushed his, and somehow, both of them came together.

Now they were holding hands and Jenn felt a rush of happiness. Neither said anything for a long time, and they both seemed content to stroll silently. Jenn would have let this go on for ages, even though her feet were getting cold from wading in the ocean.

Mark turned to check on Jack. They both chuckled as they saw him digging furiously over by a big log of driftwood. "There he goes, digging a tunnel to China," said Mark.

"He sure looks determined. Why does he do that?"

"Could be a couple of reasons. They were bred as little hunters, chasing down foxes, rodents, or other vermin."

"Charming."

"Or, in Jack's case, he might be showing off his digging skills for us. That boy likes attention."

They veered off to go check out Jack's work. He'd already dug three holes and was now tackling a fourth. Mark filled in the holes and snapped the leash on him. They continued walking toward the point. At the end of the beach, they sat on a couple of logs and pulled out their sandwiches and salad. Mark put the leash around the log, giving Jack room to move around without wandering off.

As they ate their lunch and looked out to the ocean, Jenn pointed out a heron and some ducks, paddling in the water. She pulled out her camera and zoom lens, snapping pictures of the birds at every angle, without getting close.

But the showstopper was watching the tiny piping plovers at a distance. Weighing in at only a few ounces, they were gray and white with a black ring around their neck. A small group of plovers entertained them with their miniature bodies running in spurts, stopping and starting, flying and pecking in the sand at the shoreline. They darted around as if the word "skedaddle" had been invented to describe them.

"It's like watching the Mother Nature Network here," said Mark.

"So true. Those little birds are too amazing."

"Cookie?" he said, holding a bag open for her.

"Should we wait until the end of the walk?"

Mark looked at it and bit into a chewy oatmeal chocolate chip. "You can. But I'm having one now. And I'll do my best to save a couple for the end. Damn, those are good."

They cleaned up the picnic and stowed the garbage in their knapsacks. By the time they got back to the parking area, they'd been gone for a few hours. Jenn's lungs were filled with fresh, clean air and Mark looked happily tired from physical work. Even Jack had reduced his activity level from frenetic to contented.

"Well, should we get on the road and head back?" Mark said.

Jenn nodded. "I had a great time."

"Me too," he said, leaning over and kissing her. They stopped for a moment and he stepped back. "Is this okay?"

Instead of answering, she replied with another kiss. When they stopped, she looked down and noted a beautiful seashell with wisps of white, black and purple. She took her camera and shot a picture of it, then looked up at him. He smiled at her and rocked back on his heels lightly. At that moment, the late afternoon sun shining on him caused him to close an eye, as if he were winking at her. She snapped at the right moment and caught his expression, which she found intoxicating. Then he put his hand on hers and turned the camera for a selfie with the two of them. When they looked at the photos on the screen, she felt like she saw love blossoming between the two of them. Everything felt right in the world. She crouched down and picked up the shell.

"Taking home a souvenir?"

"Yes. Whenever I have a special day at the beach, I like to have a little reminder. It goes into my glass bowl on the coffee table," she said.

"Well, I'm honored," he added, leaning for a kiss, and then another. Then he straightened up and said, "Right then, I think we should be on our way before I get other ideas."

Funny, I was thinking the same thing. Jenn couldn't think of the last time she had been so relaxed or had so much fun with a special guy. Was Mark the real thing, or some guy on his best behavior?

She decided, no matter how fast she wanted to move things forward with him, she would take her time. For once.

When he pulled up in front of her building, Jenn rustled around gathering items. She didn't want the special day to end. "Hey, do you want to come in for a drink and a bite?"

Mark shook his head. "Sorry, I've got a commitment with my family."

"No worries, just a thought. I had a great time today, Mark," she said, lifting her knapsack onto her lap.

"Me too," he said, leaning over to kiss her. "I'd like to see you again."

Jenn beamed. "Sure. When?"

Mark looked ahead in the car, then returned to her gaze. "Anytime, of course. But I had an idea."

"What's that?"

"Charlotte is turning thirty in a few weeks and we are holding a big family celebration that coincides with Thanksgiving. Would you like to be my date? I want to make us official to my family."

"I'd love to, but ... is that okay with everyone?"

"Well, it's okay with me, and that's all that matters. Even my foster son, Andrew, is flying here from Toronto with his partner Kim. He doesn't come back home very often, so it feels like the perfect time to celebrate everything. I couldn't be more excited."

Jenn thought about all the holidays she had either spent alone or cobbled together with friends. While she always had fun, she missed the fun and chaos of being around family. This filled her with warmth and anticipation. "I'm in! Tell me what I can bring."

"Let me check with Nicki because she's hosting. I'm thinking pumpkin pie because we all love it, and nobody is good at it. But I'll make sure."

Jenn's eyebrows squeezed inward. "Was that Annie's specialty?"

"No, she wasn't good at it either," he laughed. "She was the queen of roasting and dressing. Nicki took over that role."

"In that case, I'd be happy to make the pie. I even have a gluten-free version with a crust made from pecans."

"Jeez, you are making me hungry," joked Mark. "I'll get back to you. That's in two weeks. In the meantime, let's play some pickleball."

"Sounds good. Text me on Thursday," she said, giving him a quick kiss and Jack a little nuzzle.

"Later!" he shouted as she shut the door.

Jenn walked into her place and dropped everything in the hallway. Her cat Mocha came out to see what the fuss was about and meowed for her dinner. She scooped her up, nuzzled her softly and walked into the kitchen to open a can of food. She set Mocha down, and the cat meandered in and out between her feet while Jenn put out the food. Mocha then abandoned Jenn to pick away at her meal.

Revved up, she texted Maggie to tell her about her official "coming out" date with Mark. Maggie replied with a barrage of emojis. She was likely preparing a meal and too busy to talk. Then she messaged Kyle and told him about her Thanksgiving plans. It was in the middle of the night, so she knew he'd have his phone shut off. But he'd be excited for her. He once explained the pressure of being an only child and the guilt he felt when he couldn't attend family functions.

Jenn opened the fridge and stared at all the ingredients. She could put on some rice and cobble together a stir-fry from what she had.

She was so keen about her first family get-together with Mark that she decided to make a practice pie because it had been so long since she baked. She smiled. Finally, it felt like someone lovable was coming into her life.

Chapter 28
Mark

THE NEXT MORNING, MARK was in great spirits as he thought about all the fun things coming up, especially with Jenn in his life. He always lived in hope of having more time with his grandchildren, so he'd always try to be there whenever there was a need, hoping the time would expand to include more engagement as the kids got older.

He was on his way home from the grocery store and in a moment of enthusiasm, he swung by Nicki's home. Usually, he didn't stop by spontaneously during the workday because she worked from home and he didn't want to interrupt her. He had discussed having lunch with her, and she said she usually grabbed a bite at noon, encouraging him to stop by then. Since it was twelve thirty and he saw Charlotte's bike to the side, he figured it was a perfect time for a visit.

He parked the car and bounded up the steps, ringing the doorbell. He could hear Nicki and Charlotte talking and laughing in the kitchen. They had missed the doorbell because they could be loud and rowdy when they got going. He stuck his head inside the door and called out, "Hey, it's me."

"In the kitchen," the two girls shouted simultaneously, then laughed. Mark loved that they were so close, even though they were very different. They worked well together.

Mark arrived and gave his daughters big hugs, gently nuzzling his granddaughter, Katarina. "Hello, my little darling," he said, kissing the top of her head. "Augustus at daycare?"

"Yes, thank heaven," laughed Nicki. "I'm in the middle of projects and I need to focus."

"Well, I won't stay long."

"Don't be silly, we've stopped for lunch," Nicki said, handing him a plate. "There's plenty of salad. Help yourself."

Mark added some salad to a plate and took a seat at the island where Nicki usually ate standing up. They chatted about all kinds of things, and he savored every bite of his salad and time with his daughters. He looked at Charlotte and said, "I can't believe you're turning thirty."

"I know. I'm as shocked as you are, Dad."

"I remember when you were my little girl," he said, showing her childhood height with his hand. "Still are. I shouldn't say that. It's only because I love you so much," he gushed.

Charlotte leaned over to hug him. "It's fine, Dad. I love you, too."

"I can't wait until we celebrate your birthday and Thanksgiving."

Nicki smoothed the last bit of cottage cheese on her multigrain cracker and set her spoon down. "Oh, I was going to ask you, Dad, could you pick up Andrew and Kim at the airport when they come home?"

"Of course, I'd love to do that. They can stay at my place if they like."

Nicki shrugged. "Sure, you can check with them. Who knows? Maybe they'll stay at a hotel."

"Will do," Mark said, adding it to the To Do list on his phone. He figured this was the perfect time to mention Jenn. "By the way, I'd like to bring Jenn."

Nicki's face pinched at the eyes. "What do you mean, Daddy? Bring Jenn, what, where?"

"To Char's birthday party and dinner." He saw Nicki glance over at Charlotte, whose face stayed neutral.

"Is that a problem, Char?"

Char smiled at him. "Not at all. The more the merrier."

Suddenly, he felt a little twinge of weirdness inside and knew his eldest daughter had something she was thinking but not saying. "Nick? What's going on?"

"I'm surprised. I didn't know you two were getting serious."

Mark took in a deep breath and smiled to keep things positive. "Yes, indeed. That's exactly why I want to bring her. I think I'm falling for her."

Char reached over and put her hand on her Dad's. "I'm excited for you. I really like Jenn. We have great chats at the yoga studio."

"I'm glad, honey." He turned back to them and said, "She's keen to bring something, like a pumpkin pie."

Mark focused on Nicki, who still looked a little stubborn. "What's wrong? Talk to me."

Nicki stared at her plate and picked at the cracker crumbs. "I don't know, Dad. I pictured it as a family event, with, you know, just family."

Mark felt a bolt charge through his body. "Well, she's not family yet, but she's becoming important in my life. Isn't that enough?" He saw Nicki shrug. He looked at her and said, "Charlotte is bringing Luis, and they only started dating a few weeks ago."

"Right, well... it's her birthday," said Nicki.

"Oh, I get it, you don't like Jenn—"

"I didn't say that," snapped Nicki.

"Well, you haven't said that. But you're fighting this."

Nicki gulped some coffee. "How about if you wait for another holiday like Remembrance Day in November?"

"Nothing happens on Remembrance Day, other than we go to services and a brunch. Plus, Andrew won't be here, so that means we aren't together as a family." He took a breath and looked at her. "In other words, you don't want to deal with her."

"Well, I support Jenn coming with you, Dad," said Charlotte. She gazed over at her sister. "Nick, this means a lot to Dad. Can you make this work?"

Nicki sighed and scrolled through her phone.

Mark took his plate and silverware to the dishwasher and placed them in the racks. He turned to her. "Nicki, I love you and Char more than anything in the world. But Jenn is quickly winning my heart and I want to be with her. That should be enough if I tell you that. But if she isn't welcome at the dinner, then you are telling me I'm not welcome either. I have to run," he said, walking out to the hallway.

"Daddy!" Nicki shouted as he closed the door.

⁕

Charlotte shot Nicki a look. "That was mean-spirited. Dad came bounding in here today looking happier than I've seen him in a few years. What's going on?"

Nicki teared up, pursing her lips tightly.

"Nick? What is it?"

"I don't know. Why does he have to go chasing a woman? It's pathetic."

"No, it's not, Nicki. Old people need love too. Whoops, I shouldn't call them old; he's not even sixty. But you know what I mean. I see so many lonely men and women around here. You saw what he was like on his own, slumped in his chair watching old movies and sports events."

"How can he forget Mom like that?"

"Nicki, it's been a few years. I have no doubt Mom would want him to move on. And if it were the other way around, he'd want her to do the same."

"Call me crazy. But I can't help but wonder if she's scheming or something. What's she after with him?"

"How about a good-hearted man who has a great sense of humor and is still active? Watch the two of them playing pickleball. They're having a right old hoot."

"I guess," harrumphed Nicki. "What now?"

"First, you owe Dad an apology. Tell him you were a little off today and beg his forgiveness, which he always gives. And of course, tell him Jenn is welcome and you'd love a decent pie."

"Can you do it? I mean, like, tell him what you just told me."

Char tapped her fingers on the counter. "No, you hurt him. It needs to come from you. And the longer you leave it, the worse it'll be."

Nicki sighed. "I'll text him this afternoon."

Charlotte rolled her eyes. "Pick up the phone, for Pete's sake. Texting with Dad is for pick-ups and drop-offs, not heartfelt apologies. Look, I gotta run. Let me know when the party is back on track." She hugged her sister, walked out to the yard, and got on her bike.

Chapter 29
Mark

MARK PULLED INTO THE driveway, still fuming. He couldn't believe what he had heard from Nicki. He didn't know why she had a beef with Jenn, and he also didn't like the idea of her being defiant over someone he was dating. He figured there must be a way to work through this. He opened the door and called to Jack, who bounded to the door, ever excited to see him. Mark grabbed the leash and snapped it on the dog. "Come on, buddy, we're going for a walk."

They moved quickly toward Fort Needham Park so that Mark and Jack could walk up a hill. Mark pushed hard, but Jack was still straining the leash. "Fine for you. You are running on four legs, I'm on two," Mark complained.

At the top, he caught his breath and took in the view of the Halifax Harbor. Jack was checking out all his favorite spots. Mark's phone buzzed in his pocket and he saw that Nicki was calling. He was somewhere between angry and hurt and almost didn't answer—but didn't want to behave like that. He pressed the button and held the phone to his ear.

"Daddy?"

"Hey, Nicki," he said, trying to sound upbeat, but not feeling it. "What's up?" There was a long break. Mark gave her the space to gather her thoughts or find the courage she needed.

"I'm sorry," she mumbled.

"I'm listening," he said. He wasn't letting her get away with a pipsqueak apology.

She drew in a breath. "Well, you know... I heard I wasn't very hospitable to you at lunchtime."

"And do you agree with what you heard?"

"Yes, I was out of line to talk that way about Jenn."

"Honey, I don't get it. What do you find so offensive about Jenn?"

She sighed. "Nothing. I was in a mood. And I'm sorry I hurt you."

Mark waved a little dog treat at Jack to bring him back. "Well, thank you. Apology accepted. Does this mean Jenn is welcome to come?"

"Yes. And she can bring a pumpkin pie. None of us ever mastered it."

Mark laughed. "That's what I told her. She'll be delighted."

"Good. I have to get back to work. Love you."

"Love you, too." Mark hung up. He felt better. Almost. But he decided to emphasize the positive.

⟫ ⟪

Mark dialled Jenn's number. "Hi Jenn."

"Hi, what are you up to?"

"Taking Jack for a walk. And I wanted to check in about the combined birthday party and Thanksgiving dinner."

"Am I in?"

Mark paused. He wondered if he should give Jenn a heads-up about his conversation with Nicki. He hoped everything was settled, so he decided there was no point in raising concerns about a problem that might not happen. Besides, Jenn assumed the best in people until proven otherwise. "Of course you're welcome. And not just because you can make a pumpkin pie."

"Sounds great. You said Saturday, right?"

"Yes. And I'm picking up Andrew and Kin at the airport after lunch on Saturday. Would you care to join me? It would give you a chance to get to know them a little bit."

"Sure, I'd love to."

"I know it's always tough for Andrew to come back here. He has a lot of bad memories from his childhood. But he's my foster son, and he's always welcome here."

"Understood. And are they staying with you, or at a hotel?"

"Who knows? Parents are always the last to find out what the plans are!"

"Tell me about it," Jenn giggled. "When Kyle comes home, I get bits of information and then try to put the puzzle together."

"Oh, and I should give you a heads up about Kim."

"Go on," said Jenn.

"I told her you are a home organizer, and she would love to get input from you on a few questions. They have a six-hundred-square-foot condo in Toronto that she wants to optimize."

"I love talking shop."

"She's bringing a floor plan. But she has a good sense of design, so she'll appreciate your ideas. I hope that's okay."

"Not a problem. People often corner me at parties to ask questions. Unlike you, who rejected me on my first visit."

Mark slapped his forehead. "Don't remind me! But I'll let you in on a secret: I still found you attractive even when I was giving you the gears."

"Good to know!" Jenn laughed.

"So, I'll pick you up on Saturday after lunch. I'll text you when I'm leaving."

"Perfect," said Jenn. "Don't forget we've got mixed doubles pickleball on Wednesday."

"Not a chance. I have a feeling we are headed for the winner's circle."

Mark hung up and called out to Jack to head back home. Suddenly, everything felt right with the world. He couldn't wait to bring Jenn to the family dinner.

Chapter 30
Jenn

On Saturday, Mark picked up Jenn and then headed out to the airport. She had already made the pie for the evening dinner, so she felt relaxed and on top of things.

They talked nonstop as they drove to the airport, despite having seen each other just the day before. Jenn felt comfortable enough with Mark to jump into conversations and zigzag around numerous topics. They parked the SUV at the airport lot, and holding hands, they walked indoors to the escalator where arriving passengers picked up their luggage.

Jenn stopped to chat with a neighbor who was a volunteer at the airport. She welcomed people to the province and answered questions about traveling and places to see. Airport volunteers looked distinctive, wearing bright blue Nova Scotia tartan vests.

The flight was only a few minutes late and they stood by the arrivals door like excited parents, their eyes darting around in search of loved ones.

"There he is," said Mark, trying to talk over the laughter and chatter around them. "Andrew!" he shouted and waved. Andrew turned and smiled. Mark hugged Andrew and Kim, then introduced them to Jenn.

"So nice to finally meet you. Mark has told me all about you," Andrew said warmly.

"You too," she said, noting Andrew called him Mark, not Dad. When he arrived in the Russell family as an older teenager, Andrew was clear that he wasn't looking for a new father. She sensed that Mark accepted him for who he was, with no expectations.

"And lovely to meet you, Kim," she said, smiling and hugging her.

"What an adorable couple you make," said Kim. "You look young and fit."

"Thanks," said Jenn and Mark together, followed by a laugh.

"Kim is buttering you up so that she can get your input on reorganizing our matchbox condo," said Andrew.

"How dare you!" she said, feigning shock.

Jenn liked how the two of them interacted. And chatter seemed to flow with everybody—no effort required. Andrew spotted their bags moving on the conveyor belt and walked over to pick them up.

The trip back to the North End was fast and they landed at Mark's place in a record thirty minutes from the airport. After touring the new and improved house that Jenn and Mark had worked on, they stopped for refreshments.

Over tea and snacks, Jenn asked Kim about the condo plans. Kim pulled out the floor plans and started asking Jenn about the placement of furniture and storage. Andrew announced he was entirely uninterested in the topic of interior design, so Jenn suggested that he and Mark go into the living room for a chat.

She and Kim quickly jumped into a rapid-fire exchange about her ideas. She got out her pencil and started working on the plans. They carried on and laughed while they worked. An hour later, Mark and Andrew walked into the kitchen. "We're almost finished," said Jenn.

Mark raised his eyebrows. "Wow, it seems like you've been talking forever."

"Yes and no," Kim said. She showed them the marked-up plans, which didn't register at all with Andrew and Mark.

Jenn looked at her watch. "Holy moly, I have to go home to have a shower, change and get my pie!"

Mark placed his hand on her shoulder. "How about we pick you up around six thirty and we'll head to Nicki's and Ethan's house?"

"Sure thing," said Jenn. "I want to fit a walk in, so I'll walk home now." She kissed Mark and said goodbye to the others. They'd see each other again in a few hours, which sounded fun. She looked forward to seeing how the whole family interacted.

Chapter 31
Jenn

JENN WAITED OUTSIDE HER condo, watching for Mark. She wore a delicate, sleeveless blue dress that made her feel good and kept her body cool in crowded rooms. The highlight accessory was her once-in-a-lifetime splurge: designer sandals. Yes, they looked like a million bucks, but like many of life's minor tragedies, they were decidedly uncomfortable. She called them her "sitting shoes" and only wore them when there would be minimal walking. Tonight was a family dinner, so they were perfect. By the look on Mark's face when he spotted her, it was the right choice. She had noticed his enthusiasm whenever she wore a dress, and he would tell her she had nice legs. She couldn't remember the last time she'd heard that comment.

Jenn smiled as she watched Mark circle the driveway and pull up to the door. She was holding a gift bag with a bottle of wine and the pie. Kim and Andrew jumped out to help carry the items and let Jenn sit up front with Mark.

"Very nicely maintained building," noted Andrew as they passed a flower bed.

"Thanks," said Jenn. "They do a good job here looking after the property."

"And don't you look lovely for the occasion," said Kim. "Lucky you, Mark."

Mark and Jenn exchanged a smile. "Tell me about it," said Mark. "She's definitely done something magic to me. I even ironed my shirt for tonight."

"Isn't this fun?" said Jenn, buckling into her seat and turning to the two in the back. "I don't have a big family, so I've always envied people who get together with relatives."

When they arrived at Nicki's and Ethan's and rang the doorbell, it triggered dog barking and Augustus shouting for his granddad from the inside. Jenn could see Mark's excitement, preparing to hug his grandson. He'd told Jenn that he wanted to do more with Augustus and take the kids out on more adventures. Nicki said she wasn't against it but, they had busy schedules, and Mark had to find a way to fit into the time slots.

Nicki swung the door open and waved people in. Everybody stepped inside, hugging and passing items to take to the kitchen. Nicki hugged Jenn, which helped Mark relax. Everything felt great until Nicki scanned Jenn's outfit and stopped at her sandals.

"Oh dear," said Nicki. "Those heels are a tad high. They could dent my imported cork flooring. Would you mind wearing these?" she said, reaching into a basket without waiting for an answer. She handed Jenn a pair of knitted slippers.

Great. Granny slippers. Best-laid plans to make a good first impression on the family with her sandals. She glanced at Mark.

"Don't worry, you still look beautiful to me," he smiled, as if trying to find a way to diffuse the situation.

Jenn shrugged. Her younger self might have questioned the request, when others kept their shoes on, but she decided it wasn't worth making a fuss. It was only the entrance that was important and that was kiboshed. *Whatever.* Mark squeezed Jenn's hand as they entered a spacious open-concept kitchen. She discreetly surveyed the space, with Kim pointing out the marble counters, the hanging racks with every type of cooking pot imaginable, and the light fixtures that shone a soft amber glow on the counters and backsplash.

"This is such a beautiful home, Nicki," said Jenn, handing her the pie. "Did you work with an interior designer when you were building?"

"No," said Nicki, setting the wine on the counter. "It was my design."

"Well, you have impeccable taste."

"Thank you," said Nicki. As she received the pie, she looked puzzled.

Jenn wondered if there was a problem—she sensed Nicki aimed for perfection in everything. "Nicki, if you are looking for the whipping cream, it's in the carrying container. I'll whip it closer to the time."

"Hmmm," Nicki mused, checking it from all angles as if she were the chief judge of a television baking show. "The crust looks a smidge burnt. Should we still serve it? I've got an artisan cheesecake in the freezer."

Jenn's jaw clenched when she heard the words "a smidge burnt." She felt she had to defend it without sounding defensive. "No worries, Nicki. The crust isn't burnt; it's made out of crushed pecans. That's why it's darker than a white flour crust. I wanted to make a gluten-free crust for Andrew."

"Oh," she said in an unconvincing tone, as she set it on the counter.

Kim appeared from around the corner and said, "Oooh, is that a pumpkin pie with pecan crust?"

Jenn nodded. She was starting to doubt herself for bringing it.

"That looks fabulous," gushed Kim. "I saw Chef Sondeson make that on his TV show, and I've always wanted to try it. It looks identical to his pie, and it went viral."

"Really?" Nicki's eyebrows lifted. "That's cool. Well, let's keep it in and I'll let you know when to make the Chantilly cream." A timer dinged, and she moved back to her massive stove to tend to a dozen different items.

Kim winked at Jenn. They stood at the end of the island while others bustled. "Did you see that on a chef's show?"

Kim shrugged. "I drop in comments like that to stay one step ahead. I knew it would appeal to her." She picked up her glass of wine. "Cheers," she said to Jenn, clinking the crystal glasses ever so gently. "Don't worry about Nicki. She comes off as finicky and a little shallow, but she's okay."

"Thanks." Jenn smiled. "Now all I need to do is find out what Chantilly cream is."

She swirled the wine in her glass. "A fancy word for whipping cream with vanilla added."

"Oh, I already do that, so we're all set. Thanks, Kim." She wanted to hug Kim for being so supportive. Nicki ranked people in a particular pecking order of respect, and Kim was at the top due to her beauty, successful art career, and international recognition. Nicki seemed in awe of Kim and never questioned her authority on matters of artistry.

Kim leaned a little closer and added, "Her tone can also get a little snarky when she's had a few glasses. The worst comments are usually aimed at Ethan, but she can be an equal opportunity nitpicker about everybody. Except herself, of course."

"Well, I'm sure she'll be fine tonight. Mark said it's been a long time since everyone has gotten together, and it seems like there's a great vibe here."

Kim smiled at Andrew across the kitchen island and he walked over to chat.

Mark and Jenn moved through the room, saying hello and meeting Charlotte's boyfriend, Luis, who admitted that he'd become a big yoga fan after meeting Charlotte.

"I know the feeling," chuckled Mark, looking at Jenn. "I've developed a passion for pickleball since Jenn's introduced me to it." They chatted about Charlotte's work and the many benefits of yoga, which Mark agreed might help to improve his flexibility. When Luis invited him several times to come to a class, Mark finally admitted having a fear of farting during class, which had everybody in stitches.

A short time later, Nicki and Ethan invited everybody to grab a serving dish and take it to the dining room. The large room accommodated ten people, with ample space for more guests. Nicki had decorated the table and room in a gorgeous autumnal theme, with beautiful leaves and earthy tones. Each place had a name with a pretty plate underneath. Everybody gushed how gorgeous it looked, and Nicki looked pleased with how it had come together—until Augustus discovered his place.

"I wanna sit by Grandpa!" he sulked and made such a fuss that Mark asked Nicki if Augustus could join him and Jenn.

"I guess so," replied Nicki. "But first, I have to get a photo for my Instagram post. I want a photo with a proper seating arrangement; and before the kids are wearing dinner on their faces and clothes."

"Here's the Norman Rockwell moment," Andrew whispered to Kim, which Mark overheard and sent his special "referee warning look" to him.

After five minutes of photos, Augustus jumped up from his seat. Out of respect for Nicki's efforts to make a beautiful setting, Jenn suggested that everybody pass their name plates to the correct spot. Kim teased her for being on "organizer" duty during dinner, which made her laugh. Augustus looked delighted as his granddad lifted him onto the chair with a booster and beamed as his grandfather cut up his food.

Jenn got a tear in her eye to see how patient Mark was with Augustus. Soon she'd be a grandmother and she hoped that Kyle and Achara would move back to Nova Scotia so that she could enjoy the same activities with her grandchild. When everybody settled, Jenn lifted her glass and said, "Thank you to Nicki and Ethan for hosting this amazing family get-together." They toasted the hosts and settled in for a delicious meal.

After a fabulous dinner, everybody lingered at the table. They agreed they needed time to let the meal settle before having dessert. Augustus had run off and was playing in the living room when Ethan told him it was time to go to bed. Augustus fussed and then asked if Grandpa could read him a story. Mark jumped up and invited Jenn to join him for the reading. Jenn wondered if she'd noted a slight twitch on Nicki's right eye when Mark invited her to read, but she figured she'd imagined it and assumed everything was fine.

Augustus was quite excited, and it took a bit of time for Mark to calm him down once he got in bed and under the covers. After three short books, he drifted into a deep sleep. Mark took Jenn's hand and they tiptoed out of the room to make sure they didn't awaken the sleeping boy, who could suddenly turn into a bundle of energy.

Downstairs, Jenn could hear laughing and loud talking. "Sounds like the young ones are enjoying themselves."

"Yes, and I suggest maybe we have dessert, then excuse ourselves and head to my place," he said, brushing her with a light kiss.

"Sure." Jenn gave him a quick hug and they headed downstairs to the dining room.

"Just in time for dessert and an after-dinner brandy," Ethan said, holding up two bottles. "Nicki is serving the pie."

"Yes to pie, no thanks to brandy," said Mark.

Jenn and Mark sat down in their chairs, joining a lively conversation about the meaning of art. Jenn could see that Andrew and Kim were very well informed about contemporary art, and she knew little about it, so she chose to listen. Mark leaned over and whispered, "I haven't a clue what they are talking about."

Looking over at Jenn and Mark, Kim said, "Great, you're back. Andrew has some news to share and I wanted him to wait until you two were back."

"Wait, let me get a sip of brandy so I can focus on his news," said Nicki, pouring some into a snifter. She waved the bottle at everybody as an invitation for a drink, but nobody else wanted one.

"What's up, Andrew?" said Mark, sipping on his sparkling water.

Andrew took in a breath. "Well, four of my paintings have been accepted into an art show at a gallery in New York."

Everybody cheered, toasted and offered congratulations.

"When?" asked Mark.

"Next spring."

"Andrew, this is incredible news," said Mark. "I'm so proud of you!"

"Yes, well done," added Jenn.

"Thanks," said Andrew, nodding.

Jenn sensed that he was a bit of an introvert, so he was not exactly vying for attention from the crowd. But he did look happy.

Mark asked him more about his work and his career progress, which enlivened Andrew as he warmed to the subject. When he finished his story, Mark said, "Do we get an invitation to the opening in New York?"

Andrew looked surprised. "You'd like to come?"

"Of course," said Mark. "Any good family news is a reason to celebrate."

"Who's we?" Nicki asked.

Under the table, Mark's hand rested on Jenn's thigh. "Jenn and I." He looked at her and said, "That is, if you are into it."

"You bet," Jenn said. "I'd love a weekend with you in New York," she said, lacing her fingers through Mark's.

Nicki sipped her brandy. "That's six months from now. A bit presumptuous, don't you think?"

"How so?" Mark asked.

"Well, assuming you two will still be... a thing," said Nicki.

Jenn didn't like where this was going, but she stayed quiet. While Nicki wasn't out of control, she appeared to be feeling the drinks.

"I sure hope so," Mark said, draping his arm over Jenn's shoulder. "And with any luck, we could be more than a 'thing.'"

Charlotte piped up from the end of the table. "Here's to you and Jenn," she and the others cheered, except for Nicki.

Nicki stiffened. "We should talk about this, Daddy. What do you mean by more than a thing?"

Mark took in a breath. "Hon, we're having some fun together. Besides, I'm old school and don't want to get into a heavy conversation with the entire family."

"Why not?" she said. "Everybody's wondering, but nobody is brave enough to ask."

"Speak for yourself, Nick," said Charlotte. "I'm happy to see Dad enjoying himself with Jenn. And let them decide how they want it to grow."

Jenn could see determination on Nicki's face. The rest of the family had some experience with this type of behavior, but it was new to her.

"What are your intentions with Daddy?" Nicki asked, staring at Jenn.

How about hot sex? Jenn felt like retorting to wind up Nicki, but she realized that could cause trouble. Calmy, she replied, "I'm not sure what you mean by 'intentions', Nicki. Can you help me understand?"

"My father is quite a catch. He has several women at Mom's church hot on his heels."

"I'm popular with the over-seventy and pious crowd," quipped Mark.

Andrew chuckled and sipped his wine. "You go, Mark."

Nicki ignored everybody's attempts at humor. "*And* you have assets."

"I do? That's news to me," joked Mark.

"You know what I mean. A nice house and a pension."

"Nicki. Stop being rude right now."

"Time to go home, Nick," joked Andrew.

"I am home," she said defiantly.

Enough is enough. Who needs this scrutiny? Jenn felt ire rising in her body. She stood up and placed her napkin on the plate in front of her. "Thanks for the dinner. It sounds like your family has some issues to sort out, so I think I'll head home."

The conversation halted. "Jenn," said Mark, standing up.

"See you all later." She turned and walked out of the dining room, with Mark calling from behind her. She felt humiliated and wiped a tear. She knew Nicki had had a problem with her since day one, but she couldn't imagine it would be about Jenn being a gold digger.

"Jenn, wait."

"It's okay, Mark, you stay with your family."

"No, let me at least drive you home," he said, taking her hand and pausing. "Please."

Jenn shrugged and said, "Whatever."

In the car, she sat quietly, her big hopes dashed.

"Jenn. I'm sorry about Nicki's comments. She sometimes has an edgy tone when she has a few drinks, but that was unacceptable. I will talk to her when I go back."

Jenn sat quietly.

Mark turned into her driveway and put the car in park, turning off the engine. "Jenn? Say something."

"Nicki's trying to drive a wedge between us so that it won't work out."

"Why?"

"You'd have to ask her. And she may not be able to explain. But I know one thing: I'm not going to make you choose between her and me. I know your children mean everything to you, in the same way my son means the world to me. So, I'm not going to put you in the horrible position of making a choice."

He looked down at his lap. "What does that mean for us?"

Jenn paused. "I'm not sure, Mark. I've reached a point in my life where I want peace, love and fun. I can see that until Nicki finds a way to process 'us,' she's going to try to make us miserable. I need time on my own to figure things out." She leaned over and kissed his cheek, then reached for the door handle.

"But... what does that mean?" said Mark. "I know how I feel about you. I don't need time to think about it."

"And I know how I feel about you. But I won't allow Nicki to make me feel small and insignificant... or worse, like a gold digger." She got out of the car.

As she passed by the windshield, she saw him look stunned and even a little distraught, but she couldn't risk creating a huge family mess. She figured taking some time apart would help them both decide if they wanted to be together. Once she was inside her building and through the security door, she saw Mark pull away.

She ran up the stairwell to avoid meeting anybody on the elevator and let herself into the condo. Tossing her bags on the floor, she slumped on the sofa and cried her eyes out.

Chapter 32
Jenn

JENN FELT SO FRUSTRATED by the evening that had started with so much promise. She loved the banter and the laughs. And she felt like she could fit in with every single person in the family, except Nicki. But Nicki was a huge force in the family and she could make day-to-day interactions miserable for everybody.

Why, oh why? She complained to her cat as she slumped into her reading chair. Mocha meowed and jumped up on her lap, purring to comfort her. Sometimes life didn't seem fair. She had finally found a man who dovetailed with her interests, sense of humor and sports hobbies. Jenn knew it was always a bit of work to date someone who had children and ex-spouses. But she'd found ways to work with families in the past—even when the relationship didn't work out. And there were lots of those situations. Even though Halifax was a city of over half a million people, it still felt small at times. There were many pockets of people she knew around the city. And especially with a business like organizing, Jenn often bumped into her exes and children. But it was never a big deal.

She wondered if she should reach out to Nicki and ask to have a coffee with her. She could invite Nicki to talk about her fears and issues with Jenn's and Mark's relationship. While

Jenn wasn't wealthy, she had worked hard all her life and saved her money. She earned a comfortable living; she owned her home and car. She could take vacations. More importantly, she liked the freedom of being self-sufficient so that she could do whatever she liked, including walking away from a relationship that wasn't what she wanted. She had done that in the past, including parting ways with wealthy men. If her heart wasn't in it, she wouldn't stay.

Jenn wanted the chance to assure Nicki that she wasn't after Mark's assets. But on the other hand, it was none of Nicki's business and the thought of having to defend herself irked her.

She knew if she pushed too hard on this issue and drove a wedge between Nicki and Mark, the whole thing could implode. They needed a timeout. Deep inside, she felt she should be patient and wait for the dust to settle, but she missed Mark already, and it had only been a day.

She had plenty of work to do in preparation for the television series and vowed to throw herself entirely into the project. That could help to take her mind off Mark. She would even offer to take on some tasks for Maggie, who was always run off her feet. Jenn took in a deep breath. She felt better figuring out a solution to her woes—and she committed to jumping back into work tomorrow with a renewed sense of purpose. *Dammit!* Why did she still feel bummed out? She petted and nuzzled her beloved Mocha, who never let her down.

Chapter 33
Mark

MARK SAT IN HIS recliner, staring at the television, which was blaring. He pressed the mute button. It had been less than a week since the showdown at Nicki's. Andrew and Kim had returned to Toronto, and Mark felt let down after they left. They told Mark how much they loved Jenn and made him promise not to give up on her. They offered to talk to both Jenn and Nicki to sort things out, but Mark sensed that Jenn needed her space and he didn't want to push any further than he had. But he was miserable and felt himself slipping back into his former slumpy self.

He and Nicki hadn't spoken since the dinner, and Mark knew he should take the high road and reach out, but he dreaded sorting through the mess. She texted him and said she was traveling to Toronto on business for a few days and would be in touch. He was relieved to have a break before the "big talk" and sensed Nicki was too.

He leaned over to tickle Jack, who was curled up by his feet. Mark watched as Jack looked up, then trotted out to the kitchen. He fetched his leash from the shelf, returned to Mark's chair and dropped it by his feet. "Well, I can take a hint," Mark said, patting him and promising to take him out after the hockey game.

He yawned and turned the volume on again. Sports commentators whom he usually enjoyed sounded like they were blathering. But he sat there anyway, unmotivated to do much else. Suddenly, Jack bolted upright and ran to the top of the sofa, letting out a minor woof and wagging his tail, which meant that a "friendly" was on their way.

His heart pounded. *Could it be Jenn?* She said she needed time, and a week without talking to her already felt like an eternity. He pictured her charging into the house and them embracing deeply. And instead of focusing on the irritations of the last week, they'd give in to their growing desires that were constantly dashed due to what Mark described as "one damn thing after another."

He checked the window. It was Nicki. He felt let down because that meant that they'd have to have the conversation they were both dreading. He walked to the kitchen door as she was walking in.

"Hey Nicki," he said without giving his usual hug. He was hurting inside. "What's up?"

"Not too much. It's been a hectic week and I only got back yesterday."

"Come on into the living room," he said, walking into the room. He watched as Nicki entered and started to sit down, then stayed standing.

"It's dark outside. Why don't you have any lights on?" She walked over to a side table and turned on a lamp.

Mark shrugged. "So, how was Toronto?"

"Oh, the usual. Everybody's in a hurry."

"Par for the course." Mark noticed Nicki shifting and spinning her wedding ring. He sensed she wanted to say something, but couldn't find a way in. She fidgeted for a minute; he stayed quiet to give her the chance to speak. Her eyes were darting around, but no words came out. He put his hand on hers.

"Daddy—"

"Yes dear."

"I heard that I owe you an apology."

Here she goes again, trying to sound innocent. "And do you agree? Or are you saying you were too inebriated to remember and someone had to tell you?"

"No," she said, blowing a raspberry. "I wasn't out of control, but I didn't need another brandy after dinner."

"Well, I have a question for you: do you regret what you said to Jenn and me, or do you still feel that way?"

Mark watched as tears welled up in her eyes. *Oh god. Not crying.* He could take a lot of hard knocks in situations, but seeing a family member crying, especially one of his daughters, got him every time.

"No, of course not," said Nicki, dabbing her tears and showing signs of regaining control. "What started as a pointed question by someone who should have stopped while she was ahead grew into aggressive questioning."

"More like an interrogation," added Mark.

Nicki nodded. "I know. And it was none of my business."

"I agree. Nick. And I love you. However, I felt very hurt by your comments. And Jenn was humiliated. She barely spoke on the drive home. Why would you lash out and try to hurt her so much?"

Nicki lifted her shoulders and let them drop. "I don't know." She sat down for a minute, then looked at him. "Have you discussed it with her since the party?"

"No. Jenn said she'd be in touch when she was ready. I have to respect her wishes. But I sure miss her."

"Sorry."

Mark nodded.

"How can I make it up to you?"

"Well, first we need to figure out why you behaved that way. I think there is something inside you that doesn't like seeing Jenn and me together. And I sense the ridiculous gold-digging comment was simply a way to inflict hurt and try to drive her away. You were successful at both."

"Yeah," she said, looking at the carpet.

Mark took her hand. "It seems to me that you are fighting something inside. On the one hand, you and Char have been bugging me to move on, with you always pushing toward the church ladies, who aren't my type and never will be. When I finally meet somebody I care about, you—"

"You're going to forget Mom," she blurted. "I see the way you look at Jenn."

Mark drew in a deep breath. "I could never replace your mother. That would be too weird. If you don't believe me, you should watch that Hitchcock movie, *Vertigo*."

"Who's Hitchcock?"

"Alfred Hitchcock was called the master of suspense. In the movie, a man tries to replace his dead wife with a woman who looks exactly like her, which is very creepy, and it's actually a scam. Never mind, let's not get sidetracked. My point is that I loved your mother very much, but she's gone. I won't ever forget her. How could I? I see her in you and Charlotte. Jenn doesn't want to replace Annie as your mother; you are all grown up. Well... except when you have too many glasses of wine."

Nicki stood up, then sat down. "Daddy, I need to tell you something."

Mark braced himself. He was freaking out. What if she were seriously ill? He couldn't cope with losing another loved one, but he needed to stay strong for her or himself. "You can tell me whatever it is."

She took in a breath. "The truth is that I've had a hard time coping with losing Mom. She was so young and was such a vital part of our lives. I think about her every day, what I'd be telling her and sharing with her. I dreamed of her as a grandma looking after the kids and loving every second of it. I miss her so much!" she whispered.

"Me too," Mark said. He moved over to the sofa and put his arms around her and leaned her close to him, letting her cry. And she cried a river. He discreetly put out his left hand to pull the tissue box closer and handed her a wad.

"Sorry," she said, mopping her face. "Where did that come from?"

"Deep inside. That's why you had problems—the fear, grief and anger were all stockpiled inside."

"I know it seems like I'm great and busy making everybody happy. But inside I'm so freaking sad and I can't seem to shake it. I miss Mom so much."

"I understand, honey. I've been through my own tough time. You know that."

She hiccupped and continued dabbing at her eyes. "How come Charlotte isn't that way?"

"We all process grief differently. Char has also dealt with some tough days. She came over here and we cried together on several occasions."

Nicki sat up. "And you didn't invite me?"

"Well, it just happened. It's not like we organized crying jags."

"I wonder why Charlotte didn't tell me how she felt."

Mark took in a breath. "She tried a few times, but said you changed the subject."

Nicki twisted the tissue. "It's hard for me to talk about it."

Mark picked up her hand. "Well, this is a good start."

"Start? I've opened the floodgates!"

They both laughed and he held her close for a minute. "Have you thought about getting some grief counseling, Nick?"

"I'd feel stupid; it's been a few years since she passed away."

"Hon, grief takes as long as it takes. Everybody is different. Maybe you'd feel more comfortable talking to a professional instead of a family member. That's what I did."

"Really? Who did you talk to?"

"She was a counselor through the school system. But you could find someone else quite easily. Will you think about it?"

"I'll give it some thought." Nicki pulled another tissue and finished dabbing her face. "Daddy, I do want you to be happy. And I know Jenn seems to be someone special for you. I think you should carry on."

"What's this, the papal blessing?" he joked. "I've been nicely trying to tell you to butt out, not give permission."

"Well, you vetoed some of my boyfriends when I was younger."

"I'm your father. They were dickheads. Big difference."

"Would you like me to apologize to her?"

Mark stood up and stretched his arms out to help her stand up.

"Maybe in the future. For now, I'd like to sort this out my own way."

"Okay. Is there anything else I can do?"

Mark stared off into the distance. Was this the time to confront his big beef with her, or would it be too much? *What the hell.* "Since you asked... I want to spend more time with Augustus without having to apply for a timeslot."

Mark saw her open her mouth to reply and he held his hand up to stop her. "I'm not finished. I've asked so many times to do something spontaneously and you turned me down because he had an event, or a freakin' playdate. Hell, I'd have taken him to the playdate. He's a highly active and curious boy. I'd love to let him run rampant in unstructured play and not worry about a stern lecture from you. You forget I used to handle a classroom full of energetic boys."

"Hmmm," she said, her weight shifting from one side to the other. "It's how my friends and I do things. I don't know why. I guess we share what we do all the time because we want to protect them."

"Right. And mostly that's good. But how do you expect him to stand on his own two feet if he doesn't make a few mistakes, skin a knee once in a while or lose a game now and then?" He sighed. "That's why I stopped asking to hang out with Augustus. But I resent only having a Saturday morning slot."

"Well, thanks for your input. I'll try to do better."

"It's not about doing better, Nicki, it's about relaxing. Let the little guy rip now and then."

"I'll do my best, but you'll have to be patient."

He hugged her. "You got it."

"I do have one idea for you."

"What?"

"We are organizing some after-school sports for the kids, and we need coaches. There's T-ball and soccer. Would you be interested?"

"Are you kidding me? I would love that."

Nicki picked up her bag and they headed to the kitchen door. "I will give your contact info to the coordinator and she can call you."

"Great, because I've got time on my hands." Mark watched Nicki head out the door. He was relieved that they had been able to talk through her feelings about Annie. While he didn't expect a full improvement—she was who she was—he figured she'd at least be civil to Jenn. He reached for Jack's leash, then remembered the dog had dropped a big hint at his feet in the living room. "Jack. Walk?" Jack bounded out to the kitchen with the leash in his mouth. Mark felt buoyed that the obstacle blocking him and Jenn might be solved, except now he had an even bigger challenge: he had to win her back.

He decided this called for courage, perseverance and even a little goofiness if need be. And he had to convince her of their potential for love before some other jerk weaseled his way into her life.

He looked at Jack and said, "Cue sappy music, dog. Mark Russell is going to win his love back or go down in humiliating defeat."

And he knew exactly where to bump into her, accidentally on purpose.

Chapter 34
Jenn

Jenn arrived at the Halifax Forum as the sun was coming up. It was going to be a long day shooting the next segment of the TV show *Clutter Bye Homes*. This was the fun part, where a family saw firsthand how much stuff they had accumulated in every square inch of their home—they were about to see it all on display. Some families had lived for years surrounded by items stored haphazardly and couldn't find anything, so they bought the same items repeatedly. The families would learn to bob and weave around piles everywhere in the house.

Six families were selected for the season, with a different family featured in each episode. They had bravely stepped up to admit they needed professional help to rid themselves of too much clutter and disorganization in the home. No matter how horrifying the mess or lack of organization, Maggie and Jenn never shamed them about their living space. Their role was to improve the lives of everyday families who were doing their best to get by in life.

The Bradford family of Halifax was the focus of this episode, featuring forty-something parents, Jeremy Bradford, and Samantha Fong-Bradford. The crew shot footage in their home where Jeremy and Sam talked about their lives with their two boys and two girls, ranging in age from twelve to nineteen. Plus, there was a beloved Lab named Oaf, who galloped through the house eating items of indeterminate origin, knocking things over with his tail or shedding large tufts of fur in every corner.

The show host would spend time at the beginning of the segment introducing the viewers to the family, and building empathy for them. They'd talk about their chaotic lives and how much they'd love to have a better functioning space for everybody. One of the boys said he didn't care about how the house looked, while the teenage girls said they were too embarrassed to bring friends over. Both Sam and Jeremy blushed when their daughters said that.

Sam was a nurse who did shift work, while Jeremy worked in sales and had to travel frequently. The only thing they had well organized was their family calendar on the fridge, and by their description, everything else was sheer chaos. As Sam described it, life consisted of dropping off and picking up kids 24/7, preparing meals, doing dishes and laundry, then collapsing from sheer fatigue at the end of the day.

While they were very unhappy with the state of their house, they hadn't found a way to conquer the mess. Sam said she had attempted to do a spring clean for five years, but it had never materialized. The kids pushed back when she tried to get rid of stuff, so she eventually gave up. Plus, everybody was adding new activities and gear, without clearing out the old equipment. As a result, every conceivable space in the house was full, including the attic and basement. The camera zoomed in on them laughing when they all had to lean as a group to close the garage door. It couldn't accommodate another sheet of paper, let alone a car.

Everyone agreed that it was time for a major cleanup. That's when they applied to be on *Clutter Bye Homes*.

In exchange for being featured in the show, the show's team would come into their home, remove everything, then bring in specialists to clean, repair and paint the interior of their home, including building organizing systems. Their motto was "Four days to restore domestic peace." As a motivator, the featured family would be put up in a luxury hotel for four days while the team carried out home improvements unimpeded.

This is where Jenn and Maggie came in, along with a team of specialists who couldn't wait to tackle and reorganize the house. They all got satisfaction in seeing families transition out of chaos into a space that was clean and smartly organized. Often, there were tears when the family returned to their home.

The entire contents of the Bradford family home had been packed up the day before into moving trucks and taken to the arena. A team managed by Jenn and Maggie had organized everything into zones of themed items—toys, books, videos, clothes, cosmetics, kitchen goods, electronics, sporting equipment and games from their twenty-five-hundred-square-foot home, plus garage.

Once all the items were organized in the arena, the family would arrive the next morning with the camera crew documenting their response. For most participants, this was a mixture of deep shock, embarrassment and laughter.

After recovering from the shock of seeing their home contents fill most of the arena's surface, the family would then start the task of paring down their goods. Jenn was always fascinated by how people behaved: some looked as light as air as they chose things to be sold or donated. Others stared at every little item and tried to justify keeping it. But Jenn and Maggie had perfected the art of helping people to understand the importance of clearing out and getting rid of things they no longer loved, wanted or needed.

Each family had agreed in advance to get rid of at least fifty percent of what was in the arena. At the back, there were four designated areas with large signs: Keep, Sell, Donate to Charity, and Landfill. For the "Mammoth Sort Out" segment led by Maggie and Jenn, each item had to be decided upon by the household's owners and delivered to one of the designated sections. Once that was done, the items being kept for their home were packed up and returned to the house, while the other items were sold or given away.

Jenn put on her headphones and looked for Maggie in the distance on the arena floor. They waved excitedly at each other. They were on their fourth episode, so they knew what to expect—long hours of crazy activity. Yet they both found it exhilarating and they loved the families they were helping. They busied themselves organizing the house items in the arena for the big reveal when the family arrived.

Jenn had her mile-long list of things to do. She looked at her watch and then glanced around in search of her assistant, Tasha, who was supposed to be there at 6:30 a.m. When Jenn and Maggie were interviewing for the job, Tasha had sold them on her insistence on punctuality and willingness to work as many hours as possible to earn money for college. Within a couple of weeks, her enthusiasm waned and she was showing up late and gradually announcing she had to leave early.

"Have you seen Tasha?" Jenn asked as she walked to Maggie and gave her a quick hug.

"No, but I'd like to. We've got so much to do," said Maggie.

"Me too. I've got a zillion things and, in a few hours, she has to do the drop off and pick up of VIPs at the airport." Jenn was losing faith in her assistant but was far too slammed to do anything about it—she'd have to make do. "I texted Tasha and reminded her that we needed her help right away. But I haven't heard back."

"Funny, when she's working, her cell phone is velcroed to her palm and she never stops texting. But when we need to reach her—"

"No response," Jenn interjected. "Well, I'm headed over to the books/DVDs and electronics section to tidy up. How on earth can one family have twenty-seven cell phone chargers?"

"Beats me. I'm about to tackle Sarah's collection of seventy-five dolls that she's outgrown but hasn't acknowledged yet."

"That alone would clear out the spare bedroom," laughed Jenn. "Everything on track for the family's arrival at 9 a.m.?"

Maggie nodded. "Manny's been in touch and they are raring to go."

Jenn got busy organizing the various areas. An hour later, she heard a text come in and saw it was from Tasha. "Finally," she muttered to nobody. Her face fell when she read, "I quit." She marched over to Maggie, who set some dolls down and waited for Jenn to arrive.

"Your face looks like a red balloon about to burst."

"Tasha just quit, by text. Can you believe it?"

"Doesn't surprise me," said Maggie. "Is there anybody else we can bring in who can jump in and do nearly everything with minimal instruction?"

"I started texting friends, but it's only 8 o'clock on a Saturday, so I can only text the ones who will be up this early."

"Worst-case scenario, we work twice as hard and fast."

Jenn nodded. "We've done it before." As she turned back toward the electronics, she noticed a group of lively people laughing and chatting as they found seats in the stands. "Who are these people strolling in?"

Maggie shrugged. "Maybe they think there's a hockey game on."

"Okay, there's been some miscommunication. It was supposed to be the Bradford family arriving and the big reveal of the mountain of stuff in their house. I'll go check with Manny."

Jenn wandered over to Manny, who was yelling instructions to some of his crew with his left hand while texting with his right. "Hey Manny, people are wandering in and hanging out in the stands. What's going on?"

Manny grinned. "Well, things have taken a bit of a turn. Sam Fong-Bradford posted a social media update to her friends. She told everybody what was happening at 9 a.m. Then it got shared umpteen times and before you know it, people asked if they could come and watch. She told them it was fine with her, and she just told me now."

Jenn texted Maggie and told her to come over so they could brief her. "Won't the family be embarrassed to let their friends see the stockpile of crap from their home?" asked Maggie, once she was updated.

"Apparently not," said Manny. "Family, friends and neighbors love the idea and are asking for first dibs on the items to be sold. My only question to her friends is: don't you people have anything better to do on a Saturday morning?"

"Yes and no," said Jenn, laughing in sync with Maggie. "There's a mixture of interest, curiosity and nosiness around here. They all know they have the same style of mess in their house, so there's no judgment."

"Well, they'd have to stay in the stands until everything is sorted. Can your shooting crew manage it?" Maggie asked.

Manny nodded. "To be honest, I had never thought of allowing the public to be part of the shoot, but it's sure generated a ton of buzz on social media. That will help us. We have to sell this series to a lot of outlets to make a profit."

Jenn noticed one of the crew members had turned on the speakers and soon lively music was filling the arena. She looked at Manny. "Okay, if that's your decision, fine, but we may need help from your team if the crowd gets squirrelly."

"That's what I love about you two—you are so flexible." Manny hi-fived Jenn and Maggie, then ran off to tend to something else.

The two of them exchanged surprised glances. "What-ev," said Maggie. "I guess we can make it work."

"Not our circus, not our monkeys," joked Jenn.

Maggie laughed. "Besides, if it gets out of hand, it's Manny's problem."

They returned to their tasks. Jenn was amazed by the growing number of people in the stands, but she noted it was adding to the fun. Then she thought about all the tasks she had to do and she still hadn't found anyone to go to the airport. As she picked up a cardboard box full of old cell phones, she heard a familiar voice call her name. She looked up. "Mark! What are you doing here?"

"Funny thing. I was out doing errands and driving past the Forum when I saw the production trucks, and I knew you had your big show at the arena today. I wasn't going to bother you, but there was a hand-printed sign that said, 'All Welcome', so I thought I'd drop in."

"Yeah, they decided to open it to the public, so it's a little nuts right now."

"You look stressed. You okay?"

Jenn sighed. "Well, my assistant quit an hour ago, I didn't know about the public coming, and somehow, I have to find someone to go to the airport to pick up VIPs."

Mark paused. "How about me?"

"Me what?"

"I could go to the airport," he said, standing up straight. "I can pretend to be the chauffeur. I'm even wearing a shirt with a collar and my finest perma-press chinos."

Jenn's face twisted slightly. "That's so nice of you, but you'd have to have a bunch of credentials."

He smiled. "I know. You forget I was a coach for years. I have a chauffeur's license, security clearance and auto insurance for transporting people. I specialize in driving unruly teenage boys, but I can also drive normal people."

"Can you drive a passenger van? There are two to four people plus luggage."

"I've driven a bigger van loaded with eight continuously hungry teens over to Prince Edward Island."

Was this crazy? They hadn't spoken all week, but here he was looking game for anything. "You don't mind?"

"I'd love to help."

She waved Manny over and introduced them. "Manny, this is Mark. He's going to the airport for the VIP pick-up. Can I get your van keys and the signs for the VIPs?"

Manny looked him over, staring at his shirt, pants, running shoes and a knapsack. "Well, you don't exactly look smart in that outfit."

"I'm smarter than I look," Mark replied, winking at Jenn.

Jenn could see that Manny didn't get the humor. "Relax, Manny, this is Nova Scotia," said Jenn. "Nobody cares about dress codes."

"This shirt has a collar and I ironed it, so that's almost a wedding outfit," said Mark.

Manny took off his designer blazer and handed it to Mark. "At least put this on when you are greeting the VIPs off the plane. And no drinking slurpies or whatever it is you people drink out here."

"Craft beer," Mark said, rolling his eyes at Jenn.

"Thanks a million for doing us such a favor," she said to Mark. "Remember to take the new bridge; the McDonald is under construction today."

"I don't recall a new bridge," said Manny.

"It was built in the seventies, so it's newer than the McDonald," said Jenn.

"OMG, that's crazy," sighed Manny, handing Mark the keys.

"Well, I'm off," said Mark, surprising her with a kiss on the lips. Jenn knew that was for Manny, who was obviously irritating the hell out of Mark. "Thanks," she said, returning the kiss knowing it would please Mark.

"I'd tell you to get a room, but we're too busy," Manny clipped, turning to the next person waiting to speak to him.

Mark took Jenn's hand. "And when I get back from the airport, I'll help you with whatever you need. No job too small."

Jenn looked around. "Crowd control with a microphone or a bullhorn. It's turning into a party around here."

"No problem," said Mark. "I'll practice my gym teacher voice on the way to the airport. I'm used to barking orders and regaining control of large spaces."

Wow, my lucky day. Jenn looked over and saw Maggie give her the thumbs up, then mimed doing a rapid heartbeat. Jenn had told her how much she wanted to see Mark. Her phone started pinging, ringing and buzzing at the same time, bringing her back into work mode. She couldn't wait for him to get back.

Chapter 35
Mark

When Mark pulled into the Forum, the VIPs were engaged in a raucous conversation filled with banter and laughter in the back seat. After flying first class from Toronto and enjoying a few cocktails, the three guys arrived in a happy yet sloshy mood, and Mark noted they were finding everything hilarious.

During the trip back from the airport, Mark had learned that they were film producers working on several projects, including a pitch to Hollywood: A sports mockumentary about the rise of an unlikely celebrity athlete and his hilarious missteps to stardom. As soon as Mark heard the description, he said, "That's a mouthful. Why don't you call it a *Jockumentary*?"

Two producers exchanged glances. "That's amazing!" the first one gasped. "I'm writing that down. Well, I'll text it to myself because I'll never remember it."

Mark felt a ripple of pride flow through his body. He had no experience with films, but he figured these chuckleheads wouldn't compliment him if they didn't mean it.

"What else have you got?" said the second one. "The working title is not getting anyone excited either."

Mark glanced in his rearview mirror, deep in thought. "Hmm," he said, "How about *110 per cent*? Years ago, when athletes were being interviewed about their performance in a game, they'd say, 'I gave 110 per cent!'" The guys howled. They wrote that down too.

Must be the booze that's making them so agreeable, Mark thought. With short attention spans kicking in, they asked Mark if he had watched Ted Lasso. "Of course!" he chirped, "I'm a coach." They spent the rest of the trip shouting and interrupting their favorite lines from *Ted Lasso*, which Mark had memorized. When he arrived at the front door of the forum, he texted Manny, who came running out to greet his guests, behaving like a total suck up.

Mark opened the side doors on the van, pouring the group out onto the entryway. They were still carrying on. They shook Mark's hand vigorously and then one of the producers put his hand on Mark's shoulder and gushed to Manny, "This guy is brilliant. He's got the coolest ideas for our new doc!"

"Oh yeah? Like what?" Manny asked, glancing dubiously at Mark.

"Can't remember," one shouted. "But it was super hot. I sent myself a text to remind me for later." With that, Manny smiled at them and turned to lead them inside.

"Manny, here's your jacket. Didn't need it, Bud." Mark smiled as he tossed him the rolled-up blazer.

Once inside the Forum, Mark jumped in to help Jenn and Maggie and suddenly things started falling into place. They laughed and joked about the excitement growing, and Mark beamed to be part of such fun. Jenn had assigned him to help with "fans in the stands" control, as she described it. The Bradford family was about to arrive, so she needed to clear the space.

"Copy that," Mark joked. He would have done anything for Jenn; he felt so alive around her. He walked over to the microphone by the penalty box and tapped it to see if it was live. "Okay, everybody, listen up. The family is about to arrive, so please move from the floor up to the stands."

He was surprised when they did what he asked. "While we're waiting, let's get a little wave going in the stands. If you are here to cheer Jeremy, do a wave." In one section, a bunch of bubbly people set their coffees on the bench and jumped up to do a wave haphazardly.

"C'mon, you can do better than that! Who's here to support Sam?" A group of women jumped to their feet and cheered loudly. "That's better," Mark shouted. "And how about the kids in the family?" Another group stood up, but a bunch of teenage boys booed their friends, just to be jerks.

Jenn came over and nudged Mark. "Good job," she said. "Everybody's laughing."

"Who knew?" said Mark. While he was used to herding sports teams, he had never thought of himself as an emcee who could rally a crowd.

Jenn pointed to the main door. "The family is pulling up. Why don't you keep going? It's like color commentary at a sporting event."

Mark beamed and gave her the thumbs up. "Ahhhhhww right everybody, the doors have opened. Please give a warm welcome to *Team Bradford*. And don't make fun of them for having so much crap to get rid of. We're all in the same boat!"

The crowd clapped, stomped and shouted at the family as they walked in. While the family members were stunned by the arena full of their stuff, they laughed as they noticed family and friends waving madly in the stands. Mark thought the parents looked like politicians at a rally—nodding, waving and giving thumbs up to their friends as they walked. The teens looked ready to die of embarrassment until they saw neighborhood friends waving at them. Suddenly, they perked up and responded to the attention.

After Mark explained to the family and crowd what was going to happen, the Bradfords got down to business and started moving things to the piles at the back. Jenn arrived by Mark's side as he stood by the mic. They stood talking, and then Jenn said, "You're a natural."

Mark said, "Nah, any monkey could do this."

"Nope," she replied. "I know talent when I see it." Jenn leaned toward Mark and touched his arm. She pointed to the stands. "I noticed a few people cheering when they put an item in the charity section. We could encourage some more cheers like that to keep them occupied."

"Great idea." Mark watched as Jeremy grabbed a box of CDs and DVDs and started walking toward the drop-off stations. He leaned into the mic and shouted, "Hey everybody, where do you think he's going to drop this box: in the sell area or the charity?" A small group yelled, "SELL, SELL, SELL." While another chanted, "Char-a-*tee*, char-a-*tee*." It was clear to Mark that they didn't have strong opinions; they enjoyed the revelry and turning it into a game.

Off to the side, he noticed Sam pick up a duffel bag full of hockey gear and mime holding her nose because it was so stinky. She had a determined look on her face, as if she couldn't wait to get rid of it, and started walking quickly, making a beeline for the landfill section.

Mark seized the moment. "Check this out, everybody! Sam's got a break away carrying the smelly hockey bag full of gear that no longer fits anybody, yet they refuse to part with it. Looks like this might be a sore point in the Bradford household. And she resents having to store this at home." Sam looked at Mark, gave him the thumbs up and shouted, "Got that right!"

Buoyed by the feedback, Mark continued. "Wait a minute! Jeremy and the boys have noticed she's heading to the goal zone, but they are down at the other end of the arena. If they can't catch her before she gets there, she gets to choose whether it's to sell the gear, donate to charity or do not pass go, go directly to landfill. What will it be? And it's young Nate racing up from the side. I think he wants it to go back home. He's running hard, and he might even be offside, but this boy won't stop."

Mark gauged the crowd as everybody stomped and cheered. "Sam appears headed for the landfill drop-off spot while Nate is sneaking up on the side to cut her off at the pass. Nate is heading for a roughing penalty if he gets too close to that duffel bag. People, this is a tense situation! Sam has officially faked out her exceptionally talented hockey-playing son, and she's about to biff that unwanted bag...wait for it...not the landfill, people—SCORE for Char-a-teeeeeee!"

The fans in the stands erupted, high-fiving each other. Someone in the arena had turned on the PA system and sounded the foghorn that was used when a goal is scored in a hockey game. Jenn, Maggie and Mark hugged each other, pumped up on caffeine and donuts, excited to see the event take such a lively turn. For the next hour, Mark jumped onto the mic now and then to wind up the crowd.

When the family finished, they had a pile of things in the sell section, most of the items in the charity section and only a few hopeless, broken items destined for the landfill. Their friends cheered for them when they donated or recycled goods.

At center ice, the good-natured family of six stood and hugged each other in a huddle, getting lots of cheers from the crowd. Mark interviewed them as if they had won an international sporting championship and invited everyone from the stands to come down and congratulate them.

By the time they wrapped up, Maggie had to race home to be with her family. Manny went off with the crew.

⇢⇢ ⇠⇠

Mark and Jenn went to a pub on Agricola Street for a bite and a drink. They chatted endlessly, replaying all the fun moments of the day. Jenn praised Mark for his hilarious and entertaining commentary, but warned him that sometimes a ton of footage is shot and only a bit is used. He said it didn't matter, but inside, he hoped some of it would show up.

Finally, he felt like he needed to address the elephant in the pint-sized pub. "Jenn, I know I was supposed to wait until you contacted me. I'm sorry. I couldn't wait any longer." He hated to ruin the moment, but he knew he needed to tackle it.

Jenn nodded. "I missed you."

"Me too. I think I figured out things."

"You, or Nicki?"

Mark shifted in his seat. "I know Nicki's been a pain. I talked to her. She's stubborn, but mostly she's still grieving about her mother and she feels like I'm going to forget her and focus entirely on you."

"That's not going to happen," said Jenn, sipping her beer.

"I know. I made it clear that wasn't the case."

"I'm glad you two talked. I heard from Char and she's happy for us. Andrew and Kim also texted me. So, I was hoping Nicki would understand."

Mark took a drink. "She does now. Jenn, you're the best thing to come into my life. I feel so alive again. I am no longer that pudgy, bummed out lump sitting on the sofa, passing time. Thanks to you, I'm a pickleball player, cyclist and hiker...and—"

"And a budding, hammy emcee on a reality show."

"Is that what you think?" he joked. Then he took a deep breath. "Look, I know we both have our quirks and fears about relationships, but I want to try. Do you?"

Jenn gave a minor nod. "I'll do my best, too, but I need to know you have my back no matter what."

"I don't want to live without you, Jenn. That's all I know. And I'd like you to give me a chance to woo you."

"Woo me? Okay," she said, with a warm smile. "How do you plan to do that?"

"Oh, I can't tell you. It's a super big surprise."

"Does that mean you have nothing planned yet?"

"Hey, no fair. But I will have something spectacular cooked up at my place. Are you free on Friday night?"

"Yes."

"Great. Come to my place around 6 p.m. and we'll take it from there."

"Where are we going?"

"You'll see."

"It doesn't involve a do-over of the recliner, does it?'

"Nah. That's for old folks. We're a young-ish, hot couple."

"Right on," she replied. "Should I bring anything? Wine?"

"No thanks, got it covered." They paid their bill and stood up to leave.

"Do you want me to bring food?"

"Nope," he said as they reached the door. He held it open for her.

As she brushed by him closely in the doorway, she whispered, "My jammies?"

He kissed her, pausing briefly on her lips. "Definitely not."

Chapter 36
Jenn

Jenn turned up the volume on her stereo and sang as she hustled around her place getting ready for an evening with Mark. She had no clue about his plans other than showing up at his place, but felt charged up in anticipation. Knowing him, it would be something a little unusual and lots of fun.

On the downside, with him organizing the surprise, she had no idea what to wear. A while back, when they had dreamed about things they wanted to do together, Mark had suggested a camping trip to Kejimkujik National Park, or Keji as everybody called it. She didn't think he'd do that without including her in the planning because it required special gear and outfits. But still she drew a blank.

All she knew was that he told her pajamas were not wanted, which gave her a shiver about what might unfold. Their chemistry fired up when they were near each other and she felt relieved that she still had it in her. There had been long stretches of not dating and even longer patches of not sleeping with a guy, and at times, she wondered if all that excitement circulating in her body had disappeared. Now she knew that was not so.

She opted for a t-shirt dotted with delicate flowers and a pronounced scoop neckline. After trying on three pairs of jeans umpteen times, she settled for the pair that was a wee bit tight when they first came out of the dryer. This usually annoyed her and she'd spend ten minutes doing deep knee stretches to loosen them. But tonight, they felt perfect. While she didn't wear make-up, she added her favorite shade of I'm-ready-to-party lip gloss.

Even though Jenn loved the idea of being spontaneous like she was in her youth—and she dreamed (well, hoped and prayed) for a grand seduction this evening—she had no idea what was planned.

As a mature woman, stumbling through her fifties, she now suffered from being far too organized and practical. In short, she didn't like to do things without a "what if" plan. She couldn't help it; that's where she'd landed in life. Sighing, but accepting who she was, she tossed together an overnight bag with a change of clothes and some toiletries in case things got a little wild.

She'd stow the overnight bag in the back of her SUV. However, if it turned out to be a normal evening where she'd visit and leave around midnight, Mark would be none the wiser. Sometimes she drove herself crazy overthinking things with Mark.

⟫⟫ ⟪⟪

When she pulled into his driveway, it looked a little too quiet and unnerving. Did he change his mind? A soft light glowed in the living room, but otherwise the house brooded in the dark. And no Jumping Jack was bolting to the top of the sofa to greet her. *That's odd.* She got out of the car and walked up the steps. There was a little handwritten sign on the door that said, "Jenn, for full instructions, please step inside." Relieved, she turned the door handle.

Another low-wattage lamp in the kitchen gave it an ambient evening feel. "Mark?" she asked softly. No reply. *Hmmm.* She walked a little further. She felt that something looked different, but she couldn't put her finger on it.

She glanced around, her eyes landing on the side wall in the kitchen with the big fancy chalkboard. Then it struck her: the famous To Do list was gone. Jenn was amazed he had found the courage to erase Annie's final list of tasks from three years ago. He and Jenn had discussed it a couple of times, but he confessed to her he couldn't bring himself to do it. She assured him he'd know when the time was right. After that, she stopped asking.

Her heart thumped when she saw the new message on the board. He had drawn a big heart in the center with an arrow going through the heart and scrawled, "Mark loves Jenn." Then in the corner, he wrote "Very True," which made her laugh because that's the message they'd write as kids in public spaces.

This was a major step—Mark announcing his love for her. She felt the same way about him, but had held back because she knew he was still dealing with the lingering grief over Annie. While she'd felt there was no rush for Mark to tell her this, the message triggered a burst of excitement—and bonus, she didn't have to beat it out of him!

Underneath the chalkboard, there was an envelope on the counter with Jenn's name on it. She opened the envelope and read the message: *Dearest Jenn, Please follow the rose petals on the back steps—your suave lover awaits.*

"Sounds good to me," she announced out loud. She spun around and walked out of the house. At the bottom of the steps, she saw the wild rose petals increasing and a bottle of champagne in a planter full of ice. There was a tent set up at the end of the trail of petals.

"Hello," she said tentatively as she made her way across the lawn.

"In here," he announced from the tent.

"Oh my," she gasped as she opened the tent flap and saw him seated cross-legged on a sleeping bag, with a big grin on his face. Inside, the space was decorated with flowers and fairy lights. She inhaled the wafting scent of the fresh flowers.

He waved his hands like a magician who had made a romantic setting appear. "You like?"

"Need you ask?" she replied, accepting his hand. She crouched down and sat beside him. "Wow, what's this?" she pointed to a low table.

"Smart little snacks, so we don't have to run back and forth to the house all evening. We have a fine selection of dips, breads, cheese and charcuterie—and a treat grilling on the barbecue."

"This is amazing," she gasped. "I love the sparkling lights, the food and all the details you've thought of. Thank you, Mark!"

She leaned over and rested her head on his shoulder. He took the cue and slid his arm around her. They sat quietly for a few minutes. If she could have frozen this moment forever, she would have. He made her feel so special and she felt at peace. Everything was perfect.

Finally, he released her hand and gently pushed back a few strands of her hair while gazing close up with the most serene smile on his face. "We have a lot to talk about," he said. "But first, shall we sip a little bubbly?"

Jenn nodded and he handed her a champagne glass and reached for the bottle in his camping cooler. "Nice Nova Scotian champagne bucket, there, Mark."

"Nothing but the best for my big crush. And watch this. I am about to open this bottle without causing it to spray everywhere."

"Well, aren't you Mr. Cosmopolitan."

"I watched a couple of videos." He chuckled as he calmly twisted the cork side to side, while easing it up the bottle neck with the little wire cage holding the cork intact at the top. The cork finally completed its journey out of the bottle, creating a gentle pop. He removed the cage and poured the bubbly into two glasses, then set the bottle in the ice bucket. "To us," he said, clinking Jenn's glass.

"To us." Jenn nodded. She tilted back the glass and took a generous sip, enjoying the sudden effervescence that flowed through her body. Jenn couldn't remember the last time she'd had champagne. Several sips later, she found everything quite amusing as she and Mark chatted.

When her glass was empty, Mark held up the bottle and said, "Top up?"

"Wow, it's hitting me fast, but why not?" she said, holding her glass. He filled it, then added some to his glass.

"That's part of the plan because we are going to start our evening with some scallops wrapped in bacon, followed by sloshy Scrabble." He reached for the game, unfolding the board and shaking the velvet bag full of letters.

"Oh really? Is it like it sounds? We get sloshed while we play?"

"Aren't you clever—you cracked the code," he said, getting up. "Please stand by while I fetch the scallops from the barbecue."

Jenn looked around, puzzled. "Wait a minute, where's Jack? If he smells scallops grilling, he'll go crazy."

"I dropped him off at Kevin's this evening. I couldn't risk interference from a pint-sized pooch that would insist on being the center of attention."

Maybe I will need my overnight bag after all. "Makes sense," she stated matter-of-factly, even though inside she wanted to yelp, "Yippee!" Much as she loved Jack, she and Mark needed some "couple time" without concerns about interruptions from children and pets.

Mark returned to the tent with a small plate of delicious-smelling grilled scallops and sizzling bacon wafting in the air.

"Scrumptious," Jenn gushed as she popped one into her mouth. "I'm impressed."

"Thanks. I didn't even need a recipe or a video. Wrap a slice of bacon around a scallop and stab with a toothpick, then grill briefly." When they finished the last two, he looked at his slightly greasy fingers and said, "Points off. I forgot napkins."

"No problem, I have some wipes," said Jenn, reaching into her cavernous carrying bag. She handed him a towel. "Can't help it. Organizers are always digging around places that are dusty and dirty." She took one for herself and soon they were ready for Scrabble.

They settled in and were carrying on as they filled up the board and drank the champagne. Late in the game, when it looked like there was little room to maneuver, Mark disrupted the moment by placing a string of nine letters across to the right-hand side.

"Well, who's the smarty pants for coming up with a nine-letter word?" she said, turning her head to read it. Her eyebrows shot up and she looked back at him. "Whoa, that's quite the loaded word," she laughed.

"What?"

"It's oozing with innuendo."

"Yes, that was my intention. And by the way, I just *scored* thirty-six points. No pun intended."

"Oh, I get it," she said, digging in the bag for more inspiration. "This is Sloshy Scrabble morphing into Slutty Scrabble."

"Great idea. Shall we start a new game with that theme?"

"I thought you'd never ask," Jenn said, folding the board and while Mark held the bag, she eased the tiles back inside and gave them a good shake. They had one more top-up of champagne.

"Gotta watch it with the bubbly," she said, still sipping. "It goes down a little too easy."

"What's wrong with that?"

"What was it that the writer Dorothy Parker said? 'Three martinis, I'm under the table. Four, I'm under the host.'"

"Ha," laughed Mark. "I don't know Dorothy Parker, but I like her thinking."

They were soon playing an impaired but focused game of Scrabble. Each word made them laugh harder.

"Is that really a word?" Mark asked as he read it. "Sounds like slang to me."

"Whatever," laughed Jenn, "This game has degenerated into pure filth."

"And loving it," said Mark. Then he added one more long thread of letters.

"Wait a minute," she smiled as she read the phrase silently. "That's a suggestion, not a Scrabble word."

"Uh-huh," he replied, moving the Scrabble board to the side and patting the sleeping bag for two. "Let's finish this game later."

Chapter 37
Mark

WHAT THE HELL DID I do? Mark's chest tightened like it was in a vise. His arm was underneath Jenn, holding her close, and she was curled up in his embrace, her face a beautiful expression of love. He didn't want to move and upset the moment, yet he had the urge to curl up in a ball on his own and rock back and forth. While he'd been thinking and dreaming about this moment with Jenn since the first time he laid eyes on her, what had just happened was too much for him.

It was the first time he'd slept with anyone since Annie's passing. A wave of guilt washed over him, even though he knew he needed to move on from his late wife. They had enjoyed a solid and safe marriage. They'd trundled into a few ruts like many couples who had been together for decades. Yet not once had their marriage teetered toward implosion. They knew the other's reply before they opened their mouth and knew how they'd behave in most situations. They also used numerous conversational shortcuts, which made things... well, predictable. Not bad by any means, just predictable. Sometimes that was comforting, other times, not so much.

Over time, their relationship had shifted from a lively married couple in their early years to a more relaxed friendship. It was somehow never discussed, and neither seemed to mind. And most importantly, they still got along. Mark noticed Annie had become a little bossier over time, with a driving urge to maintain control of situations. Yet he had his jokes and jabs to signal when she was pushing things too far, and she understood when to back down.

But overall, if he'd been asked about the status of their marriage late in life, he'd have said without pause, it was good—no, make that damn good. By the time they got through the career years, the raising children era and welcoming grandchildren, they were more like best friends, with a random romp in the bedroom once in a while.

Jenn had turned his life upside down. He had no expectations, so this whole shift into a relationship with her had caught him off guard. Mark found his brain bouncing around with thoughts like, "Yee haw! Sex again!" followed by, "What on earth am I doing?" He never dreamed he'd feel that intensity of love again and it freaked him out entirely.

Jenn shifted and moved around. Mark removed his arm, which had gone to sleep. He checked his watch; it was four in the morning. He had never felt more awake. Employing full stealth movement, he eased himself free from Jenn and turned over to face the outer wall of the tent so he could stare off into space.

"Mark?" she whispered.

Dammit, she's awake. He paused. "Yeah?" he managed.

"You okay?"

"Sure," he said, reaching for her hand, but staying turned away from her.

"Could have fooled me."

Mark sighed. He had no idea what to say. "I'm good," he mumbled. "How about you?"

"I feel amazing," she whispered. "This is the best I've felt in years." She touched his shoulder. "But something's changed with you."

"Yes... No... I don't know what the hell. Sorry."

"No need to apologize," she said. "But I feel a *it's-not-you-it's-me* moment coming on."

"Possibly."

She sighed. "I thought we'd shared something special tonight."

"Yes, we did, Jenn. But I don't know what to think." There was a long, dreadful pause. Neither spoke. Mark knew he should say something more; he was in danger of ruining things... again.

"Would you like me to leave?" she asked. "I know we sometimes need our own space." She began to rustle around, gathering items.

Mark gasped. "No, please no. I want you here, Jenn," he said, rolling onto his back and staring at the top of the tent.

"It sure doesn't seem like it."

"Your leaving is the opposite of what I want. I'm just a little rattled."

"Then you need to talk to me," Jenn said. "At this very moment, I'm lying here wondering if it worked for you. I am fifty-five. I know I'm not exactly a big catch. My body still works, but gravity has shifted things in a southerly direction. I'm getting sneaky streaks of gray hair. And worse, my skin is losing its elasticity as we speak—and I'm getting rings around my neck like a damn tree."

"I never noticed," he said quietly, but he still couldn't turn his head toward her. "And if I had, I wouldn't care."

'Well, that makes me feel better. While I'm in my late fifties, most days I feel fit and raring to go, like I'm in my forties—until I look in the mirror. Then I gasp and wonder: When did I start looking older?"

"Now you're fishing for compliments," he said. He heard her tiny laugh.

"Seriously, though. I'm lying here wondering if I was good enough last night. So, tell me what you're thinking, or I'll assume the worst. And, I'll be leaving."

Mark turned to her, face-to-face. "It's the opposite. That was mind-blowing with you last night. I've never felt like that before. And that's what's freaking me out."

"Oh," she said. "I don't know what to say, other than I felt the same way."

"Really?" Mark asked.

Jenn nodded. "Look, it's a little awkward discussing the past—and I don't want to know about Annie. None of my business."

"Thanks," said Mark. "It feels weird, and I don't want to compare."

"Then let's not," she smiled. "It's not like I want to revisit the highs and lows of my past. How about we start from zero with us and accept it for what it is?"

Mark reached for her hand. "Good idea."

"And one more thing. If we are going to do this, we need to feel comfortable discussing things with each other. No secrets, okay?"

Mark looked her in the eye and touched her cheek. "Got it. And in the spirit of sharing, you were amazing last night."

"You too," she said, giving him a little elbow. "Must be all that cardio work you're getting from pickleball."

Mark smiled at her. It was hard to believe that only a few months ago, he'd been slumped on his sofa. Now he felt more alive than he had in years.

"Care to pretzel with me?" Mark asked.

"What's that?"

"Like spooning, only better. I made it up. It's a new tradition for us." He slipped his arms through hers and curled them here and there. With a few adjustments and her giggling the whole time, they entangled themselves and quickly fell asleep in each other's arms.

Chapter 38
Jenn

THE NEXT MORNING, JENN stood at the stove, patting the bacon on a folded paper towel and stirring the scrambled eggs in the pan. After Mark had started cooking the eggs on high heat, she'd reassigned him to bagel duty at the toaster. He sliced them evenly, without incident and popped them in the toaster. Then he waited and watched the toaster as if it were the most important task in the world.

There was a bit of noise and shuffling outside, including some tiny barks.

"Jack's back!" Mark shouted as he walked to the kitchen door. Kevin knocked and pushed the door open, letting Jack burst into the middle of things. He leapt into to Mark's arms and Mark petted him, but he was too wriggly, so he set him back down. Jack lay on his back and let Mark spin him for a few rounds. "Well, who's happy to see me?"

"No kidding," said Kevin. "I think he was peeved at you last night for abandoning him, but it's all forgotten."

"He smells bacon, which he's not getting," laughed Mark.

"Hey, Kevin," said Jenn, waving a spatula at him. "Coffee's on. And you are just in time for breakfast." She noticed Mark shoot his brother a *don't even think about it* wink.

"Thanks, but I have stuff to do at the house," said Kevin. "I wanted to return Jack because he was so antsy this morning. We had a long walk already. He's good to go."

"Thanks a million, Kevin," said Mark, walking him to the door.

"Anytime, bud," he said, punching Mark in the arm and smiling. "See you, Jenn."

"See ya later."

The bagels popped out of the toaster. Mark flicked them out and raced to the plates on the table.

Jenn arrived with the eggs and loaded up the plates, while Mark fetched the bacon from the oven and added pieces to the plate, tossing one crumbly bit to Jack. They topped up their coffee and sat down. Jenn felt happy to be lounging late in the morning (well, 9 a.m. was late morning for her), savoring the moment with Mark. This is what she'd been missing in her life—sharing "nothing special" moments with someone she cared about. Even though Mark was a terrible cook, he pitched in to help, and when he asked how he was doing, she replied, "You take instructions well."

After they had cleared the dishes and poured one last cup of coffee, they did a couple of word puzzles, getting a little competitive in the race to answer quickly.

Mark set down his pen and looked at her. "You remember last night when you first arrived and I said there are some things we should discuss?"

"Yes, we got a little distracted," she smiled. "Please continue." She had no idea what might be on his mind, but she was going to assume the best.

Mark paused. "Kyle's and Achara's wedding."

"Yes."

"That's in a few months, right?"

Jenn nodded and sipped her coffee. "Late November. Why do you ask?"

"Do you get a plus one?"

"Of course." For months, she had tried to convince a few friends to join her, but they were non-committal.

"Would you like a date to accompany you?"

Jenn was caught off guard. "You... you mean you?"

"Yes, well, I was thinking it could be fun and I've always wanted to travel overseas, but if that doesn't work for you—"

"I would love that, Mark!" she blurted because she was worried that if she didn't, he would talk himself out of it. "Are you sure?"

"Jeez, you make it sound like I'm making a big sacrifice. I'd love to travel to a new destination with you and attend your son's wedding."

Jenn threw her arms around him and kissed him rapidly on the cheek and neck. "OMG, I can't tell you how happy I am to have you come on this trip."

"I'm not a sophisticated traveler, so don't get too excited."

Jenn waved her hand. "It's not that at all. We'll have our cell phone with GPS, a translator, and whatever else we need. No, it's all about us doing something together. And Kyle's my only child, so this is a huge milestone, and I never dreamed I'd share it with someone I love."

Mark stood up from the table. "Well, that leads me to the other thing I wanted to discuss with you."

Her brain was still bouncing around like a pinball machine as she thought about them going to Thailand for her son's wedding. *What else mattered?* "Sure, what's up?"

He walked to the cupboard, opened the door and took out a neon yellow plastic pickleball with holes in it. He walked over to her at the table, holding out the ball, and flipped it open. He had doctored the ball to give it a hinge in the middle. Inside was a tiny velvet box.

Holy, moly. "Is this what I think it is? A pickleball proposal?"

Mark nodded. "Pickleball has a special meaning for me."

"Why is that?"

"Playing our first game together. That's when I knew I was falling in love with you."

"Seriously? What did I do?"

"Aside from being an excellent player, you were confident and self-assured. More importantly, you didn't try to protect my ego by letting me win. I liked that. As a gym teacher, I spent my career helping kids build confidence and learning how to win and lose. I especially enjoyed coaching girls to be strong and competitive when playing sports. You had no qualms about trouncing me—as it should be, especially since I was being boastful before I learned to play," he chuckled.

Mark's expression changed to worry as he held out the pickleball with the ring box. She didn't know whether to laugh or cry. Apparently, she was doing both. "You know you are a serious goofball popping the question this way."

"I think you find me kinda sexy when I'm a total nerd."

He then picked up the tiny box, his large hands fumbling while he pulled it in every direction. Finally, it opened. "Jenn, I love you and I want to spend my life with you. And even though I'm feeling younger than ever since I met you and we started playing pickleball, life is racing by at breakneck speed these days, for Pete's sake. At least that's the sensation I have. So, I want us to fit in as much as we can."

"Aren't you romantic yet practical at the same time? But I agree. So, what are you thinking?"

"We can get married or live together. We can live here at my place, your place or find a new home and start over—it doesn't matter to me as long as we're together. Shit. Now I'm rambling and offering far too many choices."

"Spoken like a true teacher, offering multiple-choice questions on an exam."

"Jenn, will you put me out of my misery and choose one?"

"I choose *D* all of the above." Jenn smiled and moved over to sit on his lap. She could see he was still fumbling around in his thoughts.

"What does that mean?"

"I definitely want to be with you. But could we take a little time to figure out the next steps? I'm sure it'll become obvious in time, but once we make the decision, we'll know we've got it right. Think of it as the escape hatch in case one or both of us get cold feet."

"Now, who's the romantic?" laughed Mark. "Look, I know we both arrived feeling skittish about committing to someone again, for different reasons. But sometimes, you have to have faith and take the plunge, or you could miss out on the best moments in life."

Jenn didn't have to think hard about all the moments she spent without a partner—the lonely evenings, the weekend breakfasts, the Sunday lounging—to know that Mark was exactly who she needed and wanted. It just took her a few years to get there. "You are so right, Mark. Let's do this."

"Perfect." He pulled a vintage ring out of the box. "In the meantime, think of this ring as a place holder to celebrate whatever it is that we vaguely agreed to but didn't quite nail down from the multiple-choice questions."

"It's beautiful," she said, holding out her hand as he slipped it on her finger. "It looks like an emerald and a cluster of diamonds."

"Yes. It was my grandmother's."

"Wow, even better. I love it."

He kissed her hand. "Yes, it's perfect with your sparkling brown eyes."

Chapter 39
Jenn

Three Months Later—The Wedding in Thailand

Mark and Jenn stood outside on the deck of the wedding venue and set their drinks on the table. The sparkling light from amber lanterns and colorful beads wove a magic spell. Even after a week, Jenn still felt the thrill of being somewhere exotic.

"Wow. That was the most beautiful, romantic and moving wedding," said Jenn. "To see my son look so in love and happy is amazing. My heart is full."

"Everybody was so friendly. I loved the food, especially the coconut curry. We are going straight to a Thai restaurant when we get back to Halifax."

"It's going to take a few rounds of pickleball to melt this trip off my hips."

"Don't worry. I'll get us in shape. And, I'll soon be beating you regularly on the court."

"Fat chance," she said, nudging him.

"You know what? While I'm having fun here, I'm happy to be going home to start our lives together."

"Me too, although I'll be sad to leave Kyle."

"Understood. But it sounds like you're scheming to bring them back to Halifax."

"With any luck, they'll be home in nine months to a year."

"That's exciting. Would you keep your condo for them?"

"If they want it."

"Does that mean I have to wait a year for us to be together?"

"No, because hearing about their plans got me thinking. My cousin Mandy in Shubenacadie has a daughter, Aliyah, who is studying to be a health care worker. She's a single mom and she can't find, let alone afford, an apartment in Halifax. She lives with Mandy and uses her car to commute on weekdays, so now Mandy is without a car. It's not good for anybody. Since I own my condo, I'd like to let her and her son stay there at cost until she finishes her studies in seven months."

"You'd move in with me?"

Jenn smiled.

Mark picked up his drink and clinked it with hers. He put his arm around her shoulder. "I can't tell you how happy that makes me."

"Just one thing, if we move in together in your house," she paused. "I'm not sure how to say this—"

"You don't want to sleep in the main bedroom."

Jenn nodded. "Is that okay?"

"I get it. And it's an easy fix with a few renos. Especially since we have an organizer in the household. You're not trying to drum up business, are you?"

"Ha," she laughed. "Good thing I don't take things personally. You tried to fire me at the beginning."

"You're not going to let me forget that, are you," he joked. "Seriously, I can't wait." Mark kissed her on the lips, then the back of her neck. "Did I mention how ravishing you look in that outfit?"

"Three times," she smiled, waving a fan in front of her face and fluttering her eyelashes. She had bought it at a market for her hot flashes while traveling, but liked that it also did double duty for flirting.

"What color would you call it? Pink, purple, red?"

"Fuchsia. And it's silk."

"I love the color and the feel of it," he said, slipping his hand into an opening at the back.

"Careful, there's only one brooch holding the entire outfit in place."

"I like it even more. Do you want to head back to the hotel?"

They clasped hands and stepped into the quiet street. The warm air carried a gentle mist, with random drops of rain. Several taxis offered their services, but they waved and said they'd walk. Walking hand-in-hand down an alley, they heard a karaoke bar in full swing. The place was packed, and the singer was thrilling the crowd every time he nailed a note.

Mark smiled. "Wow. 'Brown Eyed Girl.' I love that song."

"Me too, it was a favorite at weddings when I was growing up."

"He's doing a decent job."

"You're not going to join in with an off-key version, are you?"

"Nah, I don't want to scare you off too early in our relationship."

"I've got a better idea."

"What?"

"Well, we just attended the most beautiful wedding with my son and daughter-in-law and we're still in wedding and partying mode. Except I didn't expect to hear this song in Thailand. Do you think the universe is sending us a hint?"

"I've never been in touch with the universe. What's the message?"

"Let's dance!" She caught his hands and tugged lightly.

"Aren't you worried about raindrops on your dress?"

She shrugged. "It'll dry. Besides, for the first time in, like, forever, I want to share a spontaneous moment with you and not worry about spots on my dress."

Mark started to move with her during the song. A few of the revelers opened the window and waved to them. Soon, others leaned out and applauded, turning a disco light to shine on the street. Mark loosened his tie, which got hoots and hollers. They both laughed.

He danced like a robot that had been short-circuited with four megawatts of electricity. Over the noise, he shouted to her, "Question: Are you embarrassed with me busting my Dad-dance in public?"

"Not in the least," she yelled back.

"Good. As Charlotte would say, 'Dad, own your dance style.' So, here I go," he replied, twirling her.

"You know, I'm starting to appreciate you, dance quirks and all," Jenn said as she watched him move to the music.

"Cool. And you, my dear, are officially a badass dancer." He winked at her as if to say, "Yup, I'm a crap dancer, and isn't this fun?"

Life's short, let's dance, Jenn decided. *And who cares if everybody's watching?* Together, they pranced and strutted like they were reigning champions at a Throwback Thursday eighties dance contest.

Jenn looked at him and felt the happiness she had been missing all these years. Mark was the guy she'd dreamed of: grounded, smart, always ready for a laugh—especially at his own expense. He wasn't pretending to be a superhero trying to change the world or plotting to take it over. He was more what she would call a local hero: A great Dad, grandfather, coach and now her life partner. He was romantic when it mattered, and clearly he loved her for who she was, not for who she should be. He was the one she wanted to spend her time with.

Curious onlookers from the bar poured into the street, gathering in a circle to encourage them, as if they understood this was a special moment for the couple. And when Mark leaned toward Jenn to kiss her, the crowd whooped.

Just then, they heard one song finish and a new one start. As soon as the horns kicked in, they recognized one of their favorite Motown tunes, "Dancing in the Street," which brought cheers from the crowd. The singer walked out of the bar and waved to everybody to join him in a big dance circle, filling the street with happy revelers. It was a place where age didn't matter—everybody just accepted one another and cheered their dance moves.

At that moment, Jenn felt almost ageless. Yes, she looked in her fifties on the outside, but inside, she felt like she did in her thirties or forties. Maybe it was the pickleball, or perhaps it was Mark who made her feel young. Maybe both. Either way, what did it matter? She drew in a deep yoga breath that she had learned to use to ground herself in the moment.

The refreshing drizzle with its delicate bouquet, brushed her skin like confetti made from rose petals floating toward the earth. She paused dancing to wrap her arms around Mark, feeling overjoyed and wanting to capture this feeling forever. How many times in her life did she have an extraordinary moment, only to realize afterward she hadn't been fully present? She'd missed so many amazing details.

Not this time.

Jenn would recall every millisecond of this rare evening: every taste, smell, color, sound and touch exchanged with Mark. She didn't need a selfie, a video, or a social media post to remember it—she had every detail recorded in her mind. As they wrapped up their hug, Mark didn't say a word, but his smile told her that he understood exactly how she was feeling.

And so, they danced in the rain.

Acknowledgements

Sometimes I get an idea for a novel. It just shows up in my head like an uninvited house guest who makes their presence known and doesn't say when they are leaving. Usually, I ignore the idea unless it makes a nuisance of itself, vying for my attention, or my mind starts thinking about where the idea might lead. Here's what was rolling around in my head in the winter of 2025:

Seeking love later in life creates an invisible tension deep in the soul, hovering somewhere between holding back to avoid getting hurt again and surrendering to the exhilaration of it all.

This novel could have easily been a drama. After all, by a certain age, many of us have accumulated endless experiences, emotional scars and quirky habits that affect our future dating behavior. Worse, we sometimes undermine attempts at love to avoid getting hurt again—and so, the cycle continues. That's rich drama for a writer, but for me, there was a problem: I kept picturing it as a romantic comedy. I especially liked the idea of making readers laugh at that moment of recognition when we realize we've either been there or we've done that.

When I'm in full-on writing mode, I am amazed by the support from my family, fellow writers, friends and loved ones.

I'm lucky because they offer endless practical help, inspiration, moral support, marketing ideas, cheerleading and good laughs.

So, here are some people who have shown exceptional support in some way. Thanks to Kelly Hennessy and Cathy Jacob, co-founders of the writing group "Word Salad." For 13 years, we've helped each other develop and succeed with projects. And we've reached a stage where we are candid about each other's writing, yet still show our love and support. Kelly was especially helpful with this book, reading it in draft form and questioning everything that needed to be challenged.

To the early draft readers: Tanya Brown, Kelly Hennessey and Reisa Muir for providing detailed feedback. You dedicated many hours to reading the manuscript and did so enthusiastically, even though you are all so busy. Many thanks.

Elizabeth Peirce is an editor and proofreader extraordinaire. You are calm, thoughtful, extremely competent and attentive right down to the last comma. You dedicate yourself entirely to the project at hand and offer great suggestions. Any errors that were missed are mine. Thank you, Elizabeth.

Renée Hartleib, a fellow writer and indie publisher (and pickleball friend!), is always there to brainstorm ideas about my book and offer solid advice.

Thanks to Peggy Issenman, with Peggy & Co. Design in Halifax, for designing my book cover. You tackled a book genre that was new to you and made it sing and dance in short order.

As always, thank you to the Brown family: Dale Brown, Reisa Muir & Al Muir, Connor Muir, Tanya Brown & Ric Hamilton. Your unwavering support means the world to me. And in loving memory of my Dad, Floyd "Brownie" Brown and my Mom, Christina (Stronach) Brown. I was fortunate to have such loving and caring parents, who always encouraged my creative endeavors (including a few crazy ones!).

I love the extended Stronach and Bent families in the Annapolis Valley, and the Pugwash descendants of the Brown, Tuttle and Macpherson relatives as well as the families of Lorraine & Richard Lalonde, Greg Brown & Heather Brown, Warren Brown & Diane Salo, Ann Liebenberg and Shelagh Greenaway.

In loving memory of Robert Crockett, my partner of nine years. And it's terrific to have the Crockett stepchildren and their families in my life: Rigel Crockett, Ariel Janzen and Zella Crockett; Laurel Crockett, Drew Rector and Luke Rector; Joe Zsebenyi, Aidan Zsebenyi and Ryan Zsebenyi, and Tami Lee Malin. Plus, Sue Crockett, Jeanie Crockett, Mary Crockett, Michael Fuller, and Dave & Randi Adler.

Thank you to Sue Slade, manager of Dartmouth Book Exchange, for hearing my idea early on and encouraging me to keep writing the story. You go above and beyond to support local authors and engage readers. It's amazing.

To Bookmark in Halifax: your commitment to local writers is incredible. Thanks also to Room 152 in Dartmouth (Trina and Morgan) and Otis & Clementine in Tantallon. Appreciation goes to Halifax Public Libraries for carrying my books, and the efforts of event organizer Darcy Johns. Thanks to all the book clubs that have invited me to be a guest author. They are well-read, engaging and fun. I love the unique culture of each group.

Special thanks to my Saturday morning fitness group for starting this whole pickleball lark. We meet at 7 a.m. for our weekly fix and fun (which sometimes requires drawing chalk lines on tennis courts. LOL!). Over the past 15 years, we've evolved from running, cycling, swimming, and triathlons to arrive more recently at pickleball. While we've been through many of life's ups and downs, our friendship and fitness commitment remain strong. Thanks to Susan Smith & Steve Smith, Shawna O'Hearn, Malcolm Boyle, Dave van de Wetering, Lisa Tilley & Mike Tilley, Peter Harrison & Gisella Alecce Harrison, Kim Thomson, Dawn Langstroth, Louis Brill, Glynis Woodman, Tracy Cipryk & Peter Rumscheidt; and the early members, JK Keeping, Vicki Balcom, Andrea Power & Jim Power, and group founder, Gerry Walsh.

Also, thanks to my Halifax pickleball friends and connections at the Canada Games Centre and St. Andrew's Rec Centre, Vienna Ostrynski, Renée Hartleib and team.

Sometimes people do special things, or inspire me in some way. Thanks to: Gayle Lunn & Eric Cranfield, Dana Dean, Nancy Dorey, Matt Higgins, Cheryl Lowe, Monica MacDonald, Shelley Murphy, Bill Niven, Erika Williams, Kim McDonah, Lynn Coveyduck, Taylor Allyn, Patricia Cosgrove, Katherine McGinnis, Sheila M. Kelly, Shaylyn MacAulay, Sue Murtagh, Trudie Richards, Joe LeBlanc & Steven Smith, Alan Stanbridge, Cheryl Beck-Whitehouse, John & Rozanne Webb.

A portion of my book sales will be donated to selected charities with a humanitarian focus.

About the author

Gina N. Brown has written three novels, including *The Sugar Bowl Feud* in 2024 and *Lucy McGee's Moment of Truth* in 2021. She is also the founder of NovaHeart Media, an independent publishing platform. She lives in Halifax, Nova Scotia, where she swims, cycles, skates and plays pickleball. Visit novaheart media.com.

Book Club Questions

1. DATING AND FORMING a relationship seem to get tougher as years go on. What do you see as the biggest obstacles for fifty-somethings Mark and Jenn?

2. When the book starts, Mark's life has changed, but he isn't dealing with it very well. When Mark and his wife retired early, his dream was for them to travel and do things while they were still young enough to enjoy them. But when his wife dies suddenly in an accident, he finds himself floating for a couple of years and can't get any traction. How do you think that impacts his chances of finding new love?

3. Jenn is divorced and craving love but can't find the right one for her. Why do you think that is?

4. When it comes to dating and relationships, women of a certain age sometimes feel invisible as time goes on. Is that something you've experienced?

5. When it comes to second chances and late-in-life romance, adult children can either help or hinder their parents' romance. Have you either experienced this yourself or heard about it from friends? What happened?

6.   Do you think Mark's daughter, Nicki, was justified in her actions of trying to block her father's romantic relationship? Why or why not?

7.   As people age and try to start a new relationship, they bring baggage to the table. Sometimes the obstacles feel too significant for the couple, and they end the relationship before it has a chance to flourish. As a result, they end up alone and miserable when they could have been enjoying a relationship. What, in your mind, are the most significant problems for Jenn and Mark to resolve?

8.   Who do you think changed the most in this book, Mark or Jenn? And in what way?

9.   The divorce rates for first marriages are around 41 to 50%; for second marriages, 60-67%, and for third marriages, around 73%. Why is love so hard for everybody?

10. If you've been married for a long time, or know of people married for a long time, what do you think they are doing to stay in love?

Your reviews help!

WHETHER YOU BOUGHT THIS book from an online retailer or borrowed it from a library, many platforms offer the opportunity to review the book. I would encourage you to do so—whether it's taking a moment to write a sentence or two or simply clicking on the stars. Both help the author tremendously!

Why? Because readers read reviews before they buy. Reviews also help search engines rank books higher in the listings, where they will be more visible. Thanks for supporting an independent author!

Stay in touch

Thank you for reading this book. If you would like to learn more about the author, sign up for updates or check out other books published by NovaHeart Media, please visit novaheart media.com.